Old Heart

Old Heart

PETER FERRY

UNBRIDLED BOOKS

UNBRIDLED BOOKS

Library of Congress Cataloging-in-Publication Data

Ferry, Peter.
Old heart / by Peter Ferry.
pages ; cm
ISBN 978-1-60953-117-1
I. Title.
PS3606.E777O43 2015
813'.6--dc23
2015003685

1 3 5 7 9 10 8 6 4 2

Book Design by SH ▪ CV

First Printing

TO ASA, LIZZIE AND GRIFFIN

You think I was always old,
don't you?
Well, I wasn't.

ATHENE MACGRUDER AT AGE 86,
STUCK ON SIDEWALK ICE WITH HER
WALKER

Behold the summer grass,
All that remains of the
Dreams of warriors.

HAIKU BY MATSUO BASHO FOUND
AT SITE OF A MAORI BATTLE THAT
TOOK PLACE IN 1700 ON THE
BANKS PENINSULA NEAR CHRIST-
CHURCH, NEW ZEALAND

Part One

Frenchman's Lake, July 6, 2007

D ad's gone," Brooks said into the telephone.

"What do you mean? He's dead?" said Christine.

"No, no. He's just gone. He's not here."

"Oh, my God, you scared me. 'Course he's not there. He told us he was going fishing with Mike and Irma, remember?" And there was at least the tone of remonstrance in that last word, as if she were reminding him that he'd been drinking that day. "They probably aren't back yet."

"Yeah, except I stopped in True Value on my way over here, and there was Mike McIntyre, so I said, 'Hey, how was the fishing?' and he didn't know anything about it."

"You're kidding."

"I'm not."

"Well, could we have misunderstood?"

"No," said Brooks as if saying, 'I hadn't had that much to drink.' "Besides, his big suitcase is gone and half his clothes including winter ones and all his pills and toilet stuff. Cleaned out. And his keys were on the kitchen counter. He never leaves those keys."

"What in the world?"

"I'm telling you, I think the old fucker pulled a fast one on us. I think he's taken off."

"How could this have happened? This is your fault. Damn you, Brooks! If you hadn't pushed him so hard ..."

"Christine," Brooks said very slowly, "he's had a stroke."

"You don't know that. You do not know that!"

"Like hell I don't."

"Roger Daugherty gave him a clean bill of health."

"Right. You really think Dad went to see him?"

"Why would he lie, Brooks? He's never lied about anything."

"That's just the point. He's never done any of this weird stuff before. They're behavior changes. Go on line; look it up. Google TIAs. He may have had a bunch of them."

"Okay, okay," said Christine. "Maybe you're right, but Jesus, it's all beside the point. The point is he's not there. He's gone somewhere. So what do we do now?"

"We find him. We go get him. We bring him back."

That's what they said then. That's what they told me later. That's how the great chase began.

Lake County, July 5, 2007

Tom Johnson looked at the broken front seat of the big taxi through the open door.

"Goddamn this piece of ... crap," said the big driver. Tom read his name from the license on the dashboard: Daniel Pecora. "Pardon my French, sir."

"No problem."

"Sometimes the elderly don't like cursing."

"Doesn't bother me," said Tom.

"So what are we going to do now? I guess I could have them dispatch another cab for you, but it might take a while."

"Why not?" Tom was about to say; he'd allowed for plenty of time. But there was something a little pathetic in the tone of the other man's voice that gave him pause. "Well," he said, "can you drive it?"

"This? Well, I don't know. Let's see." He got in and eased the car forward, then turned into the street. He sped up a bit, then braked. He did it again. He backed up to where Tom was standing. "I don't think the seat's like, loose, you know, unanchored. It's just broke."

"Then let's go to the airport."

"Well, I'm game if you are, sir."

"I'm game, Daniel." Tom got in the back, closed the door, caught a last glimpse of the lake as they turned onto the road, and looked at the town one final time as they passed through it. *I'm game all right.* He imagined Brooks and Christine trying to piece things together after the accident. Where was he going? Why Paris? What in the world was he thinking? Then his cell phone rang and he asked Daniel to turn the radio off for a moment. "Morning, Christine. Yes, lovely party, dear. Best ever. Best pig ever, too. Thank you for everything. It was a perfect day. Me? Halfway to Devil's Lake already. No reception up there, so don't worry. I'll be home on Friday. Call you then. Okay, sweetie. Me, too. Me, too. I will be."

Tom turned the phone off. He pushed the back with his thumbs until it slid away, picked the SIM card out with his fingernail, replaced the back, rolled the window down, and flipped the phone out like a tiny Frisbee. He watched it skip once on the shoulder and disappear down the bank. Then he saw that Daniel Pecora was watching in the rearview mirror and had a surprised look on his face. Tom smiled.

"None of my darn business," said Daniel.

"Our little secret," said Tom. It was already the third one they had shared.

He had spent the three hours prior to the arrival of the taxi crossing every *t* and dotting every *i*, packing and repacking his suitcase, writing the letter, reading it, rereading it, addressing it, putting the stamp on it, going over and over his lists until each item had several check marks beside it, making sure that nothing could go wrong. And then the very first thing had gone wrong. Daniel Pecora was gigantic, a man so wide that Tom didn't ask him to carry his bags as he had planned to but lugged them into the garage by himself. "Back her up," he told the cabbie. "Back her right in here four or five feet." This so the neighbors would not see him leaving with luggage. "Pop the trunk," he said.

"Can't," said Daniel, hoisting himself with great effort out of the seat and the car. "Thing's broke. Gotta use the key." It was while getting back in that the big man broke the seat, and it was in examining it that Daniel unintentionally tilted it back and Tom saw what lay beneath it: a rodent's nest of crumbs, crusts, peels, shredded food packages, bottle caps, and cans.

It wasn't anything, really, until Daniel Pecora said, "You weren't supposed to see that," and then it became a dark, awful fat-man secret.

"That's all right," said Tom. "If it makes any difference, I'm wearing diapers."

"Diapers?"

"You know, Daniel, Depends."

So now they were floating down the interstate, for the old Chevy rode like a boat with its bad shock absorbers and loose steering, as if on small waves and wandering from lane to lane, Daniel perched on the wobbly, shifting seat, Tom steadying it with both hands from behind.

"I'll get you there, sir!" said the fat man.

"Good man, Daniel."

"Some drivers don't like the elderly. Not me." And then, in the spirit of the momentary confidentiality that had blossomed between them, "How old are you, sir, if you don't mind my asking?"

"I'm eighty-five, Daniel."

"Eighty-five? Well, I never would have guessed that, but now I know you'll understand what I'm going to say: I like old people. Know why? They got something different about 'em, like me, if you know what I mean."

"Well, I do," said Tom. What he didn't say was "You're fat and

I'm old," but it was true, and somehow that was enough for them
to like each other and joke a bit at least for this hour.

Tom took out the letter, unfolded it, and read it one last time.

Dearest Brooks and Christine,

*By now you've discovered that I am gone. Please rest easy. I am
healthy and happy and doing exactly what I want to do. I know it
is not what you want me to do, but that's just the point. This is my
life, whatever is left of it, and I want to live it on my terms. You
were simply never going to leave me alone. It was Hanover Place
or nothing, and you were right, of course. You were doing what you
had to do, and now I am doing what I have to do, because, you see,
I do not want to live in Hanover Place or any place like it. I just
don't. I'd rather be dead, and this is better.*

*What is this? Well, I'm off to see the world, but if you try to
follow me, the trail will end in Paris. Let me save you a lot of time
and trouble. I have covered my tracks very well. I am not using
credit cards. I am not purchasing tickets beyond Paris in my name.
I have closed out all life insurance policies, bank accounts, mutual
funds, and annuities and converted everything to cash, which I
am carrying in the form of foreign bank drafts. All records of these
are secured by legal confidentiality. My pension payments will be
forwarded directly to me, and all related information is legally
confidential. The same goes for health insurance payments and
reimbursements, all of which automatically come out of and go
into a confidential foreign bank account. I have left no forwarding
address. I have taken everything I want and need and given away
most of the rest to your kids, including my pickup, the pontoon
boat, my tools, and your mother's pearls. What's left, do with all of
it as you wish. Save nothing for me. I am not coming back.*

Being your dad and Tony's has been the greatest honor and

achievement of my life; nothing else comes close. I shall think of you every day and always with absolute love; please do the same of me.

    I love you both.

    Dad

Tom sealed the letter, looked up, saw that Daniel was again watching him, and smiled.

"So," said Daniel, "sounds like you had yourself quite a little party." He said this somewhat wistfully, like someone who hadn't been invited.

"Yes," said Tom, "quite a little party."

Frenchman's Lake, July 4, 2007

Tom really hadn't thrown the Fourth of July party himself for several years; his family and friends had. We'd brought the tub of iced pop, the keg of beer, the corn and cakes and pies, and the great bowls of potato salad, pasta salad, slaw, and baked beans. We'd even dug out the fire pit and roasted the pig all day long, slowly turning it and turning it so that people could come and watch, could inhale the rich, fatty smells, could feel the water running in their mouths. Tom just officiated. He was the high priest of Independence Day. All day long he sat in one of the two Adirondack chairs at the top of the broad lawn that rolled down to Frenchman's Lake, looking craggy and magisterial while sub-alterns attended to him, delivered things—cups of tea, glasses of beer, plates of food. People came to greet him or thank him, to sit in the other chair for a moment or two and chat with him. One of those people was my mother, his daughter, Christine, who brought him a slice of watermelon. "Lovely," he said. "Can I have a little salt?"

"Not supposed to use salt. Which reminds me, did you take your meds?"

"'Course. Took 'em first thing. Always do." But in fact he hadn't taken them, and later, after he'd softly closed his bathroom door and was standing in front of the mirror looking at his pill organizer, he discovered that he hadn't taken them the day before, either, or the day before that. So he took them all right then, took three days' worth, a whole handful, not so much because he thought he needed to or was concerned about his health as to prevent Christine from finding them still in their little compartments. But that was later because right then he did not want Christine to know he'd forgotten or to see how hard it was for him to get up from the Adirondack chair.

For the year since my Uncle Tony's death, he had wondered if the day would come when he couldn't get out of his chair at all (Tony sometimes used to grab Tom's hand and pull him up), when he couldn't move himself far enough forward or push himself all the way up into a standing position. It occurred to him now that this was no longer a concern. Funny. He had worried about it. That someone might see him struggling and use it as evidence of one thing or proof of another. He had never even thought of that when he had bought the chairs in kits at the lumberyard ten years earlier and assembled them one breezy summer afternoon out on the lawn with Tony's help and Brooks stopping by.

"Oh, my God!" Brooks had said. "It's such a cliché!"

"What?"

"Adirondack chairs on a rolling lawn. It's a bad book cover, Dad." This from a guy who hadn't had a real job in two years, whose dyed hair you could spot from two blocks and whose muffler you could hear from six. Remembering now, Tom once again marveled (is that the word when you are annoyed?) at his younger son's almost total lack of self-awareness. "I think I'm in a greeting card. For God's sake, Dad, promise me one thing. Promise you won't paint them green."

So he had painted them bright pink, a coat of oil-based

primer one day and then two of shockingly pink pink over the next two days. Actually, Tony had painted them and with meticulous, timeless care, his tiny pointed tongue protruding in concentration, his stubby little fingers clutching at the brush as he knelt in the grass and talked to himself, sang, "Love, love me do, you know I love you" over and over again. Up on the porch, Tom watched and called out from time to time, "Atta boy, Tony. Spread that stuff on as smooth as silk." A couple of days later they became the Ironic Chairs because Tony got the words "Adirondack" and "ironic" mixed up. When I was studying French in high school, I called them the "chaises ironique" and my sister, Carly, called Tom and Tony the "chers ironique," and the legend was born.

Tom and Tony sat in those chairs for the next nine years, Tony's short legs never quite reaching the ground, Tom's long ones usually crossed, one foot dangling. They sat in them all summer, of course, and all fall, as early in the spring as they could, and even on selected winter days when the temperature moderated, the sun shone, and the wind died down. The neighborhood kids whom they let fish from the dock always waved and called them "the big man" and "the little man," and one once said to Tony, "You're almost little as me."

"That's 'cause I got Down syndrome," Tony explained with something like the patience a parent shows a child. "It makes you little. 'I'm little but I'm old,'" he then said, paraphrasing his father and quoting Harper Lee.

"How old are you?"

"Fifty-one. My birthday was on April sixteenth and we went to the Museum of Science and Industry. You ever go there?"

"No."

"Gotta go. They got a Nazi submarine."

Brooks could be facetious one moment and supercilious the next, and Tom was embarrassed to admit that he couldn't always tell or perhaps trust the difference, which was to say he never really knew how much Brooks objected to the chairs, if at all. He wondered now, as he had so many times, if he'd have felt differently about his second son if they'd called him Bill or John. The name "Brooks" had been Julia's choice, and Tom had always thought it pretentious. Or would Brooks even have been a different person? Would he have gambled less? (That was another thing Tom wouldn't worry about after this day.) Brooks seemed always to be trying to fit his name or make it fit him. Not Tony. He'd been a Tony every day of his life. There was no other name for him. Nor Christine, for that matter, who had seemed to him as a girl beautiful and fragile in about equal proportions, like a piece of crystal. At fourteen she was a willow, thin as a girl wants to be thin, with fine features, mother-of-pearl skin, and hair that curled of its own accord. By twenty-four she had fretted herself plain; she had a horizontal crease across her forehead, her fine features had become a little sharp and her skin a little pallid, her hair no longer curled on its own, and she was now thin as a girl does not want to be thin. She was habitually harried. She still had a good heart and always meant well, but sometimes she lacked the time and patience to do well.

The day was hot and sunny. A perfect Fourth of July, as if he'd ordered it, and perhaps he had. It was, after all, his day; he thought for a moment that perhaps even God might recognize this, might owe him just one day. But no. God owes nobody anything. He knew that. Had always known it. Had lived by it since when? The war, perhaps; could any soldier believe otherwise? Was it then that he first fancied himself a "cheerful fatalist"? Had first made his constant companion the knowledge that any moment, this moment, might be his last? Life is short and hard, pass the beer nuts, please. But hadn't people always known this? When had it changed? When had people begun to believe that they have a right to happiness? In Rousseau's day? In the land of the free and the home of the brave? Maybe in his own lifetime. Maybe since the advent of penicillin or x-rays or social security or health insurance or malpractice suits or emotional distress. Tom had always known that one day Roger Daugherty would not say, "Fit as a fiddle" or "You're in perfect health." Roger, about whom Tom had been skeptical when he'd taken over the old man's practice. Too young. Wet behind the ears. He'd decided to try him out on something easy: a physical exam, and Roger in that tiny examination room listening through the stethoscope, saying, "Do you smoke?"

"Yes."

"Hmmm."

And Tom later, putting his shirt back on, saying, "Tell me, Doctor, did you know that I smoke from something you heard in my chest or because you saw my cigarettes in my shirt pocket?"

Roger had hesitated. "Well, I saw the cigarettes."

"I know I should quit, but it's hard."

"Tell me about it."

"You smoke, too?"

"Trying to quit."

Now Tom hesitated. "Want one?"

Roger thought. "Sure." He got up to open the windows and turn on the fan. Tom shook out two smokes, and they sat there together, knees practically touching, using the wastebasket as an ashtray. He must have been about forty then, Roger thirty and fresh out of residency, but that had sealed it. Roger had been his doctor ever since. Now they were both old men.

"Mr. Johnson?" someone was saying. "Bryce Heinz. You probably don't remember me. ..."

"Well, of course I do, Bryce."

"Please don't get up." And then he was meeting his former student's wife and two teenaged children and the student was telling a funny story about something Tom had said in class one day.

"I just wanted to stop by and say hello."

"Well, I'm so very glad you did, Bryce."

Now the lawn was filling up with people, Christine or someone had put on a CD—was it Creedence Clearwater? He could never tell (he probably would have chosen the 1812 Overture or the Brandenburg Concertos, but he'd lost the privilege of playing music at all because two of his neighbors had complained that he played it too loud especially in the early morning although a third liked to awaken to Tom's music especially Debussy because it allowed her to feel that in a world of calamity and distress, there was also some grace).

In the lake young guys with their girlfriends on their shoulders were engaged in chicken fights, and Tom was thinking about diphtheria. He had read in the paper way back on New Year's Day that it had been the leading cause of death in the United States one hundred years ago, and Tom did not know what diphtheria was. He had intended to look it up half-a-dozen times and never had. This was probably what Christine and Brooks meant by lapses in memory. But Tom had always been absent-minded. No, it was his getting lost in the woods that really concerned them. Of course he hadn't really been lost in the woods; he'd been lost in thought. He'd been working on his plan, but he couldn't tell them that. Besides, he'd often gotten lost. It had been Tony's old dog, Al Jones, who'd always known the way home. He'd followed Al Jones for years. And if he hadn't stepped in the creek and finally been coming out of the woods all wet and muddy just when Christine had stopped by after dinner, she would never have known.

Diphtheria. If he could get out of his damn chair, he'd go look it up right now. Or if he had the energy; was this what Roger Daugherty had meant by "losing strength"? What if he really couldn't get up, and no one came by or looked out a window and a storm blew in and lightning crackled all around? Would he raise his face to the pelting rain? Would he be willing to die this way? Tom was testing himself again, and as was always the case, he knew he wouldn't know the answer until the moment. And then there was what he was going to do the next day. He knew he would regret it sometimes. He knew there was a chance that he'd regret it altogether, that it would be a mistake. He had tried to be objective. He thought his odds were good. If he could just weather the bad days. If he could just keep his eye on the ball. If he could remember the alternative. Of course it was a wild hare, but wasn't that exactly the point? In truth, he wasn't quite sure; it all seemed so big.

What he was entirely sure about was that despite all the people who covered his lawn this day, despite the letters and phone calls and marriages and promises and prayers and all the many and constant attempts not to be alone, he was. First and foremost, before anything else and after everything else, he was alone. It was a fact. It was his fact. It was what he knew and always had known. He'd known it as a child at his brother's funeral amidst the flowers, robes, music, scented air, and stained glass, all of which were elaborate lies carefully designed to deny the thing that was so viscerally apparent, so blatantly obvious to him even then. And all his life he had wondered if it was a fact he would abandon, knowledge he would compromise when he was old and sick and death was near. He wondered if he would find himself in a church pew searching for some solace in the ancient words and smells and rituals. He hadn't yet.

His brother had died of a burst appendix at the age of twelve. What year was that? 1930 or '31? Tom had been eight. Diphtheria, influenza, diarrhea. Simpler ailments for a simpler time. With so many childhood dangers lurking, he wondered if parents then could afford to love their children as much as parents did now that babies came with warranties: three years or thirty-six thousand miles. Don't worry about measles or small pox or polio or tuberculosis or diphtheria, whatever that is; we've got those covered. Did his parents love him a little more or a little less after Paul's death? Love was riskier then. A little riskier. Did they love him at all? They didn't kiss him much. Didn't hug him. Didn't really touch him after a certain age. Perhaps they were afraid. Perhaps they weren't. Perhaps they simply knew what people had always known until very recently. Pass the party mix, please. And had it been easier when you'd had more children and loved them each a little less? Perhaps he had loved Brooks not too little but too much. (The thought momentarily relieved the guilt he seemed to always carry with him.) Had he doted and smothered and coddled until the boy thought he deserved it all: happiness, success, prosperity, even luxury, seventy-six point eight years, a full head of blond hair, and erections on demand?

Someone sat down heavily in Tony's chair. It was Brooks, and Tom's heart sank a little because he was wearing the Brooks smile, the one he always wore when, even though you'd said "no way," "absolutely not," said "no" a thousand times in a thousand ways, he was going to ask you again. He was the most relentless person Tom had ever known. Self-centered and relentless. And now here was another grand scheme, an insurance deal he was working on with Claude Collier that would revolutionize the home health care industry, and if they could just get their foot in the door of one major health care corporation, like Premia, for instance, and Claude had contacts. ... Tom put his hand on Brooks's forearm to stop him. He didn't want to hear this.

"Brooks, listen to me for a minute. I called Paul Sianis at Coldwell Banker and told him I wasn't going to sign that contract tomorrow."

"Oh, Jesus Christ, Dad, why'd you go and do that?"

"Because I'm not going to sell this house, Brooks."

"Oh, for Chrissake, Dad, we've been through this. ..."

"Hush, now. Listen to me. I didn't say I'm not leaving. I am. I said I'm not selling, and the reason is that I'm going to give this house to you and Christine. Fact, I already have. All you two have to do is go into Jerry Santoro's office and sign the papers. It's all arranged."

Brooks and Christine would own it jointly, but Tom wanted Brooks and Marian to live there. He'd explained it all to Christine. But there was one condition: they had to live there ten years before the house could be sold. By then, he reasoned, the house should be worth a great deal of money. Tom talked about buying the place after the war, when it was the only house on this road, about paying twelve thousand dollars for it and wondering how he'd ever make the mortgage payments every month, about the money he and Brooks's mother had saved and invested, about how he would be quite comfortable, about his good teacher's pension. "Now, I know you weren't very happy about the size of Tony's estate, but there was method in my madness," Tom said. "I used up his money so we wouldn't lose so much of it to taxes, and now you're getting the house instead. It's worth more anyway, and a lot more if you take the taxes into account." What Tom didn't say was that this way Brooks couldn't blow the money, or gamble it away, not for a while at least.

Through all of this, Tom was aware that Brooks was quiet, and after he finished, there was more silence. Finally Brooks said, "Know what's worried me?"

"What?"

"What we'd do with these damned ironic chairs. Now I guess we don't have to do anything."

"Except sit in them."

"Perfect timing, too. You're number one on the list at Hanover Place. I didn't tell you that, did I? They called a couple of days ago."

"Hmm," Tom said, "someone must have died."

"Now, Dad, please don't start. ..."

But he wasn't about to. It was a diversionary tactic, just a little ground fire to make Brooks think Tom was still fighting. In point of fact, the battle was over. It had gone on a long time, but it was over. Tom was tiptoeing away under cover of darkness, rowing with muffled oars, and Brooks had no idea. Neither did Christine, of course, and that he regretted, but it had to be.

The battle had started long ago, when Julia had died. Julia turning her face to the wall, closing her eyes, breathing ever less deeply and often. It had been the act of turning away. He'd been standing there talking, making small talk, and she had simply rolled over as if to say in the plainest terms what they both knew: We have wasted our lives on each other. In that sense it was dismissive, impersonal, perhaps even cruel. In another it was intimate, an acknowledgment of the secret only the two of them shared completely, and for just a moment hope had formed and burst again in his heart like a soap bubble: ephemeral, glistening, and doomed. Or perhaps it was just the act of a woman so worn out by dying that she had no time for pretense or delusion. Whatever it was, it had left each of them utterly alone: he standing there, she lying there.

What he was left with was the house and Tony, and almost immediately Brooks had started in about selling the house. Had Tom suspected an ulterior motive even then? At any rate, he was appalled; he was only seventy-four at the time. The arguments were the usual ones: too much upkeep, too much yard work, out here all alone.

"I'd rather be out here all alone," said Tom, and at that time it was true, "than any other place in the world." But he wasn't all alone, of course; he had Tony. His sidekick, his soulmate, his pal. And then when he didn't anymore, well, then he *was* all alone and then he did have time on his hands and then the house did seem suddenly large and empty. And then he really could go looking for Sarah van Praag, as he'd always told himself he wanted to. But I'm getting ahead of myself.

"Oh, come on, Dad, think about it. Chance to be with people your age. Socialize. They say it keeps you young. Who knows? Maybe meet someone." Why was Brooks always saying these things? He lacked knowledge not only of himself but of Tom, perhaps of everyone. Somehow he'd always treated Tom as a generic commodity, as if he must feel as all other parents, teachers, old people feel. It raised Tom's ire that Brooks could be so stupid about his own father, or perhaps uncaring. Maybe it just hurt him.

"Brooks, I'm a curmudgeon. I don't like people."

"And what about Tony? Wouldn't it be good for him to be in a more social milieu? Everyone would love him. Besides, there'll come a time when you're going to need help with him."

Social milieu! He'd finally put an end to it, at least round one of it, with Christine's help. He had just the two of them—no spouses, no kids—to dinner. He wowed them with his paella Valencia, softened them with Spanish wine, amused them, charmed them, and then, while Tony was doing the dishes and singing "She Was Just Seventeen" in the kitchen and they were oohing and ahing over his flan and espresso, he said, "Look, you two, I went through a bad time when your mother was dying, and I know there are probably hard times ahead with Tony, but right now I'm in a very good place. I'm on one of those little plateaus of happiness and good health that comes along every so often, and I am enjoying it thoroughly." He said that he had Tony, Al Jones, music, books to read, this place that he loved, the lake to swim in and sail on, the forest to walk in, and his family all around. "I'm strong, I'm healthy, I'm happy. Please let me be. Please."

Christine looked under raised brows at Brooks. "He's right, you know." And they let him be until Tony died, and then it started again.

"Dad, you already know about ten people who live there."

"Yeah, but do I like any of them? And what about Al Jones?"

"He's a dog, Dad."

"He's the best damn dog in the world, and I'm not going anywhere without him."

"He's incontinent."

"Don't exaggerate. He has an occasional accident."

He was holding his own until the "incidents" that occurred after Tony's death and after Al Jones got too old to take long walks. That was what Brooks called them: "incidents." The first was an automobile accident. Tom glided through a stop sign and was broadsided. Neither vehicle was going very fast, so the damage was minimal. Problem was, the stop sign was at the end of Tom's street less than a block from his house; he'd been stopping at it for almost fifty years. This time he didn't.

"I didn't see it," he said.

"How could you not see it, Dad? It's practically in your yard."

"I just didn't, okay?"

Incident number two was the time Tom got lost in the woods. "Dad," Christine said when she saw him wet to his knees, his boots caked with mud, "what in the world!"

"Don't even bother to ask."

"But Dad, I have to ask." And of course she did have to ask and to wring her hands. It was part of her. It was in her genes. So now she came with him whenever she could for his walk in the woods. Sometimes he tried to outpace her just to prove a point, but usually they just walked and talked, and the first time they did, he realized that it had been a long time since it had been just the two of them like that, since their conversation hadn't been cluttered with details. Once he took her soft, cool hand and held it a long time as they walked, and once he asked about her marriage, and she blushed and said, "We're fine, Dad. We're good. For a while we tried to be great, and that didn't work out so well, but as long as we stick with good, we're okay." Then she smiled at him a little wistfully, and he looked at her a little differently. Had she grown wise and strong in time, and had he missed it?

The third incident was actually a series of incidents that had to do with snowmobiles and Jet Skis, both of which Tom loathed because they were so noisy and disturbed his peace. Almost since both vehicles had been invented, Tom had been trying to get them banned from the lake, as they had been from several others. But also almost since their invention, snowmobiles had become a working-class institution, and Jet Skis had been celebrated as "poor men's yachts," and since there was a blue-collar town at one end of the lake and a summer community consisting of trailers and shabby cabins at the other, Tom was derided and dismissed as an elitist. He made matters both better and worse when he saved a Jet Skier's life.

It was a weekday summer morning about ten o'clock, and Tom was sitting on the dock in a lawn chair, reading. Around the bend came a Jet Skier going fast and much too close to the shore. Tom put down his book and yelled at him, to no avail. Then he watched the boy, who, it turned out, was fourteen, lose control and plow into the neighbor's dock. Tom stood up, looked, and listened. A moment later he heard a gurgled "Help me." Tom let himself down into the waist-deep water and slogged the hundred feet to the accident. The boy's legs were trapped beneath the heavy machine, which had turned onto its side and become wedged beneath the dock. His arms were free, and he was flailing but sinking. Tom got behind the boy, put his hands under the boy's arms and across his chest, and rested the boy's back against his own legs and body so that he could keep his head above water. Then he began to call for help. It was almost an hour before the garbage collectors came by and heard his now weakening pleas. By then both Tom and the boy were shivering and exhausted. The local weekly put Tom's photograph on the front page and called him a hero.

Unfortunately, they also interviewed him. To the question "What can be done to prevent accidents like this one from happening in the future?" Tom answered, "Keep hillbillies and half-wits off the lake, and ban Jet Skis altogether. I think that in order to operate a snowmobile or a Jet Ski on Frenchman's Lake, you should have to meet one or both of these qualifications: first that you have an IQ of at least 75 and second that you have less than 75 percent body fat. That should pretty much eliminate the problem." With that public statement, Tom's status moved from eccentric to crank, and the affair became an official "incident."

And incident number four, which Brooks came to call "the last straw," had to do with his income taxes. It wasn't that Tom didn't do the tax return. He did. He filled out the forms neatly, completely, and accurately, all before April first, and he even wrote his check for two hundred forty-three dollars. {Then he put the stamped envelope aside and forgot about it. Christine found it on May 6 while sorting through a stack of mail. "Dad, didn't you send your taxes in?" she said.

"'Course I did. Had 'em in by April first."

"What's this, then?" She held up the envelope.

The IRS fined him, and it was agreed that Christine would come by once a month to look over the bills and help him balance his checkbook and that next year they would hire a professional to do his taxes. It was humiliating. If it had happened twenty years earlier, it would have been a good joke, maybe even one he told on himself. "So I did 'em early, set 'em aside, and forgot to send 'em in. What a moron." It was also the first time that Brooks mentioned the term "power of attorney," causing Tom's heart to sink into the deepest pit of his stomach and his mind to flood with fear and paranoia. Had it come to that? Was he that far gone?

"Just sign it over so Christine can help you keep track of things, Dad."

"No way. Never."

On the phone his lawyer, Jerry Santoro, had said, "Oh, hell, Tom, they can't make you do it unless you're a lot worse off than you are. Not to worry."

"Well, I do worry."

"Tom, look, you're fit, you're strong. I know men ten years younger ..."

"That's not what my children think." He resisted adding "or doctor."

"Children don't think, Tom, you know that. You still out there on the lake sailing your boat?"

"Sometimes, but they want me to stop."

"Don't stop, Tom. Die at the tiller! That's what I say!"

He felt a little guilty because he hadn't sailed in almost two summers and really wasn't even sure he could anymore. Or was he just buying into Brooks's propaganda? He found himself thinking more than once about Wayne Rasmussen. He even said his name out loud once, and it sounded so odd and foreign on his lips that he thought perhaps he had never said it in all these years, not since the first time. He had been fifteen then. His father had gotten him his very first job working on a delivery van at Christmastime for Walter Flowers, the florist. Walter's son Walter Junior was seventeen, and it was his job to drive the delivery van and call out the next address from a routing list on a clipboard that hung from the rearview mirror. It was Tom's job to locate the next delivery, which he would then run up to the door of this house or that while the van idled in front. The only time Walter Junior got out of the van was when they had multiple deliveries at the hospital or the county home. Then he would walk ahead with the clipboard while Tom pulled a wagon full of flowers behind. Tom didn't mind the hospital, but he dreaded the county home, which had been converted from a shabby old hotel called The Monroe and was full of people slumped in wheelchairs sitting at odd angles in dim corridors and the smells of stagnation, decrepitude, old flesh, dying flesh, dead flesh that no disinfectant could ever wash away or disguise. It was a smell with which for the rest of his life Tom's association was immediate and absolute, like burnt hair, vomit, shit, and spoiled food.

"Wayne Rasmussen." Walter Junior said his name as they went up in the elevator. "Room 412."

Wayne Rasmussen was a man notable not so much for being old as for being ill. You could see the veins and very nearly the bones through his skin. He was sitting upright in a hospital chair, and all four limbs were tied down.

"Mr. Rasmussen? Got a little Christmas flower for you," said Walter Junior.

"Nice," said the old man as Tom put it down on the night-stand. "Nice. You wouldn't happen to have a little Christmas cigarette for me, would you?"

"Well ..." Walter Junior hesitated.

"Make an old man mighty happy. Only pleasure I got left. Hell, look at me, I'm nine-tenths dead already. Ain't hardly nothing left of me. Won't do no harm."

"Sure," said Walter Junior, tapping three smokes out of his pack.

"Now, just untie my right hand here."

"Well ..."

"Can't smoke without my hand here."

"Of course."

"Walter ..." said Tom.

"Shut up," said Walter Junior. They left the old man smiling and inhaling deeply. They delivered the last of the flowers and went back down in the elevator. Out on the sidewalk a small crowd had gathered around a fallen body. Tom thought someone must have slipped on the ice, but the person was dressed in a hospital gown. His legs and feet were bare. Someone looked up, and then they all looked up at an open window.

"Must'a just sat there on the sill and tipped over backwards," someone said.

Tom heard a siren. The man had hit a no-parking sign, and bits of him stuck to the pavement, the ground, and the sign. Back in the van, Tom sat in the drop seat on the passenger side. "That was Wayne Rasmussen," he said.

"So what if it was? He was nine-tenths dead anyway. Didn't you hear him?" Walter Junior was shivering so violently as he said this that Tom was afraid they would crash.

"You shouldn't have ... we shouldn't have ..."

"Don't you ever tell anyone, you hear? Don't you say a god-damn word. If you do, I'll say you did it."

"Me?"

"My word against yours."

And so he didn't tell anyone, at first out of fear, then out of shame, then perhaps out of habit, until the day he told me. But he decided that day at fifteen that he would never end up in a home for old people. Never.

Chicago to Paris, July 5 and 6, 2007

On the plane Tom thought about all the people he loved from whom he was moving away now at half a thousand miles an hour, at nearly ten miles a minute. One thousand one, one thousand two, one thousand three ... Grandchildren he'd never see again. Great-grandchildren he'd never see at all, never hold or tickle or kiss. Perhaps this was all a grand mistake. Could he just step off this plane in Paris and onto another and be home again before anyone knew? But the die was already cast, his property disposed of, the letter mailed. And then there had been my last phone call, the one I had thought long and hard about before making. It was spring then, and spring can be such a cold season in that place.

"Tom, listen," I said, "I feel as if I need to tell you something. I overheard Uncle Brooks and my mom ..."

"I know, I know," he said. I imagined him taking off his reading glasses, pushing his book away and trying to ignore the fact that the rain outside his window was turning to snow and that he'd just caught himself reading the same page for a third time. "He wants me to sign over power of attorney. Well, I'm not going to do it. I—" "No, it's something a little more serious than that," I said. "He's talking about guardianship. He wants to be appointed your legal guardian."

"My guardian? Oh, my Lord."

"Tom, he says you're losing it. He says he thinks he can prove dementia. Says he can document it."

"That's ridiculous, Nora. That's nonsense."

"I know, I know. But don't forget he plays golf with half the judges in the county."

"I'll be damned. I can't believe this."

"Just to let you know, my mom said no. She said she wouldn't stand for it."

But that was all before Tom got stuck between the wall and the toilet. He dozed off sitting on the can in the middle of the night; anymore he sometimes had to sit there a long time, and it was dark and he was groggy and he fell asleep. Groggy. Or senile. He wondered if one condition could simulate the other. He awoke with a start when he slumped to the side, found himself off balance and disoriented, put the palm of his left hand on the seat between his legs and tried to push himself up while reaching in the dark for the sink. But the toilet seat he'd been meaning to tighten for weeks shifted, his left palm slipped, and his right hand failed to find the sink because that sink was in the downstairs bathroom and this one was across the room. This time he lost his balance altogether and fell harder against the wall, sliding down it until he was wedged between it and the cold porcelain of the toilet. He had a brave little laugh, sitting there half naked in the pitch black, but then he couldn't move. He wiggled and inched and squirmed, but he was stuck and he stayed that way the rest of the night. He slept in starts, dreaming once of the old man named Wayne Rasmussen sitting on a cold windowsill and letting himself fall backward. Then, when he couldn't hold it any longer, he urinated on the floor beneath himself. By the morning his discomfort had turned to pain, and when he finally heard someone downstairs, he croaked, "I'm up here."

Later, after my mother had burst through the door and gaped at him, turned away from him, said, "Oh, my God," been unable not to gasp, after the firemen had greased his sides and worked him free, the ambulance had taken him to the hospital, the doctors had wrapped him and rehydrated him, and he was resting in the emergency room, he tried to make a joke. But my mother said, "No! Don't! Don't even try to pretend that this is funny, that this is nothing, that this could happen to anyone, that you're not an old man. You are old, Dad. I'm sorry. This is just irrational. You shouldn't be mowing your lawn; you shouldn't be out on your boat. You shouldn't be living out there all alone while I lie awake in bed worrying about you. You're not able to do all these things anymore; I'm sorry. My God, Daddy, you could have died!"

"Okay, Christine," he said. "Okay, okay."

"Why can't you just move into a nice retirement home like everyone else's parents? Why can't you think of someone other than yourself? I mean, do we have to ..." She didn't go on, but she didn't have to. It was that unfinished sentence and the use of the word "irrational" that told him he had lost, that she'd crossed over to Brooks's side, that the clock was now ticking and his days as a free man were numbered. He would have to act soon if he were to act at all.

But what if she were right? Was all of this self-indulgence? Delusion? Demented hubris? Was he torturing or was Christine overwrought? Was he paranoid or was Brooks conniving? "How the hell should I know?" he said the next day, badly bruised and heavily bandaged, as he stood at the window looking out at

Frenchman's Lake while a light rain fell and Haydn played. "How in God's name should I know?" And if he didn't know, if he really didn't know, he should at the very least appear to go along with them. So he let Brooks buy him a cell phone and painstakingly teach him how to use it, and he dutifully answered their calls every day. He agreed to sell the house, and he agreed to put his name on a waiting list for Hanover Place, "a retirement community for active seniors with thoughtfully designed independent apartments and tasteful, elegant common areas, gardens, and grounds." He even agreed to sign the forms giving my mother power of attorney in his affairs. But he didn't sign them. Not yet. "Wait 'til we sell the house," he said. "It will be easier for me to keep it until the paperwork is complete so one of you doesn't have to run out here every other day." He did all of this as if he had suddenly seen the light, and perhaps he had. He acquiesced, he apologized, he accommodated, and he planned.

In truth, none of the "incidents" really worried Tom or mattered to him. The only one that did was the one Uncle Brooks and my mother didn't know about; I was the only person he told. He found himself one day standing with a shopping cart in the frozen-foods aisle without any idea of what he'd come to buy. Of course he'd often entered a room and been drawn up short because he didn't know why, but when he'd gone back and discovered the pan on the stove, the open book, the shoes awaiting polish, he'd remembered. This time he didn't. He never knew what had sent him to the grocery store that day or why there were three frozen pizzas and a can of hairspray in his shopping cart or why, when he went out to the parking lot, it seemed to be on the wrong side of the building or why then he couldn't find his car, and when he did, it didn't look right; it didn't seem to be his car. He told himself that it was because he hadn't slept well the night before.

He told himself it was because he'd drunk a caffeinated cola. He told himself these things, but he wasn't convinced.

Somewhere high over the Atlantic, when darkness had settled around them, when the dinner dishes had been cleared, the movie shown, the lights dimmed, and the man next to Tom was reclined and snoring lightly, Tom pushed his seat back, pulled the cotton blanket around him, and listened to the drone, felt the occasional shudder of the great craft. As he dozed he recalled falling asleep at night in the backseat of his parents' car when he was still young enough to do so but old enough to know that he would not be much longer. He remembered listening to them as they talked in soft voices. Sometimes he could hear a song on the radio. Sometimes it rained and he could hear the rhythmic swish-swish of the windshield wipers. He felt then, he felt now, a sense of peace and safety in the warmth and soft lights of the night missile.

And what was he moving toward, if anything at all? Sarah's soft, rich voice? Her smiling eyes? Her self-knowledge that seemed to allow her to be so damned certain of everything, including him? Could any of that have survived all these years? He did not want to get his hopes up, so he made himself think about, fell asleep thinking about, Tony's ashes, which very early on the morning of the Fourth of July he had scattered from his pontoon boat on the waters of Frenchman's Lake. They had created a silvery wake that had ridden the surface before very slowly disappearing beneath it.

His hotel room had doors that opened onto a railing above a narrow, nondescript street (if he craned his neck, he could see a café down at the end), a wooden floor that creaked, a tarnished brass bed that sagged, and a faded print that hung askew. It did not have a bathroom. The toilet was down the hall, but it had no tub or shower. "That's all right. I'm not staying long." The room was very inexpensive. That was important. He did not want to waste his money. He would rather go to hear the string quartet in Sainte-Chapelle that he'd seen a poster for or have a second glass of wine with dinner than have a television he'd never turn on, an air conditioner he didn't want, or even a shower.

It was still morning. He washed his face and went downstairs. The two Algerian brothers who ran the hotel nodded to him. "Bonjour!" They seemed somehow honored to have him as a guest. Was it his age? He went to the corner café and sat outside at a small table. The street had been washed and smelled damp and warm. The smell stirred some ancient memory or association with springtime: exhilaration, perhaps abandon. For a moment he was thrilled, and the feeling rose through him to his head, and he felt delightfully free.

He carried with him a new translation of *Madame Bovary*. He had always wanted to read Flaubert's novel in France. He opened it at his bookmark and drank tea as he read about Charles and Emma. *They talked first of the patient, then of the weather, of the periods of bitter cold, of the wolves that roamed the fields at night. Mademoiselle Rouault did not find it much fun living in the country, especially now that she was almost solely responsible for running the farm. As the room was chilly she shivered as she ate, revealing her rather full lips that she tended to nibble when she was not speaking.*

Tom took the Métro to the Arc de Triomphe. He stood a long time looking at the great monument. Then he turned and looked across the town and across the river to the Eiffel Tower. It was more odd and graceful and wonderful than he'd imagined it would be. He spent the rest of the day walking slowly down the Champs-Élysées and through the Tuileries and thinking about Brooks. All afternoon on the Fourth he had thought about Brooks. As he had watched his second son crossing back and forth in his motorboat, Tom had thought about their many battles over the years, about the many promises Brooks had made and broken, about the fresh starts, the new deals, the last chances, about how Brooks had never changed even a little, had only gone through the motions, gone to the meetings, worked the steps, carried the literature, and kept right on gambling. He thought of the file of his correspondence with Brooks over almost forty years now that he had recently leafed through. Did the fact that he'd always made copies, some of the early ones with carbon paper, say more about Brooks or about him? There were the proposals, the bargains, the incentives, the attempts to understand, to find common ground, to meet halfway. All of it achingly familiar and similar. Had he never changed, either? And yet there Brooks was, spending the afternoon of the Fourth pulling tubers and skiers across the lake (Tom *had* wondered how many beers he'd had). Brooks the coach, the scoutmaster, the tutor, the Sunday-school teacher, the ne'er-do-well ("Brooks, you've got it backwards; first you find a vocation, then an avocation"). Brooks who somehow cobbled a life together out of plans, schemes, projects, poker games, pipe dreams, ponies, odd jobs, ten-dollar Nassaus on the golf course, occasional employment, workers' comp, unemployment insurance, and the money his mother had left him, most of which was gone in those same schemes, projects, and pipe dreams but a good bit of which had been gambled away or simply wasted. Living in apartments, moving in the middle of the night, always almost in legal trouble with the IRS or the attorney general's office but not quite. Old cars, "great deals," a community college for Charlie and an apprenticeship for Lou, hanging around golf-club locker rooms, surviving on Marian's meager income as a teacher's aide and depending always on her health insurance even, especially, when she had breast cancer. Now both boys had jobs, homes, and families, and Brooks had a motorboat that was sure to be repossessed next month ("Hell, the summer's almost over anyway"). And then there was the time when he got fired and took his whole family on a Caribbean cruise ("What better time for a vacation?"). That was just it; he could turn misfortune and misery into a good story or a bad joke, and pretty soon, almost against your will, you found yourself laughing along with him even if you were shaking your head. Once Tom had asked Marian not quite playfully why she'd stayed with him all these years, and she had said, "You know, Tom, he can always make me laugh, and he's so good with the boys." Had anyone ever said that about Tom? Had anyone ever said, "He's so good with Brooks"? And earlier that very day, when Tom had asked about Marian and Brooks had said, "Cancer-free five years now, thank the good Lord," Tom had found himself envying his son's joy and relief. "We just got the results Friday."

For years Tom took comfort in the fact that Brooks had never stolen from him, never cheated him. But then he tried to get his hands on Tony's money. Perhaps Julia had distrusted Brooks even before he had; perhaps that was why she had left Tony's money in a trust and made Tom, to his surprise, the trustee. Otherwise Brooks might have pulled it off. Of course Tony, flattered by Brooks's attention and proud to be a "businessman," had blurted it out. "Heart of Gold!" he'd said. "Heart of Gold Inc.!"

"What's that, Tony?"

"Going through the roof! Going to make a million!"

"Tony, what are you talking about?"

"Going to make a killing, Dad!"

Brooks had denied it, of course. "It's an investment opportunity, Dad. An excellent investment opportunity. He could double his money. Triple it."

"Well, if it's so good, why didn't you tell me about it?"

"'Cause I knew you'd thwart him. Stifle him like you always do. Hell, Dad, it's his goddamn money. Why not let him live a little?" Then it had poured out, as sometimes happened when Brooks had had a few drinks. "Because you can't. Because you have to stifle him just like you've stifled us. Ever wonder why Christine is such a goddamn nervous mess? Ever wonder why I can't pull the trigger on a big deal? If just once you had said, 'Go for it,' if just once you had believed in me instead of … instead of …" Tom hadn't answered, and he had been proud of his restraint at the time, but afterward he had wondered if there was room for pride in any of this.

And then there was Brooks the generous: giving away things he didn't own, giving gifts he couldn't afford. Brooks the foolhardy: getting kicked out of high school (Tom's high school) for smoking marijuana, flunking out of the state university no one had ever flunked out of. Brooks the athlete who could hit a golf ball three hundred yards but who wouldn't go out for the team because he didn't like the coach, didn't want to give up drinking beer, and refused to sign the honor statement saying that he had. Brooks the lover, who had to screen his calls from girls even as a kid, who rolled his eyes and made excuses and broke hearts, who sang Prince's song "Kiss" in the karaoke bar at Louie's wedding and had a whole chorus of mothers and daughters laughing, dancing, waving their hands, singing along. Brooks the husband who had somehow chosen Marian and had somehow stayed with her all these years. Beleaguered, world-weary, old-before-her-time Marian, who got teary-eyed at the wedding dancing with her husband. Brooks the salesman who could sell anything but always had bigger plans, wouldn't show up, was "let go," but with regrets and best wishes. Brooks the twelve-year-old towhead with more freckles than sense, who would laugh harder than anyone Tom had ever seen, who would rather sit at the dining room table all night and not do his homework than sit there for half an hour and do it, who told his seventh grade teacher that he didn't do homework because "I like to keep my school life and my home life separate."

And what if Tom had just let him be, had recognized way back then that Brooks was a self-deluding, good-natured layabout who somehow would get through life without a nickel, a wrinkle, or an enemy—except perhaps his own father? What if when Brooks was nineteen, Tom had allowed him to hitchhike to California or drop out and become a ski bum in Aspen? What would the real difference have been? Perhaps only the distance between the conviction that Tom had caused it to happen and the one he now held that he couldn't have stopped it from happening. And why hadn't he ever just let go and relaxed and laughed along? Sitting there on a park bench under a shade tree in the Tuileries in Paris, for heaven's sake, Tom felt suddenly very old and very foolish, the "tight ass" Brooks had often accused him of being, or James Joyce's Gabriel, who, so full of puffery and pretense, had missed the point altogether, had somehow failed to love or to allow himself to be loved, neither of which could be said about Tom's son. Brooks, after all, was loved; Marian and those boys believed as much as Brooks himself that he was always just one break away from hitting it big. Then for a moment it seemed that everything could be Tom's fault. Not just Brooks but Julia, too. Had he been too stubborn, too stupid, to recognize and accept her love?

But no, that couldn't be it, at least not all of it. Otherwise how could you explain all the people on his lawn two days earlier, all those people who had come to sit beside him in Tony's chair, to thank him, share a memory with him, take his hand in theirs, kiss him on the cheek? His colleagues, younger teachers he had worked with, former students: "I'll never forget that day in class

..." "You're the reason I became a teacher ... " "You taught me to think." His nephews and nieces and their friends stepping forward to shyly shake his hand. Wasn't that all proof of something?

Perhaps only that he was a fraud.

Tom stopped at a café in the park and had a juice and later another café and drank a beer. He watched people hurrying by. July. Any self-respecting Parisian was in Provence or Spain. These people must all be imposters or tourists like himself. And had he come all this way just to think about Brooks? Maybe he had. Maybe he needed the perspective. Or maybe he was trying not to think about Tony, who was no longer there, or about Sarah van Praag, who couldn't possibly still be there. Suddenly his whole plan seemed quixotic and more than a little crazy. But then he revisited the conversation he'd had with himself when Tony had died and he had finally been free; he'd thought about it so often for so long, and now here it was, and he was overwhelmed by the question "What do I do with the rest of my life?" Overwhelmed until he asked the next question: "Do I do something, or do I do nothing?" And then it was easy. He knew he had to go looking for Sarah van Praag just as surely as he knew that it was a ridiculous long shot. "Lost love," he once said to me, shaking his head. But what better way to spend the rest of his life than finally taking the chance he'd never had the guts to take before? Blaze of glory! And did it matter that he hadn't much of anything left to lose?

When Tom got tired, he took a cab, and back at the hotel he nodded again to the two brothers, and they to him. He lay down for an hour, then took a sponge bath and left to find an early meal before the concert. He found himself in a pedestrian square in Le Marais inhabited by friends and couples lying on the summer grass and children playing in a large sandbox. All around were colonnaded buildings and pretty cafés. He imagined this was the kind of place where he and Sarah van Praag might have come if they had come to Paris. He ate spaghetti Bolognese and a green salad because they were easy to order. He walked along the Port de Plaisance and onto the Île de la Cité to Sainte-Chapelle. "Oh, my," he said, entering the great room and looking up. "Oh, my goodness." There he bathed in the crystalline beauty of the evening light through those high windows and in the sharp, clear notes of the strings, which described the light so well.

The next day Tom was weary in his very center, perhaps ill, certainly low. Of course he was. After the exhilaration of the trip, his first day in Paris, plus jet lag. Market correction. He'd overdone it. Walked too much, rested too little, pushed himself. *Don't panic. Keep things in perspective.* Besides, he'd always known there would be bad days, but this bad this soon? He took a deep breath and wondered if he could take another. His head spun; his whole body ached. He was not sure he could even stand up. He was pretty sure he couldn't walk. *Easy. Easy. Breathe.* He lay on his back flat against his mattress, as flat as he could make himself. He was okay with the horizontal; it was the vertical that suddenly frightened him. What if he were dying? What if he died right here in this bed? "Elderly American Found Dead in Parisian Hotel." *Okay. You could do worse. Better than a Motel 6 somewhere. Better than on the street with a crowd of people looking down on you.*

All this he thought lying there while downstairs the Algerian brothers smiled and nodded, while cabs and trucks and motorbikes passed his open window and those heels clicking on the pavement were someone late for a job interview or waiting for biopsy results or about to fall in love. *Easy does it.* He was shaky when he got up, weak in the knees. He needed food. Across the street was a kabob stand. It was as tantalizing as it seemed unattainable, but he was sure he'd feel better if he ate. He washed his face and changed. He went down the stairs one at a time, hand on the wall. He sat at a tiny table and methodically ate a kabob and some fries. Much better.

Back in the lobby of the hotel, one of the brothers spoke to him in French, then held up an imaginary telephone receiver. When Tom didn't understand, the other brother was called from the tiny office behind the desk. "Yes," he said, "a man called for you on the telephone."

"Me? Here?"

"Yes."

"How long ago?"

"Now. Perhaps five minutes."

"Thank you." Tom started away, then came back. "In French or English?"

"French."

"Hmmm. Can you check me out and call a taxi?"

"A taxi?" The brother was a little surprised.

"Yes. To the Gare de Lyon. And then come for my bag, please."

In the cab, he told the driver, "Gare du Nord."

"Nord?"

"Oui, Nord." He looked at Paris out the window. All his life he had wanted to come here, and now he was hurrying away. He thought of me and how I would be disappointed. "They've found me. Thirty-five hours, and they've found me. How the hell did they do that?" They couldn't have gotten the letter. No.

But then he knew. Someone had noticed the cab and remembered its name. They had told Daniel Pecora that Tom was ill or senile, and he had caved in. They'd found the airline, found the flight, found the destination. Hired someone to call all the hotels in Paris. *Shit. Freedom is an illusion,* he thought. *No one's ever really free.*

At the station he waited in a toilet stall for his train so long that the attendant seemed concerned. Tom smiled and waved him off. "No, no." Only when the train was passing Sacré-Coeur, which he'd intended to visit that day, did he take a real breath and begin to feel a little better. And a little better yet when he ate the ham-and-cheese baguette and drank the Orangina he'd bought on the platform. He tried then to imagine his best day at Hanover Place: an early-morning walk around the grounds, a hot shower, a warm breakfast, working on his garden plot, reading the *New York Times* in the solarium. And then what? Waiting for lunch? Waiting for *Jeopardy* to come on? *No,* he thought as he looked out his window and his hand steadied, *this is better; this is right; this is what I want to do. Now, if they will only let me.*

He knew he had been easy to trace to Paris. He hoped he would be harder to find now, but he suspected that Thomas Wolfe had gotten it wrong: it isn't that you can't go home again but that you can never really leave.

Frenchman's Lake, July 4, 2007

The pig was done. The pig boys, Brooks's grown sons, Lou and Charlie, began to carve it. One of them brought a steaming morsel across the lawn on the end of a chef's fork to the pink chairs, where Tom tasted it and said it was the best ever. People began to line up at the pig, at the keg, and at the picnic tables to spoon out salads and to butter ears of corn. Now I was sitting on the edge of Tony's chair, holding a manila folder in my lap and watching my grandfather.

"Oh, Nora," he said when he finally noticed me. "Oh, my beautiful Nora."

"Oh, my beautiful Tom," I laughed, mimicking if not quite mocking him, "I think you're going blind. I've been sitting here for five minutes."

"I was woolgathering. Time-honored pastime of the very old."

"I have something for you." I held up the folder. "I wrote a paper about you."

"About me?"

"Based on some of what you told me last summer. I needed something for a class in personal historical narrative, and, well, I used your story. Just the first part of it, and I didn't use your family name, of course." I started to apologize, but then I didn't, and Tom seemed amused by that.

"You are certainly like your grandmother. So what grade did we get?"

I laughed. "An A, of course."

"Well, as long as it was an A. Is that it?" He nodded toward the folder in my hands.

"It is."

"May I see it?"

"Of course. That's why I brought it. I realized this might be my last chance to give it to you."

"Not so loud."

"And something else," I said more softly. "I thought just maybe I could talk you into writing the rest of it."

"Oh, I don't know ..."

"Or at least writing the part you didn't tell me about: the war years and Sarah van Praag."

No one knew what Tom would do with himself when he didn't have Tony to take care of, so the summer of Tony's death I was drafted to spend a few weeks with him. He was annoyed, and I was reluctant. He knew that he didn't need to be tended to, and, although he couldn't say it, I knew that he felt his new freedom impinged upon. As for me, I had just found the place I'd long been looking for. I had grown up in the suburbs and gone to college in a small town and didn't feel at home in either place, but I did in Evanston, where I was in grad school. It was only an hour from my parents' house and another half hour from Tom's, but it was a world apart. It was full of bookstores and coffee houses, of people who had conversations in German or Italian on park benches, of people who rode bikes to hear string quartets on

Sunday afternoons, of people who not only read books but wrote them. And I had made wonderful new friends there, witty people full of insight and passion, morose, cigarette-smoking fatalists, people with causes and complex belief systems, people who got emotional about Descartes or the Fabians or game theory over plates of noodles in cheap Thai restaurants. And then suddenly I was uprooted to babysit Tom, and in the summer, the best time of the year, when every restaurant and bar and coffee house in Evanston moved out onto the sidewalk, when there were free concerts in the park, sailboats on the lake, and I could ride my bike all the way down the shore to the Loop if I wanted to, when all I could see from my sunny sixth-floor studio was the sky above and a rolling carpet of treetops like green clouds below so that I hardly knew I was on earth, let alone in the city. And now that corner room, windows closed against storms, was stuffy and empty and the cellist from across the hall was coming in twice a week to water my ferns and I was stuck here in the land of the fish fry surrounded by big, fat people riding motorized shopping carts. And I was resentful.

I arrived with one small suitcase and two large cartons of books. It was a statement. So was my refusal to let Tom help me with any of it. I set up shop in one of the dormered bedrooms on the second floor that overlooked the lake. I used a card table as a desk and ostentatiously lined the windowsill with books. For the first three days I emerged from my room only for the dinners Tom cooked me. At that, I read at the table. On day three, over grilled salmon, roasted potatoes, and blanched asparagus, Tom said, "I want to thank you for coming out here to take care of me."

I didn't acknowledge his sarcasm, but the next afternoon I came to sit in Tony's chair beside Tom. Still, I read and took notes on a legal pad. In fairness, I had lots of work to do. The next day

I came again and finally put my book and pad down. When I did, Tom said, "D'you like Evanston?"

"I love it," I said, a little fiercely, I suppose, as if to contrast Evanston and un-Evanston, which was here.

"Chandler's still there?"

"What's Chandler's?"

"The bookstore."

"I don't think so. How do you know about that?"

"I did my master's at Northwestern on the GI Bill after the war."

"In education?"

"In English lit. Spent a lot of time there."

"Did you live there?"

"No, no. Tony and Brooks had already been born. We lived right here. Bought this place in 1950."

"Then you did it by extension?"

"No. I drove back and forth once a week. Took whatever was offered in the late afternoon. Made for an odd mix of classes, but then I went a couple of summers, too."

"That must have been a long drive back then."

"Well, not too bad. The roads weren't as good, but the traffic was better. It's kind of a wash, I guess, like most things."

"Like most things," I repeated, probably a bit too pointedly. "You believe that?"

"Do I believe that?" he asked himself. He thought he did. He talked about balance in life, yin and yang, the whole equal to the sum of its parts.

It should be said that a few years earlier I had been a sweet, compliant girl, and now I am—at least I hope I am—a fairly confident, fairly grounded woman. But the summer that I went to stay with Tom, I was in transition. I was just learning to be assertive, and I wasn't very good at it yet. I was practicing on Tom and other family members because I thought correctly that they, unlike my professors and fellow grad students, were either intellectually or emotionally incapable of attacking and destroying me, although in truth I didn't know my grandfather very well at all, didn't even know what to call him anymore. It had always been "Grandpa," but that now seemed juvenile or perhaps rural, so I called him "Tom," and he let me.

"Is that the organizing principle of your life, then?" I remember asking.

"One of them, I suppose. What are the organizing principles of your life?"

Well, I didn't really have any yet, at least none that were firm and formulated, so I said something silly I'd heard someone else say about life being a kaleidoscope of rotating, concentric spheres.

Tom said, "Hmm."

The next afternoon I came outside with a pack of cigarettes. I shook one out and lit it a little defiantly without asking Tom if he minded. Tom pointed at the pack. "Okay if I have one?"

"A cigarette?"

"Uh-huh."

"I've never seen you smoke a cigarette."

"I've never smoked one in your lifetime, but I used to smoke a lot of them." He took one, lit it, and inhaled it. "Whew. First pull still makes me dizzy."

We sat that way for a bit, smoking together, looking at the lake. "No book today," he noticed. "Sometimes it's hard to put 'em down."

"Sometimes," I said noncommittally, uncertain whether or not he was being sarcastic.

"You remind me of me when I was falling in love with literature before the war. Got a job as a night watchman at a factory in Waukegan and sat in a little booth all summer just reading. Read twenty-two books. Didn't understand a damn thing. Didn't night-watch a damn thing, either." Before I could take offense, which I was quite inclined to do then, he waved it away. "'Course I was much younger. Still in college. You," he said, "I'm thinking you might be looking for a dissertation topic."

I was, of course, but I wasn't going to admit that he was right. "Not really."

"What are you working on?"

"Oh, just some interviews. They're part of my research assistantship. I'm helping a professor with an oral-history project."

When he saw that I was being intentionally vague, he didn't ask any more, but another day he said, "Only oral historian I know is Studs Terkel, and I suppose he's not a real historian, but I did like The Good War."

"Because you fought in it?"

"Yes, and he got it right, I think, although the people who quote him all the time, mostly politicians, must not have read the book because they don't seem to know that the title is ironic, or else they're just stupid."

"Ironic?"

"As in 'There's no such thing as a good war.'"

"Not even World War II?"

"Especially not World War II."

"I didn't know you felt that way."

"I do."

"You were in Europe, weren't you?"

"Uh-huh."

"Where?"

"England, Belgium, Holland, Germany."

"Why wasn't it a good war?"

"Sixty million people died. Only one of them was Adolf Hitler. None of them was Hirohito."

That warm evening we ate dinner at the picnic table on the lawn, and Tom opened a bottle of dry rosé wine. Perhaps it was our earlier conversation, or perhaps it was the wine; I'd only recently been taught to distinguish dry pink wine from sweet (I remember being a little surprised that he knew the difference) and to enjoy its chilled tartness. Perhaps it was the evening or the high lacy clouds lolling about the heavens. I'm not sure what it was, but when Tom asked about my research, I answered him. I had resolved not to, of course, long before I came and several times since on the assumption that he would either be offended, like my parents, or amused. I found myself turning to him (we had pushed our plates aside and were lingering on this perfect night over the wine and cigarettes as the colors of the day flattened, faded, and sank into the darkness and the lake) and answering without hesitation or reservation.

"I'm helping a professor named Maria Donlon write a book. It's a bunch of case studies, really, that have to do with the failure of marriage in the twentieth century. Interviews with contemporary women." I went on to describe several of the women as he listened and nodded. Women who had bought into an institution designed by the male architects of our patriarchal society to fail them or even exploit them. Women for whom the social contract had turned out to be a death sentence or, if that was a little too strong, at least a form of imprisonment.

When Tom said, "Why only women?" I remembered instantly and exactly why I had resolved not to talk to him about any of this in the first place, and I cursed myself for letting my guard down. Of course he wouldn't understand. Of course he would take offense. He was a man, and an old man at that. What had Belchirre said in class that day? "They are still living in the twentieth century." He had both shocked and amazed me that the epoch in which I'd been born, everything had been born, was now gone, was truly history. And, of course, Tom belonged to it. (I was now trying hard not to.) I explained semipatiently (I suppose I didn't mind betraying a little frustration) that an institution set up by men to serve men could not, by definition, fail men except, perhaps, situationally, certainly not systematically.

"Still," he said, "might be interesting to get a male point of view, Nora." Yes, I agreed, but that would be another book altogether. This one was not about men; it was about women. It was not intended to be balanced or fair or objective. Those were all twentieth-century thinking. This was something different. This was a polemic, not a dialogue, not a discussion.

"I see," he said. "Now I see." And of course I immediately felt guilty for quite intentionally and unkindly patronizing him. The hardest part was how predictable I was with him. Embarrassingly predictable, and he wasn't at all, so that when he said the expected, I seized on it as if to make a point. It was supposed to be the other way around.

I didn't sleep well that night. I thought about my grandfather. All the things I'd assumed. All the things I didn't know. I thought about the watery blue eyes through which he had been watching me, a quiet voyeur observing my naked pretension, his long face that I realized suddenly might once have been handsome, his odd, old sense of humor; where had he learned that? His patience.

In the morning I went around the house looking at photographs of Tom Johnson. I opened photo albums and yearbooks. I studied him as a younger man and then a young man. I found pictures of him as a boy. Then I went out and sat beside him in the pink chair. "May I ask you a question?"

He looked up from his book and smiled.

"How did you meet Julia?"

"Your grandmother? Do you really want to know?"

"I really do."

He studied me for a while. "Well, let's see ..."

Now here I was sitting in Tony's chair again, holding Tom's story.

"Tell you what," he said, "I'll read it on the plane."

"You ready?" I asked. At first, he told me later, he wasn't going to tell anyone, but then that didn't seem quite right. It was too punitive or angry. No, he finally decided that he wanted one person in the world to know where he was and what he was doing, and to my surprise it was me.

"I think so. I hope so."

"Using your MP3 player?"

"I listen to it every day. Love it."

"You been going to the library to check your e-mail?"

"Often as I can."

I cocked my head. "I sent you a message."

"I haven't gotten there in a couple days," he confessed.

"You're an old dog, Tom, and it's a new trick."

"Well, I imagine they have dog trainers over there, too. Very civilized little country. I've been reading about it online."

I smiled and decided to let him off the hook. "Running away from home," I teased him quietly, "at your age!"

"Isn't that funny? No, running away is what children and convicts do. That's why children come back and convicts get caught.

I'm not running away," he said, seemingly aware that some mild petulance had crept into his voice. "Now, there's something I need to ask you." He said he wasn't going to need a car any longer, was ready to give up driving anyway. He wondered if I'd like to have his little truck. Not much of a city vehicle, he said; "You might not want it."

But I did. I could already see myself picking up Catherine or maybe Hector in it, waiting on the street, gunning the engine a little. I could imagine myself one day having a dog to ride in the back of it. I was already thinking about buying a pair of black lace-up combat boots at the Army Surplus Store.

"Title's in the glove box, signed. You can take it tonight if you want. Drive it home."

"If I do, I don't know when I'll see this place again."

"I never will." Of course that meant we might never see each other again, either, but that was more difficult to say. No, it was easier to talk about the old frame house with the big screened porch across the front, which I turned now to look at, the lawn, the lake, the cottonwood trees at the water's edge.

"How many years, Tom?"

"Fifty-seven." He'd obviously figured this out recently. "Long time."

"I remember the first time you ever saw it," I said, "or really the first time you ever didn't see it. In fact, I put it in my paper."

Nora Panco
Narrative History

Thomas J.
The Personal History of a
Man and a Marriage
1946 to 1996

GIs came back from World War II to a new world. The Depression was over, prosperity and conformity abounded, the suburbanization of the country was beginning, and the interstate highway system was soon to follow. Institutions as diverse as education and marriage were about to be redefined, as were the roles of both men and women.

Thomas J. was one of those returning GIs. Today he is eighty-four years old. He is a tall, thin man with a white crew cut that bristles, square features in a square face, a stern demeanor, an easy smile indicative of his personal warmth and wisdom but a certain edge that is sad and bitter. A retired teacher, he lives alone in northern Illinois in a rambling lake house filled with books, music, and family photographs.

The Fourth of July parade in 1946 is Tom J.'s first distinct memory of his return from the war. He and other GIs assembled on the ball diamond in the city park in Frenchman's Lake, Illinois. He remembers it as a macabre accounting that was almost more about the people who were not there than the people who were: six men from his high school class alone had died in the war.

The parade, complete with the high school marching band, the Shriners in fezzes and on little motorbikes, a couple of old tanks, and some World War I veterans on horseback, was another odd combination of mourning and celebration. As Tom put it, "We walked down the street with all of our feelings and everyone else stood along the curb with all of theirs." Tom's included exhilaration, survivor's guilt, and a good bit of residual fear.

After the parade there was a picnic in a park by the lake, and although Tom had dreamed of just such a gathering many times during the war, he found it almost unbearably anticlimactic. He was just about to leave when Julia P. stopped to say hello. Tom was flattered. Julia P. née Julia L. was two years his senior. Her father owned an auto dealership, and she drove a roadster, often with a cigarette dangling from her lips. By local standards she was a sophisticate and, with her square shoulders and long legs, was sometimes compared to Lauren Bacall. Tom had had a schoolboy crush on Julia but did not remember her ever speaking to him before the picnic. Then she did so quite familiarly. She said she hadn't been surprised when she'd heard that he'd gone to Officer Candidate School, for instance, and when he downplayed the Bronze Star he'd been awarded, she said she didn't remember him being so modest. Tom was surprised that she remembered him at all.

Julia had left college after a year to marry a football star named Buddy P., but he had died on Omaha Beach on D-day. When Tom expressed his condolences, she was touched, and he was touched in turn, so when Julia's father, mother, and two brothers came by in their locally famous Chris-Craft motorboat, she invited him to join them. They cruised around, waiting for the fireworks—the first since before the war—and Mr. L. spoke as he piloted the boat about the lake's legends; there was supposed to be the rusted carcass of a 1934 LaSalle touring car on the bottom at the south end that had been driven by some of Al Capone's men who were being chased by federal agents when it went through the ice. Mr. L. claimed to have once sold Capone a Lincoln. Tom thought him something of a blowhard. He also noticed that when speaking of his wife and daughter, Mr. L. used pronouns rather than their names.

After that night Tom was smitten, but he couldn't even begin to entertain the notion that Julia might be interested in him. Besides, he had other things on his mind. Although he had majored in English and Spanish in college, he had applied to a graduate program in history at the University of Wisconsin in Madison at least in part because he had now taken part in some of it, and he had an interview with the head of the department, Robert Whalen, the next day. The interview did not go well. The head was a busy, impatient man who was clearly skeptical about the value of the GI Bill and Tom's motives for wanting to "read history." Still, he gave Tom a long bibliography and a paper assignment to be submitted in August. Tom understood this to be a kind of entrance exam.

The next day, back at home, Julia called him and invited him for another boat ride. Tom remembers it because he had never before received a personal phone call from a woman. He went out and bought deck shoes. He assumed that he would again be part of a group, but when he got to the dock, Julia was alone. They sped around for a while—Julia liked going fast—and then anchored offshore from the house they would eventually buy and live in most of their lives. Tom didn't know this at the time, of course. He wasn't looking at houses; he was looking at Julia. She was unlike any woman he had known. She swore like a sailor, called women "dames," smoked Pall Malls, tossed the anchor into the water by herself, and, with bare feet and legs, was casual to the point of immodesty. At various times Tom describes her as salty, earthy, original, and fiercely independent. Still, there were contradictions in her that, if they didn't bother him, at least struck him as curious. Why had she dropped out of school and married a hometown hero? And after his death, why had she stayed in town? More than anything else, why did she tolerate her father's disregard? But these things probably didn't occur to him that night. That night he remembers as magical. They drank wine and lay back on the leather engine cover in the stern, looking at the stars and telling each other their dreams. He thinks he probably talked of a new world order, a second League of Nations, a great alliance of free countries that would shape the future. "I was very determined to make some kind of sense out of the war and its devastation." Of Julia's dreams he remembers little. "Perhaps that was a problem even then," he says. What he does remember is that she told him he was cute when he was saving the world.

That July was a whirlwind of a month. During the days Tom worked on his paper. He piled the dining room table high with books, journals, and abstracts, perhaps emulating Professor Whalen, certainly asserting his privilege as an adult and a war veteran. The nights he and Julia spent on the lake, often until after midnight. Sometimes they ate, sometimes they just drank and smoked, always they talked, and occasionally toward the end of the month they lay in each other's arms and listened to music from a dance club on the shore. Tom remembers wondering if they were in love. During the war he had been in love with a Dutch girl, and this was somehow different.

Around the first of August Tom showed up one night, and there were three other people on the boat: a couple named Bonnie and Chuck whom he knew vaguely and a somewhat older fellow named Briggs S. of whom he had often heard. Looking back on it later, Tom would wonder why they had been invited. Had Julia grown tired of him? Was she trying to ease away because she knew he might be leaving soon and didn't want to be hurt? Was she trying to integrate him into her life? Or was she trying to get his distracted attention and make him jealous? Whatever it was, the evening had a staged quality about it.

Briggs was from a prominent family that owned the town's only factory, one that produced ball bearings. He had not gone to war himself, and some people said it was because he had a heart murmur, others because he had been exempted in order to manage the plant, which had run around the clock to supply the war effort. Briggs had already been drinking and immediately engaged Tom in a political discussion. "I was a sucker for it," Tom remembers; this was because of his enthusiasm for the Marshall Plan, which had just been proposed. He praised it as a whole new concept. His first inkling that Briggs was picking a fight came when Briggs said something like "Here's a whole new concept: to the vanquished go the spoils." Still, Briggs was alternately flattering and aggressive. He praised Tom for his heroism and modesty while teasing him about his politics and naïveté. Tom went along in order to please Julia (it was clear that she and Briggs knew each other well) and because he was intimidated by the older, more confident man. He doesn't remember what they were drinking but thinks it might have been bourbon. As the evening advanced, Briggs got drunker and more hostile. He attacked Roosevelt, the

University of Wisconsin, and "Jew bankers." He sang the praises of Douglas MacArthur and George Patton. At some point his attack turned personal; he insisted on calling Tom "Tommy" and made fun of him for being in charge of "toilet paper and sardines" during the war because Tom had been a supply officer. In the end, perhaps fueled by the liquor himself, Tom answered back. Chuck and Bonnie tried unsuccessfully to break it up, and finally Julia stepped in. She accused Briggs of being drunk and Tom of being immature. He was surprised and hurt. He had simply assumed that she was on his side. He asked to be taken back to the dock. Julia refused and said, "Don't be childish." Tom swam ashore, holding his deck shoes out of the water. He remembers Briggs yelling after him, "Don't get those Thom McAns wet. They might run," and he remembers more than one person laughing at the joke. He was humiliated. Ironically, the "Thom McAns" (an inexpensive brand of shoes) did run, and Tom threw them away.

Tom felt as if the whole town were laughing at him. Neither he nor Julia called the other. He stayed home, licked his wounds, and worked on his paper. It became his refuge and his chance to escape what seemed to him the provincialism and narrow-mindedness of Frenchman's Lake. "I was wounded. I came back from the war thinking that I was a man of the world, and now I felt like a schoolboy again." He realized all of this when he happened by the town's high school one day and was enthusiastically received by the principal, who wanted to know all about the war and Tom's plans. He offered Tom a job teaching history on the spot. Tom's flagging spirits were buoyed. At least someone wasn't laughing at him. At the same time, he hoped he had not betrayed the distaste he felt for teaching high school when he declined the principal's offer.

Tom hand-delivered his paper to Professor Whalen, whose

only response was "Self-addressed, stamped envelope?" A week later he got it back in the mail. He still has it; he displays it with some pride and care. The early comments are terse: "Unsupportable thesis," "Expand here," "Weak source." Then they get a little more conversational: "Interesting premise—develop more fully," "See McCracken on this point in current Public Policy." Finally there is a long page of notes that ends with these words: "This is quite impressive work. With a little polish, it might be publishable. Welcome to Wisconsin, Lieutenant."

Tom went back to Madison. He enrolled in classes, bought books, rented a room that had a bay window overlooking a dogwood tree, ate the baked-ham sandwiches and potato salad his mother had packed for him, and slept in the backseat of his father's car beside Lake Mendota, dreaming about his future: Professor Thomas J., Dr. J. He imagined a leafy little college somewhere or a cluttered office like Whalen's in an old sandstone building on a major campus, papers published, a book, students waiting outside his door, conferences and symposiums.

The next day back in Frenchman's Lake his mother called up the stairs that Julia was sitting in her car in front of the house. He looked out the window. She was parked, just sitting there, hands on the wheel as if she were driving. Tom went out and stood on the parkway beside the car. Julia told him she was pregnant. She called this a "courtesy." She said he was not to worry; arrangements had been made, and it would be clean and safe. She said all of this without looking at Tom.

She also said that he was the only man she had slept with besides her husband, and that included Briggs S., whom she called a "goddamn drunk and lout." She said that Tom should have seen that. Then she wept. He had never seen her cry before; her tears and sobs erased the echoing laughter from the last night on the lake. He got into the car and held Julia. Before he had admired her for her grace, coolness, and irony; now he loved her for the sadness, loneliness, and fear he realized those things were disguising. But when he told her he loved her, she grew angry and argued with him. He had to plead with her. He had to go further. He said he wanted to marry Julia and have the baby. He said he wanted to spend his life with her and wanted them to grow old together. He said that this was why they had fought the war and men had given their lives, so the two of them could fill up the world with babies. She made him promise that he would never leave her, and he did it. She made him swear to God, and he did it. She asked him over and over if he loved her; she did not, however, say that she loved him. Tom remembers this because he was waiting for the words she didn't say. He thinks now that she didn't say them not because she didn't love him but because it didn't matter; all that mattered was that he loved her. Julia wept, and Tom held her tight, resolving to love her enough to make up for everything that had gone awry in what now appeared to be her tragic life. Only afterward did he come to realize that he had promised more than one could or should and that his promises were a form of emotional condescension that would eventually create resentment and distrust. Also that Julia had revealed things about herself she hadn't wanted to and seldom would again.

Perhaps this was why, a few days later, as they drove to Keokuk, Iowa, to get married, Tom assumed that the high emotions of the earlier day had broken a logjam when the opposite seemed to be the case. Julia was remote. She acted as if she were embarrassed by all that had happened and deflected any references Tom made to it. He remembers being concerned. He wondered for the first time if Julia was capable of love or even vulnerability. He thought of her indifferent father, of her emotionless mother, and of Buddy P., who drank beer and played softball in the city park, who flipped his bat away, who Tom once saw run over the catcher and not even help him up. Tom admitted to himself that Buddy the war hero had also been arrogant. Why, he wondered, had Julia married him? And crossing the cornfields that day en route to Iowa, Tom wondered if he was making a horrible mistake. He banished the thought. He had it, but he banished it. He chose to think that he was experiencing cold feet or the jitters. He knew that what he was doing was both necessary and noble. What he did not know was that Julia would come to see it as a smug sacrifice, a superior gesture of rescue only serving to show that the most the world was going to offer her was pity, and Tom thinks that that would ultimately make her, in his words, "definitively angry."

Despite his uneasiness, Tom was to have fond memories of that day and night, of the plain little courtroom in which they were married, of eating hamburgers afterward and playing gin rummy until midnight in a motor court near Dubuque because neither of them knew if a pregnant woman could have intercourse. In fact, so does he have good memories of the first six months of their marriage; he thinks it may have been their best time. They were performing, he says, as young people do when thrust into new roles, but in those roles he thinks they were happy, or at least too busy to be unhappy. He had been hired to teach English at the high school after all (the history positions had all been filled) and was busy staying one step ahead of his students, and she was busy setting up their house, being a wife again and preparing to be a mother. No one seemed to mind that they were suddenly married and pregnant; the war had allowed for the relaxation of the rules. They went to movies or out for ice cream with other couples, played bridge, and were invited for dinner to their parents' hous-es. They lived in a garage apartment and called each other "dear" and "sweetheart" even though the words sounded like they had borrowed them from their parents, as they had furniture, dishes, and flatware. Each was leaving something behind. For Julia, it was her first marriage. For Tom, it was the war and the Dutch girl who had broken his heart. He wanted to prove something to that girl and to himself. He wished that he could take snapshots of his new life and send them to her.

Their first fight was about the baby's name. If a boy, Julia wanted to call him Russell after her father and Tom wanted to name him Anthony after a comrade who had died in the war. For a while they jousted good-naturedly about this, but one day Julia said that Anthony didn't sound American. Tom took offense, he thinks perhaps because he had some guilt about his relationship with the dead man, whom he felt he had judged and let down; in reality, he hadn't really known the man very well and certainly not well enough to name a child after him. He made fun of Julia and her family for being big fish in a small pond and said something unkind about her father's name. She defended her father, saying that at least he would never have spent his honeymoon in Iowa. Tom was taken aback, as he had been the night with Briggs on the boat; he had simply assumed again that he and Julia agreed about something that they didn't.

One day in March a letter arrived for Tom at his parents' house. It had multiple postmarks, the first of which was June 1946. Tom read the letter standing in the foyer. He read it over and over.

Dearest Tom,

I have made a dreadful mistake. I am so sorry we had a row. I meant none of the foolish, cruel things I said. I was frightened. Please forgive me. I wish I could take away what I have done, but I cannot. I know that I will probably never see you again, and that

*is a bigger reason for me to tell you that I love you, and I always
will. If you can come back, I shall be waiting for you. I am yours,*
   Sarah

A month later Tom and Julia's baby, being breech, was born
by cesarean section. He was very small. Tom remembers seeing a
nurse holding him as if he were a broken vase. He remembers the
young doctor's fumbling attempts to explain the baby's condition. In his awkwardness he was too technical. Finally Julia interrupted him and said, "He's got a birth defect, hasn't he?" The
doctor said no, not exactly. "He's retarded, isn't he?" Julia asked.

"He has a condition called Mongolism,"[1] the doctor finally
managed to say.

Tom remembers that it was an early warm day. People kept
commenting on it. The room was hot. Someone opened the window. Tom and Julia agreed to name the baby Russell Anthony
and to call him Tony so his name wouldn't get confused with her
father's.

As an infant Tony was so small that Tom could almost hold
him in his hand and certainly in the crook of his arm. He was
amorphous and still, "like a sock monkey" with no apparent skel-
eton or muscle tone. He was content to lean against any part of
Tom, and it was Tom who held him at first while Julia recovered
from surgery. When she did begin to carry the baby around, it
was in a way that Tom calls cavalier; slung over a shoulder or later

---

1   Tony's condition was called Mongolism because one of its characteristics is an extra
eyelid fold that creates almond-shaped eyes. Others include slightness of stature, abnor-
malities in the structure of the heart, an extra crease in the flesh of the hands, and mental
impairment. The syndrome was first identified by John Langdon Down in the 1860s and
today bears his name. Its cause, an extra copy of chromosome 21 resulting in the condition
trisomy 21, was discovered by Jerome Lejeune in 1959. At that time people with Down
syndrome were typically institutionalized in childhood and seldom lived beyond thirty.
Today they are usually integrated into their families and communities, and their life ex-
pectancy is between fifty and sixty.

riding on her cocked hip almost like a duffel bag. She was the same kind of mother that she was a wife and friend and later business partner: no-nonsense. "The baby's defective, Tom," she once said. "Call a spade a spade, for the love of Mike." What both Tom and Julia knew but never said was that he had wanted the baby and she had not, that they had made an agreement from which there was no escape. "That may sound like a compromise made in hell," Tom says today, "but it wasn't." For one thing, it was based on some truth. For another, all around them Tom and Julia saw couples making astounding but functional deals to accommodate each other's delusions, phobias, and dreams. For a third, while their deal was far from perfect, it was absolutely necessary.

One night before Julia and the baby came home from the hospital, Tom smoked two baby cigars, got drunk on Dutch gin, listened to the jazz records he had brought home from the war, and wrote a half-a-dozen letters to Sarah v. P. In the morning he tore them all up and then, with a shaky hand, wrote one more. He was numb as he walked to the post office and then the hospital. From that time forward he tried not to think about the Dutch woman because to do so seemed like either self-pity or disloyalty to Julia, whom he was trying very hard to love and to change, as she was trying very hard to love and change him, a process both would continue for most of the next twenty years. "And that was a mistake," he says today, "or perhaps a red flag because what you are saying to the person you are trying to change is 'I don't like you as you are.'" And apparently they did not, although for many years they tried to. In the beginning she laughed at some of his jokes and enjoyed his roughhousing with her parents' dogs. He liked to hear her sing and watch her water ski. He appreciated her offhanded creativity in the kitchen and good nose for unusual music; he remembers nights when they sat on the floor listening to records, drinking wine, passing cigarettes back and forth, and "talking in that way that you think is intimate when you are tipsy."

They had enough such romantic moments to keep them going and to produce two more children. Brooks was born thirteen months after Tony and Christine two years later. By that time they were living in a two-bedroom apartment, and they needed a house. Julia and her mother had found one. It was a brick salt box on the second-best street in town. When Tom said it was a banker's house, not a teacher's, Julia said he didn't have to be a teacher the rest of his life. When Tom said they couldn't afford it, Julia said her father was going to help them buy it. She should have said that he was willing to help them buy it. Tom said no. He surprised both of them; he did not know how strongly he felt about being beholden to Julia's family. What followed was their second big fight. Tom remembers it now because the words said that day, with variations and refinements, became their basic script, one that they could fall into easily and almost instantly and reference or set off with a key word or two. Julia said that he was too proud, an elitist, a phony intellectual, a jealous little man who was scared of his own shadow and had a big head because high school girls had crushes on him, a reverse snob who looked down his nose at her family because they were rich and successful. Tom claims with an embarrassed smile not to remember his part of the exchange quite as well but admits it probably included such words as "philistine," "Babbitt," "bourgeois," and "materialistic." What he does remember is that that day they hurt each other in ways that never healed and that in the years to come they would spend a great deal of time trying to explain and apologize for those words but also repeating them. And he remembers laughing at his wife for the first time and realizing just how furious it made her. "I'm afraid it was a trick I used often after that."

That day the fight ended with Julia shouting, "Find your own goddamn house and live in it alone, you bastard, or with your goddamn Dutch whore!" Tom ignored the latter part, but in more or less short order he found the lake house that we sat in front of during our interviews. It was inexpensive because it was a cottage without a foundation (they would later dig one and build two additions), and in those days everyone wanted to live in the town. Only fishermen, hunters, and people who could not afford town houses lived on the lake, but Tom was able to talk Julia into it because it had a dock where her father could keep his boat and a lawn down to the lake on which it was easy to imagine children playing. The compromise was that they would let Russell L. remodel and furnish the place. Tom tried to do as much of the work as he could and to not notice how much Julia's father was spending, but in the end all that really mattered to him was that it was he who was making the mortgage payment each month. This allowed him to feel independent and self-sufficient. Still, it was during this time that Julia first used the term "my money," as in "This is coming out of my money" or "Don't worry, I'm using my money." Where that money came from and how much there was of it was never discussed, but it became clear that its use was discretionary and that she believed they could not get along without it.

At the same time her parents kept offering Tom things. For Christmas they gave him a family membership to the country club and tried to get him to take up golf. He played a few times with Julia and her parents or with Frankie and Warren, her brothers, who always made a point of talking about how much money they made and how much time they had for golf. Tom did not like golf or much about the country club except club sandwiches. "I did develop a taste for those." He used Christine's birth as an excuse to beg off from golf games, saying that he was just too busy with school, the house, and the kids and hoping that Julia's father would understand. "Russ turned out to be a hard man not to offend." But he didn't give up. One summer he talked Tom into working on the showroom floor as a salesman. Almost immediately he made two sales. Both customers traded in their Lincolns every year, and Julia's father simply sent them to Tom. Then he bought him a big cigar and took him out to lunch. He talked about retirement, a pretty little piece of beachfront property in a village called Naples on the southwest coast of Florida where he hoped to end up, and leaving the agency in the hands of Frankie, Warren, and Tom if he was interested. At that moment Tom thought he might be. "I felt like Jimmy Stewart on the other side of Potter's big desk," a reference to Frank Capra's 1946 film *It's a Wonderful Life.* But then Russ, working on his second martini, said the wrong thing. It was something like "Besides, you don't want to spend your life in the world of women and children, do you? You got too much on the ball for that. I mean, I think it's fine you put in a few years. Public service kind of thing. Sure. But for Chrissake, Tom, you don't want to be a schoolteacher your whole life."

Tom smiles wryly at the memory. "Funny thing is, until that moment, I don't think I did," but after that, the thought of working with his father-in-law made everything inside Tom feel as if it were sinking: the money, the clothes, the handshakes, the uncertainty in the other man's eyes because he was wondering if Tom's only interest was in selling him a car. Even more than that, it was living the life Julia so desperately wanted him to live; quite early on their relationship had defined itself as a competition in which they needed to oppose each other in almost everything. Besides, to his surprise Tom had begun to like teaching and to think that it might be important. A former student in a perfectly pressed Coast Guard uniform with the bill of his peaked cap pulled right down over his eyebrows came back to visit. He said Tom was the only teacher who had ever listened to him. Strangely, Tom could not remember the boy ever saying a word in class, but when a chance to teach American history in summer school came along, Tom took it. He never again played golf or sold cars.

But if Julia tried to change Tom, he also tried to change her. He clipped New Yorker articles for her that she never read, played her jazz and chamber music records, even dragged her to French movies in the city once or twice. They each managed to regularly find a way of saying, "See, this is whom I really want you to be. This is the person I really wish I'd married." And there were other cracks in the dam. A major one appeared when Tony reached school age. There was no special education yet. Six years of age was the time when children with Down syndrome often were sent away, and that was what Julia wanted to do with Tony. "Then the dinner table would be balanced," says Tom, still with sarcasm in his voice. "Two parents, two kids, two males, two females, all with forty-six chromosomes." Tom objected. They fought. In the end he prevailed by agreeing to take total responsibility for Tony, but it was another nail in the coffin of their marriage. Today he muses, "I wonder now if at that moment I'd accepted her, realized that she was telling me that she had limits, that she was asking for my support … but back then I just couldn't do that; I wasn't capable of it, I'm sorry to say. Besides, it would have meant pretty much giving up on Tony."

Instead Tony grew up in Tom's classroom, first as a little boy dusting erasers or curled up with a cookie and a carton of chocolate milk on a Mickey Mouse throw rug under Tom's desk, later as a passer-out and collector of things, a roll taker and a pencil sharpener. Later still as errand boy, message runner, member of the theater crew, and manager of the football team. Once or twice he took part in a talent-show skit, and when his class graduated, Tony was allowed to cross the stage with them. A great cheer went up that was not entirely facetious. After that Tony worked as a bagger and stocker at the IGA.

Tom admits now that he didn't know Tony well at first. He didn't know that he was a rule follower who never cursed or swore, a hard worker who was never happier than when he had a job, a tender, sensitive boy who longed for the companionship of a dog, who loved sentimental songs and silly puns, appreciated pretty girls, and was as loyal as the day was long; he became a Pirates fan when his best friend moved to Pittsburgh at the age of nine, and he rooted for them the rest of his life. In fact, Tom suspects his own motives in undertaking to rear Tony. He thinks he was probably making a statement about himself, or perhaps about Julia. "I did it for all the wrong reasons, but I was lucky," Tom says. "I think Tony probably saved my soul."

It was that summer when Tony was six that Julia started going to the dealership every day as soon as Tom came in the door from school, but it wasn't until he stopped in there for something and saw her sitting at a desk in a glass-fronted office that he realized she was working. And although he didn't know it yet, she had fundamentally changed the rules of their game: she was shooting the moon. The changes in their day-to-day lives were subtle and gradual but real. They were changes in priorities, duties, and expectations; now it was Julia who had an early meeting or a late one, who needed the car, who stayed up working at the dining room table, for whom the kids needed to be quiet so as not to disturb, who brought home chop suey or piled everyone in the car to treat them to cheeseburgers at the club. Less and less often did she and Tom share a special bottle of wine and a quiet evening. In truth, they'd stopped confiding in each other or talking about anything of much importance, but this was a fact that it was easy to overlook or ignore because they had other things to discuss, from grades to sales figures, from Little League games to dance recitals to proms and college applications. And they carried on all the formalities: Sunday dinners, Christmas mornings, Fourth of July parties.

They carried on and might have done so indefinitely had it not been for Julia's father's death. For some time Julia had been Russ's chauffeur, first because he was losing his eyesight and second because it seemed the one thing he was capable of telling her she did well. The phone would ring and she'd be out the door. Tom found this annoying and sometimes insulting, especially when it took precedence over his own work at the school, so one morning when Julia asked him to stay with one of the kids who had a high fever and go in late so she could run Russ to the airport, he refused. Worse, he lied. He said he couldn't because his students were reading assigned parts from Act V of *Hamlet* aloud, and he'd made special arrangements to use the theater and to tape-record their performances. In fact, the whole senior class was out on a field trip that day.

Julia's father drove himself, ran a red light near O'Hare, and was broadsided by a cement truck and killed instantly. When Julia showed up at the school to tell Tom, she found him sitting alone in his classroom, grading papers. She stood in the doorway, blinking and looking at the empty desks.

Tom and Julia were to stay together until her death in 1996 because "that's what people of our generation did," but their marriage effectively ended that day. They saw less and less of each other. Julia stopped cooking, and there were lots of pizzas and tubs of chicken. Communication was increasingly by notes left on the refrigerator or under the windshield wiper. Soon Julia moved into the spare bedroom. She did not even say it was because Tom snored. For Christmas she renewed his subscription to the *New Yorker,* and he gave her some kitchen utensil or other. "In the end," he says, "irony was the only form of intimacy we continued to share."

Studies of the marriages of returning World War II GIs, including those by J. P. Arnold and Cynthia Berger, Matson B. Toms, and Philip Kapstein, suggest that Tom and Julia's marriage was of a type. In *Mid-Century Marriages,* Kapstein identifies this group as survivors of the war and Depression, most of whom were Caucasian, Christian and frequently Roman Catholic, middle class, and increasingly suburban, who stayed together despite personal dissatisfaction and often unhappiness, changing social mores, and no-fault divorce laws that saw divorce rates double between 1950 and 1979. He labeled them "the Undivorced" because they were people caught on a cultural cusp.

On the one hand they were inheritors of nineteenth-century values that saw marriage in the unsentimental terms of a partnership between a dominant husband whose job it was to make money and decisions and a submissive wife whose job it was to bear, rear, and often bury children. Such partnerships were bound together more by duty and loyalty than by love. On the other hand, these people's sensibilities were shaped by the twentieth century with its growing popular belief in free will, increasing educational and employment opportunities for women, and romantic notions of life and love cultivated by popular literature, the music of Tin Pan Alley, and the films of Hollywood. These two forces were in conflict not only in the marriages Kapstein portrays among "the Undivorced" but in the individuals in those marriages. I submit that Tom and Julia J. were such individuals in such a marriage.

Antwerp, July 8, 2007

In Antwerp Tom took a room in a pleasant modern hotel on the square in front of the Central Station. He rested. He snoozed in the sunshine that came through the big windows. He thought about the beds of bright flowers in the park across the street. They reassured him. He needed a little reassurance. But in the park there was also a bench, and on the bench facing the hotel, seeming to face his very room, sat a black man wearing a Dodgers cap slightly cocked to one side, so when Tom started to make his way toward the cathedral, he went out the back door of the hotel and followed a street of sidewalk restaurants beneath big awnings. t He turned into a broad pedestrian avenue that swept around dramatically toward the center and was lined with grand, ornate buildings in the Belgian style, only now all of their ground floors were shops, banks, and fast-food restaurants with plate-glass windows and bright plastic signs. Neither this nor anything else he had seen matched his memory of this place. The cathedral had not changed since the war, of course, and yet it had because everything else had changed. It was surrounded by curio shops and tourist restaurants advertising their daily specials on blackboards, banks of tables and chairs and umbrellas, kids heavily pierced, kids heavily tattooed, Peruvian musicians, and middle-aged couples from all over the world looking at guidebooks, so that the ancient church seemed oafish and a bit ironic, like an adult sitting on a child's chair. Tom sat in front of it and had a Belgian wit-bier. It was light and spicy and refreshed him. He studied people as they passed. He did not see the black man. He looked at the cathedral and wondered if it was a metaphor for the church itself: a relic, an irrelevance, at times an embarrassment. Perhaps it also stood for his more personal conflict, the one between the past and the present, what the world wanted him to do and what he was doing.

He looked down a tiny lane that opened off the square. The more he looked at it, the more familiar it seemed. Finally he paid the tab and walked down the lane, and then another, and then a third, which was shaded and quiet and off which there opened double doors into a modest lobby. He waited at the desk until a young African woman appeared.

"Do you speak English?" Tom asked.

"Yes."

"Did this used to be the Hotel Metropole?"

"I do not know. How long ago?"

"Sixty years. Sixty years ago."

"Oh, I don't know. Who would know that?"

That evening he ate in a tourist restaurant with leaded-glass windows on the side of the cathedral. It, too, felt faintly familiar. He ordered mussels and frites, though mussels were not in season, and drank a different Belgian beer with his meal. He took his time. He thought, It's possible that this is as close as I come.

When he walked back through the square, the black man was sitting alone in a sidewalk café. He did not get up, and he did not follow Tom.. But why should he? He already knew where Tom was staying. And wasn't paranoia another sign of dementia?

The next day, pulling his bag behind him, Tom slowly crossed the square to the train station. He sat down to rest and studied the big arrivals and departures board. In line at the ticket counter, he didn't look behind him. In line hiring the porter and waiting at the elevator, he didn't look back. He went down the platform followed by the porter and checked his watch before the man lifted his bag up the stairs of the fourth car of the ten o'clock train to Brussels. Then the two of them entered the third car and worked their way back down the aisle in the direction from which they had come. Tom looked at his watch. He peeked out the door of the car and thought he saw the black man climbing onto the fourth car of the Brussels train. He stepped down and crossed the platform. "Wait," he called to the conductor, who took Tom's bag from the porter, lifted it aboard the nine fifty-six train to Dordrecht, and closed the door. Tom sat on a jump seat, breathing hard, head pressed against the wall, looking obliquely out the window as the train left the station. He saw his porter but not the man in the blue Dodgers hat on the platform as he passed; the man had to still be looking for him on the other train. Slowly his heart rate and breathing returned to normal. He held up his hand and watched it shaking. Finally he took a deep breath and looked around. A girl across the car was watching him with wide eyes. Tom smiled and shook his head. "Cops and robbers," he said.

The train crossed the border, and Tom left behind the randomness of Belgium and encountered again the uniformity of Holland. That much was familiar: the brick streets, the row houses, the shops strung together, the church at the village center, and beside it the rector's house with its small yard, its formal center door, its ornate eaves and dormers. And more: the long, straight canals, the broad, flat fields, the low farmhouses, the lambs now in midsummer almost as tall as their mothers, the windbreaks of poplars all in a row as if placed there carefully by a huge child, an old man slowly riding an old bike along a dike. But here was a superhighway, and some of the barns were free-standing metal buildings, and all the town centers were now surrounded by blocks of newer row houses with larger gardens and bigger plate-glass windows.

On the platform changing trains in Dordrecht were people with dark skin, with spiky hair, dreadlocks, red shoes, yellow shoes, listening to iPods, talking on cell phones. There were none of the fair, stolid people in colorless, shapeless woolen clothing and heavy shoes whom he had left here half a century ago.

Tom did not see the man in the Dodgers cap. No one seemed to recognize or even notice him.

Frenchman's Lake, July 4, 2007

Just before the fireworks, Mike McIntyre, who'd taught with Tom for forty years, showed up. "I was hoping I'd see you," Tom said. The two old men shook each other's hands, held each other's forearms, and touched each other's shoulders. Then they sat down in the pink chairs.

"Hell, I wasn't going to miss your last party, was I? Hey, what happened to Al Jones?"

"Bad stroke. Found him in the morning. Couldn't get up."

"That's too bad."

"Yeah. I laid him on blankets in the back of the truck. Drove him into town real slow, but there was nothing to be done. I held his face in my two hands as they put him down. He was looking up into my eyes, and then his eyes went dead."

"That's hard."

"Where's Irma?"

"She's coming. She's dropping off our goods in the kitchen."

"What goods? The party's over."

"Just some lemon squares to go with the coffee."

Irma was Mike's second wife, a former student twenty years his junior who was a deaf-mute; "Perfect wife for an English teacher," he liked to say. "Goods" was a reference to The Trea-

sure of the Sierra Madre, a movie both old men liked; the two of
them often spoke in allusion. It was a kind of game, maybe even
a kind of code that made them and their relationship distinctive.
It was also a form of intimacy or perhaps a substitute for it. This
much at least was true: their personal bibliographies had much in
common, and the older they got, the less theirs had in common
with those of younger people. In a way, then, over the years their
bond had grown stronger, and they had grown closer, but all of
that growth seemed to have stopped some time ago. Tom did not
know quite why, but though he and Mike McIntyre addressed
each other with the familiarity of brothers, he knew that to some
extent, attrition and default were at work.

"I can hardly believe this is happening," said Mike McIntyre.
"I always figured you'd be the last one of us to go."

"'Beautiful view of the stocked fishing pond, elegant country
living, atrium dining room, all the amenities of a small European
hotel ...'"

"Yeah, yeah, yeah. Come in, take a number and have a seat.
We'll call you when it's your turn to die. That's not for you. You
can't tell me it is. I think you're up to something."

"I'm not up to anything, Mike. I'm just tired of fighting with
the kids. Aren't yours after you?"

"'Course they are, but I'll be damned ...'"

Then Brooks was hurrying up from the dock. "Dad, who's going to take Tony's place?"

"Why don't you do it? Mike, excuse me for a moment. ..."
In truth, Tom welcomed the distraction. He wanted to end this
exchange, which saddened him more than amused him, because
he knew it involved deception. He had thought of making Mike
his confidant rather than me, but Mike had become forgetful and
Tom wasn't sure he'd remember not to tell where Tom had gone.

Besides, their dialogue was old and tired, a remnant of a friendship that was mostly memory now, that had grown distorted: bulbous and distended like their noses and earlobes.

So after all the bombs bursting in air, the red-white-and-blue star clusters, the booms, the comets and rockets building to the finale, it was my Uncle Brooks who stood at the very end of the dock, only a little drunk, holding Tony's baton, the one Tom had bought him, the one Tony had kept in its velvet sleeve in his top drawer the other three hundred and sixty-four days of the year (Brooks must have gone looking for it). It was Brooks who got everyone's attention, got us all standing, raised both his hands, and got us all singing. "This is for Tony!" he shouted. "Make sure he can hear you up there in heaven. Can you hear us, li'l buddy?"

Tom closed his eyes. My God, he thought, must he always overdo everything? Or is it the beer?

"Oh beautiful, for spacious skies, for amber waves of grain ..." But we really did sing it for Tony, sing it loudly and fully, because he had taken it so seriously and worked so hard at it. "... God shed his grace on thee, and crown thy good with brotherhood ..."

And it was over. Oh, some people lingered, but most began to clean up, gather their things. There were screen doors slamming, muffled voices, and the distant clattering of dishes from the house. Soon there were car engines starting and a murmured tide of thank-yous and good-byes.

Tom was the last man at his own party. Still he sat. He heard the lapping of the little night waves and the wind in the high branches of the oaks and cedars. He looked at the silhouettes of the houses on the far shore, the gently rocking lights at the ends of distant docks. He watched and listened to everything that happened on or around the lake—the parties that went on, the cherry bombs that went off, the quiet lovers on the diving platform out in the middle. He smelled in the breeze tinges of gasoline, others of smoke and food and the mingling scents of life from the water and the farms and prairies beyond. God, he had loved this old lake. It had given him such comfort. It had given him something to believe in. It had allowed him to look at the shore from a distance.

Mike had left as suddenly as he'd come, and Tom wondered now if his health was failing. And Roger Daugherty hadn't come at all for the first time in how many years? Too many to count. Roger was mad at him or disappointed in him or frustrated with him. Or perhaps frightened himself. Was that the difference between eighty-five and seventy-five? Had Roger not yet achieved resignation? Was that why he was still going to the office three days a week, still making his hospital rounds every morning, still reading medical journals?

"There's a shadow on your x-ray," Roger had said. They were sitting in the same tiny examination room in which they'd always sat. "Maybe nothing, but we should take a look." Tom had always known that one day there would be a shadow or a blur or a blip or something. There had to be, for God's sake, after thirty years of smoking, sixty-five of drinking, eighty-five of living. Something had to go wrong.

The next time the nurse led him not to the examination room but to Roger's office, and he knew he was in trouble. Roger put a desk between them, as he never had before. The desk was too big and too ornate for the plain little room; it had leather inlays. It was very strange to discover after all these years that Roger had such a desk. It was a bit like an embarrassing secret, perhaps a tattoo.

Roger told Tom that he had a condition called mitral valve prolapse, had very likely had it for years, perhaps his whole life, that it was a leaky valve that allowed blood to seep back into the atrium from the left ventricle, that now after eighty-five years the leak had become more significant, and that it needed to be surgically repaired. "They replace your valve with one from a cow or a pig. It's major surgery, and I won't pretend it's without risk, especially at your age, but other than this thing, you are fit and healthy and the surgery has become so routine that there are surgeons who specialize in the procedure, do nothing else. I'll recommend one of them. He's probably done a thousand heart-valve replacements."

"And if I choose not to have the surgery?"

Roger hesitated. "Choose not to? I don't think ... maybe my caveat was too harsh or clinical, Tom. We're talking a success rate of ninety-five percent, maybe higher, and you're in so much better shape than most people your age—"

"And if I don't have it?"

"Well, the thing will end up killing you, I suppose."

"How long?"

"Oh, my, I don't know. ..."

"Guess."

"Well, assuming the deterioration continues, I would suppose within a couple years or so, but—"

"Then not tomorrow?"

"No, not tomorrow. It will happen more gradually. But—"

"Then I don't want the surgery."

Roger was surprised. He shifted gears. "Can you tell me why?"

"Sure, and don't think I haven't thought about it. I've been thinking about it since the tests, and in certain ways I've been thinking about it for many years." He had three reasons. One was that he didn't like pain and never had. He said he would like to live all the rest of his days, however many there might be, without pain. "I know that surgery will cause me pain, and because of my age that that pain could be permanent, would at least last a long time. Will this condition ever become painful?"

"Not really. It'll just wear you down. You'll tire more easily. You'll have less and less energy. You may lose some mental acuity, but you shouldn't experience pain. Your heart will just stop one day. That's all. But Tom—"

"Second reason." He didn't like what anesthesia did to old people; he'd seen its effects and didn't want them to happen to him. He said his mind was still sharp, despite what his children might say, and he wanted to keep it that way. "The third reason, Roger, is that I've lived long enough. Eighty-five years is a long time, and eighty-six is more, and eighty-seven more yet."

"Tom, I can't guarantee—"

"I know, I know." He wondered what there could be beyond eighty-seven, or eighty-six, for that matter, but wheel chairs and drool cups and daytime TV. No, he thought, perhaps he'd had about enough.

Tom was happy everyone had come to the picnic, and now he was happy they had gone, had left him alone with his thoughts, his memories, and his lake. He examined this contradiction, turning it in his mind as he might a pebble between his thumb and forefinger. Yes, he liked to be with other people but never as much as he liked being by himself. Had Tony been the only exception to this rule, or had Sarah once been one as well? He wasn't quite sure. In fact he wasn't sure at all. It occurred to him once more that he was drawing to an inside straight, gambling everything on a long shot. But what was everything? Very little, really. The residue of his life. "Not much skin in the game," he said aloud. To his children, his friends, the world itself, even me, I suppose, he was only a diversion or a reference point or occasionally a consultant. "Dad, do you remember the name of that electrician we used to use?" He wanted to be important one more time. He wanted to be needed. He wanted to be essential. Maybe that was why Roger Daugherty kept on going to the office.

It occurred to him that he'd never see Roger again. But that's okay, he thought. That's okay. Time to say some good-byes. Finally he hoisted himself from the pink chair for the last time, went into the house, put on Schubert's Mass in G, and listened to its soaring strings as he packed his bag.

Brabant, Summer 2007

Tom stood on the wide apron in front of the Eindhoven train station amidst a thousand parked bicycles, getting his bearings. Everything was different. There were a few old buildings, but he recognized none of them. Maybe one and a distant church spire. Otherwise the buildings looked like vacuum tubes in an old radio designed by the engineers at Philips who ran the town. Traffic flowed as if on circuit boards, and the engineers themselves went by on their tall bicycles, their briefcases bungeed behind them, their ties pinned to their shirtfronts.

Tom took a taxi to Veldhoven, but the rutted farmers' lane that had once led across the fields and pastures and between the horse farms was now a highway and an overpass that quite suddenly deposited him in the center of the village in front of the church and across from the hotel. Both were still there even if the old, narrow road between them was now a wide street. These days the hotel was for pensioners and commercial travelers. He rented a plain, quiet room in the back, and the owner's son brought his bag up. That afternoon he wandered around the town. He sat in the park. He walked along the little canals, crossing and crossing again the footbridges. He couldn't find the café that had once been the town center. Very little seemed familiar.

In the morning there were fresh fruit, breads, meats, and cheeses, and the owner poured Tom a cup of tea. Tom asked him for directions to the tourist office and the public market, and the man came back with a tourist map and a pen. Tom asked if he could recommend a lawyer who spoke English.

"They all speak English," he said but wrote down a name and an address. "This is a good one. Have you been here before?"

"A long time ago. During the war."

"Are you American, then?"

"Yes. I was a supply officer. I spent some time here."

Jan Dekker, the attorney, asked him the same questions. "You know," he said, "on September 17 people show American flags. People have not forgotten, especially the old ones." He smiled. He was a strikingly handsome man with a strong jaw, a thin nose, very blue eyes, and thick blond hair that was neatly parted on the side and swept back dramatically from his forehead. He had a bodybuilder's shoulders and arms, but when he stood up he was surprisingly short. He looked like a small movie star.

"I'm looking for someone I knew back then. A Dutch woman. Her name was Sarah van Praag."

Dekker wrote it down.

"She was a teacher of English, and she worked for me as a translator. This was her address back then. I don't think the house is still there; at least, I can't find it. I haven't communicated with her since 1947. Also, I need some advice. I think I am being followed." He saw doubt creep into the other man's eyes. "I'm here, you see, against my children's wishes. I imagine they'll try to find a way to force me to return to the United States. I want to know if they can do that."

"Well," said Jan Dekker carefully, "not really unless you commit a crime. Not unless you have not enough money. If you live by the conditions of your visa, well, then, ja, you have most of the legal rights and protections of a Dutch citizen."

Tom told the young woman in the tourist office that he was looking for a room to rent for several weeks. She gave him two leads. Dickie Druyf lived on the top floor of an apartment block on the edge of town. His flat was spacious and airy with big windows that overlooked the farms and fields. Tom's room would be small but clean and bright. Dickie was a genteel man with Einstein hair and an improbably deep voice who talked too much but did so in perfect but dated public school English, as if he had learned every bit of it by watching old David Niven movies. Unfortunately, he didn't have a garden, and he seemed a little too eager.

Mrs. Waleboer had a large, fastidiously kept garden behind her row house, which Tom's second-floor room would overlook and in which he noticed a brown-and-white spaniel asleep on its side in the sun. Mrs. Waleboer was a shy, plain young woman of about thirty who wore an apron and worked in a nearby frites stand. She spoke almost no English. She and Tom toured the house and garden, communicating by smile and pantomime. In the living room she picked up a framed photograph of two little girls in pigtails. They were perhaps seven and five. She pointed toward the children's bedroom that they had looked into upstairs. She did not show him a photograph of a man, although she was wearing a wedding ring. Tom liked Mrs. Waleboer and her house but thought he would need someone who spoke at least some English. The next morning he wasn't as sure. He realized that he'd have the house to himself much of the day. Also, he had dreamt of waking up in the room that would be his, of stepping through a door the room didn't have right into the garden, of sitting in a lawn chair he hadn't seen, reading and listening to an Albinoni oboe concerto.

He went back to the young woman in the tourist office and asked questions about Mrs. Waleboer. "Her husband was a soldier. He was killed in an accident. Very sad. As for her, she is a country-woman. She grew up on a farm. She is uneducated but neat and clean, and she needs the money."

He asked the young woman to help him write a series of questions in Dutch:

"May I cook?"

"May I sit in the garden?"

"May I listen to music a little loud, for I am hard of hearing?"

"May I do laundry?"

"May I bathe each day?"

"May I drink beer and wine?"

Mrs. Waleboer stood in her doorway still wearing an apron and read the list of questions. "Ja," she said. "Ja, ja, ja, ja, ja." Then she clapped her hands once and laughed aloud. Tom liked that. He moved in that afternoon. He cranked the windows in his room open as he unpacked and listened to the Albinoni piece he'd dreamt of. Then he sat on his bed and smelled the spicy, fresh garden scents. He felt some satisfaction. He wanted to tell someone that he had an address and a phone number, but there was no one to tell. The lawyer. He called the number on Jan Dekker's card and left the information. Soon Tom would e-mail me.

Tom's reverie was broken by the sound of the children coming home. He went downstairs to meet them, to shake their small hands. Ilse was a beautiful child with big brown eyes and perfect skin. Nienke was a fireplug with pudgy arms, cropped hair, and thick red plastic glasses.

The market began to appear early Monday morning near the city center. It came out of caravans and car trunks: tables, tents, display cases, boxes and bags of merchandise. The process was nearly soundless and perhaps automatic, as if, like so many things in Holland, Tom remembered, it had been done over and over again for generations. If everyone in the country didn't quite know everyone else, they at least knew the rules: where to stand, what to bring, when to show up, what to say.

There was an aisle of clothing, an aisle for the truck farmers with piles of peppers, tomatoes, carrots, onions, peaches, pears, and plums. There were cheese vendors with their big rounds of belegen jong to oud. There were tables of tools, others of CDs and DVDs, others of bike accessories: bells, mirrors, seats, locks. There was a caravan that sold little cardboard boats of fried fish and frites, and one that sold deep-fried Vietnamese snacks with lines of tangy red sauce squirted across them. There were gypsies selling inexpensive jewelry and Ukrainians selling tie-dyed t-shirts.

Tom spent the day in the market and was in the café across the street when the market began to be disassembled late in the afternoon. Had he really thought that he would see Sarah van Praag? The very notion suddenly seemed absurd. But of course he hadn't. He had never really thought that—not even years ago, not even before Tony's death, certainly not before Julia's. No, he had told himself from the very beginning that she would not be there. She would be dead. She would be lost in time, forgotten, living in Rotterdam or England or Boise, Idaho, for all he knew. Or if she were here, she'd be happily married to someone like Dickie Druyf and have children and grandchildren and great-grandchildren. Or she would be very fat with sour breath.

Or, and this was much more likely, upon seeing her he would instantly know in his heart why they had quarreled that day and why they could never be together. Then what would that mean? That he had spent his whole life waiting for a moment that had long since passed or, perhaps, never been? That he had really been the fool and dreamer Julia had always thought him to be, that the real illusion was that he could not find a way to love Julia? That she had been waiting all through the years for him to turn to her and smile, to touch her cheek with the back of his fingers, to push her hair aside and whisper something in her ear in just that way he could never find that would make her eyes smile, her head nod, her hand touch her mouth? He could have sold cars. Why not? Other men did. Whatever made him think that he was too good for that life? He could have played golf and laughed at bad jokes. He laughed at Mike McIntyre's, for God's sake; he laughed at Tony's.

"How many cow tails does it take to reach the moon?"

"One if it's long enough."

He had laughed at that one very hard. What was the difference? And what in the world after all these years could ever have tempted him to think she would be doing the same thing in the same place on the same day of the week?

THEN HE SAW HER, or thought that just maybe he did. Maybe he wanted so badly to see her that the slim woman who had strode past the open door, whom he glimpsed in profile for no more than a second or two, looked like her in his mind or looked like he had dreamt she would look. "Sarah!" he blurted out. "Sarah van Praag!," loud enough that people at the other tables looked at him. So did the passing woman, if only for a moment, before disappearing into a bank of shoppers. No. She was moving much too fast or at least purposefully to be browsing, to be Sarah's age, to be someone who wasn't hell-bent on something. But yes, certainly; it was that last twitch of her hips before he lost sight of her that fired a sixty-year-old synapse somewhere in his brain.

He left money on the table and quickly stepped outside, but it was still too late. His exhilaration turned to frenzy as he hurried up and down the aisles of the market, chasing one woman after another whose hair was also in a bun, jacket also dark, pace also quick, and then to utter fatigue as his adrenaline waned and he realized he had lost her. In fact, he could barely make it home; his legs were heavy, his feet leaden. He stumbled and almost fell. He thought again that he should probably get a cane; he would be done if he broke his hip. *How ironic would that be just now?*

Of course he'd thought he'd find Sarah van Praag. Whom was he kidding? He'd counted on it. He'd counted on it for years, no matter how many times he'd told himself he wasn't counting on it. And by God, he'd found her; he refused to entertain the notion that it had been too easy, that it was too good to be true. Instead he focused on what to do next. His mind spun with ideas.

Absently he cooked for the first time that evening. The day before, he had gone with some trepidation to the Albert Heijn grocery store near the center of the town. He would just look, he told himself. He would push a cart around and look, get a feel for the place. But the carts were all hooked together by short chains. He tried to separate two carts. Hmmm. "Why is everything so damn hard?" he asked himself. Then he moved a few feet away and stood against the wall, waiting for the next shopper. A woman hurried up and slipped a half-euro piece into a slot on the cart, freeing it and pushed it into the store. He looked around to see if anyone was watching and shook his head, dug a coin out of his pocket, and freed the next cart. *A lot of money to use a shopping cart,* he thought. Later, when he returned it and reattached the chain, he didn't see that the coin had popped free until the next shopper caught him by the arm and handed it to him. "Oh," he said.

A similar thing happened the first time he used the washing machine. Mrs. Waleboer had pantomimed the procedure in the upstairs closet where the machine was located: one, two, three, four. She did it again. "Ja," he said, "ja." But the next day he went through the steps and the machine didn't start. He was kneeling helplessly in front of it when Ilse came by and said something he didn't understand but recognized as a question. "Ja," he answered. She reached over his shoulder, pushed a big red button the size of a quarter, and skipped away. The machine began to churn. Then he couldn't get up. He had to walk on his knees down the hall to the staircase, work himself into a sitting position, slide his legs around and down the steps, and use the handrail to hoist himself back onto his unsteady feet. *Good Lord.*

Now, after Mrs. Waleboer and the girls had eaten, he boiled pasta, fried bacon, mixed them with egg and cheese, and ate dinner with two big glasses of wine he hoped would put him to sleep. They didn't. All night he thought or dreamt of Sarah. In the morning he sat in the garden, absently rubbing the ears of the dog, whose name he still didn't know. "Good boy." He looked at the tag on the dog's collar. "Leo. Is that your name?" The dog cocked his ears. "Leo, how would you like to help me find Sarah van Praag?"

For two days he followed Leo all over town. He looked at everyone he passed. He looked in every car that passed him. He looked through doors as they opened and as they closed. He sat on benches in busy places while Leo lay at his feet. On the third day they passed into a broad green park that separated one housing block from another. There was a children's playground. There were chessboards stenciled on molded concrete tables and some men clustered. One of them said in a deep voice, "De oude Amerikaan," as Tom passed him, and he understood and a few paces farther on realized it was the man with thick white hair in the modern flat from whom he'd thought of renting a room. On his way back, he said, "The old Dutchman."

Dickie Druyf looked up and grinned at him. "You speak Dutch, old boy."

"No, no."

"You know, that's what they're calling you: the old American."

"Who?"

"People. Everyone. It's a provincial town, you see. You're quite famous. There are rumors about you."

"Really?"

"Rather. They say you were here in the war. They say you've come to look for a lost love, old boy."

Tom was alarmed, not that people would know but that they could know. Was he so transparent? He felt invaded and embarrassed. The next afternoon Dickie Druyf was in the park again, this time with his own dog. He was tossing a stick. The two men nodded to each other. After a while Tom said, "Let me ask you something. Why did you say what you said yesterday?"

The man shrugged.

"I mean, isn't it unlikely that I'd come looking for someone after sixty years?"

"I suppose."

"And that she'd still be here?"

"Yes, but then we don't move about like you do in the States, you know. I'm sure more than half the people who live in Veldhoven were born here. The old ones, at least."

Then maybe this wasn't so far-fetched after all. "Do you, by any chance, know a woman named Sarah van Praag?" Tom asked.

"Sarah van Praag? No," Dickie answered. "No one by that name."

Tom didn't want to let the man go quite yet. "May I ask you a question? Are you English?"

"No, no. Hundred percent Dutch, but I studied in England, and I worked as a translator and editor."

A WEEK WENT BY, and Tom's search slowed. Sarah was a watched kettle. He knew she was here. He knew she would reappear. And he knew he had to look away. He must be patient. In the meantime, he began to look for Dickie in the park; it was nice to speak his own language with someone who seemed like a native speaker. He fancied that the other man began to look for him, too. "Do you play chess?" Dickie asked one day. They agreed to meet the next day for a game, but when Tom got home, there was a note bearing the lawyer's name and a phone number that Mrs. Waleboer had left taped to his door. It was too late to call. He went to bed but not to sleep. In the morning he was at Dekker's door before it opened. When he was shown into the office, the lawyer came around his desk and shook Tom's hand.

"And how is your living place?"

He said he liked it. He asked if Dekker had any information.

"Ja. I am afraid you are to be disappointed. I am afraid Sarah van Praag died long ago. Only a little after the war. I am very sorry."

Tom was flabbergasted. "But I've seen her. She's here. I know she is."

The lawyer nodded his head. "Well," he said, "it's been a very long time. I think very much you wanted to see her, ja? Perhaps it was someone who looked like her, maybe even a relative. Unfortunately, I have proof." He showed Tom a copy of the death certificate. "This is her address, the same you gave. Her mother's name is the same, too. Her age is not quite right, but, well ..."

"She's dead?"

"Ja."

"I don't believe it." But even as he said it, he was thinking of how very fleetingly he had seen the woman, how much younger than eighty-three she had seemed. "How is she supposed to have died?"

Dekker said that she died of tuberculosis in the sanatorium Zonnestraal near Hilversum in May of 1949. "I wish I knew more, but it was the war, you see. Many people were sick."

Tom was stunned. When he finally pulled out his wallet, Dekker said, "There is no charge."

"But surely ..."

"I am repaying a debt of mine own, something I promise to my father that if I ever had a chance to help an American, I would make it. And now, well, ja, here it is. You set us free, you see."

Tom barely thanked the lawyer. He went back to Mrs. Waleboer's. Standing in the quiet of the kitchen, he saw his reflection in the window. He looked slope-shouldered and ancient. He had had no idea that he would feel this crushed. He had told himself over and over again not to count on finding Sarah van Praag, but apparently he had, and now there was nothing more. Nothing. He felt so foolish. More than that, he felt finished. He'd been walking down a long corridor, and he'd come to the end of it. There was no door, no window, just a blank wall. "Fool," he said out loud. "Goddamn old fool."

Sarah was dead. Sarah had been dead fifty-eight years. In 1949 Tony was two, Brooks an infant, Christine about to come along. Sarah had been dying in some dark room while he and Julia had been madly creating lives. And what about the woman in the café? He thought he knew. All the other elements had been there: the paving stones beneath his feet, the taste of Dutch tea, the licorice drops in the little bag in his pocket, the low Dutch sky and smell of rain, the way people bared their teeth to make certain sounds, pursed their lips to think, nodded their heads just once—so he had added Sarah; he had recruited someone to take her place.

He went slowly up the stairs and lay down. He slept fitfully with jumbled, awful dreams he couldn't remember when he awoke in the late afternoon. A soft breeze moved the curtains, and there was birdsong outside, but both were somehow reminders of his aloneness. This didn't make sense. He'd been alone for a year. In certain ways he'd always been alone. He was the most self-reliant person he knew. His reaction was out of proportion.

Tom found himself looking down at Saskia Waleboer, who was sitting at the little table in the garden with her elbows on her knees, rolling a cigarette. On the table lay a pen, a pad of paper, and a calculator. Tom watched her. After a time she rested her forehead in the palm of one hand, as Tom's mother used to when she was thinking or worried. Was Saskia worried? He hadn't noticed that she smoked. He hadn't noticed much of anything about her. Tom lay down again, this time with his face to the wall. He hugged himself. He slept as you do in a fever, losing track of time and place and dreaming wildly. He got up only to urinate. He lay there for twenty-six hours, and he might have lain there much longer had he not heard a cry from the garden late the next afternoon. He raised his head, listened, then put his head down again, but then there was another cry, someone yelling, "Help! Hellup!"

Tom listened again, then got up and hurried down the stairs. Ilse was bent over Nienke, who lay on her back unmoving. The younger girl's mouth and eyes were open to the sky. She was conscious but dazed; she was not crying. The older girl *was* crying and babbling in Dutch, trying to explain. Tom gathered Nienke in his arms. "Doctor?" he asked. "Doctor?" Ilse led him through the garden gate, down a long walkway, and across the next street to a house that bore a brass plaque and a name: Theo Gossens. Inside, a nurse appeared and then a doctor. It was only when Tom had laid Nienke on the examination table and backed out of the room that he felt his legs dissolve and the fierce beating of his heart. He sat down hard in a chair and waited with neither fear nor panic for his heart to stop altogether. When it calmed instead, he felt a little disappointment. *Might have been a nice way to go,* he thought, trying to be flippant, but when the doctor came to tell him that the child would be all right, Tom's eyes suddenly brimmed with tears, which he wiped away with the back of his hand.

The doctor hesitated. "Is she your granddaughter?" he asked quizzically.

"No," said Tom, "no."

Then Saskia was bursting through the office door, and there was a great deal of explaining and reassuring, all in Dutch. After some time the doctor carried Nienke to Saskia's car, and Saskia carried her upstairs and tucked her into bed, and there was much coming and going to her room. Finally Tom went back to his. He looked at his bed and thought about lying down on it again, but he didn't. He sat at the desk and looked into the garden instead. He knew what he was feeling, but he was loath to admit it. Except when he had been an adolescent and a young man, he'd been pretty much immune to depression—"No time for it," he used to say—and had taken a certain pride in that, but now this, this ... Tom was a little frightened. Where was his rational voice, the one that never failed him, that could always put things in perspective? No, he would not lie down, but neither could he move; he felt not paralysis but overwhelming inertia. He sat there until sometime later when Saskia tapped at his door and came in with a tray of food and a bottle of cold beer. "Thank you," she said in English, "thank you." When she was gone he began to cry. He felt so goddamn grateful for something.

SASKIA TAPPED AGAIN in the morning, eyebrows raised and dog leash in hand, and Tom understood that she was asking him to walk Leo. She did so the next morning, too, but the third she didn't need to. It was good. It got him up, and although he still felt like he was a bicycle whose fender was rubbing, he went. Once outside he was able to keep going for some shopping or a meal that he seldom ate all of. . He walked through the shops using an umbrella as a cane. He'd grown aware that when he tired, he shuffled. That had scared him. That had been his greatest fear: the stumble, the missed step, the dreaded broken hip. But what did it matter now? And what the hell did he mean by that? He did not want to feel hopeless, but he found he couldn't help it.

Finally he found his way to the library and mustered the courage to ask for help negotiating the computer there. He had three short e-mail messages from me. He looked at them a long time, then typed, "Dear Nora, I'll write you a letter soon. Tom." He hadn't really intended to write me. Well, he had, but to say that he'd found Sarah, not that she'd been dead for fifty years.

One day he saw Dickie and his dog and apologized for missing their chess game. "I didn't feel well."

Dickie looked at him a little too closely. "Are you well now?"

"I feel fine."

But when they parted, Dickie turned back to ask, "Did you find your friend?"

"What friend?"

"The woman."

"Oh, no. She died years ago." Tom wondered if he hadn't answered a question other than the one that had been asked.

The two men began to meet in the park with their dogs. Tom welcomed the distraction. It gave him a few minutes of relief, even bemusement. Dickie had a theatrical manner that involved lots of facial expression and the exaggerated use of his hands, and he often spoke as if what he said had been written and rehearsed so that now and then Tom found himself trying to place a line or a speech and wondering if Dickie did all the same things when he spoke Dutch. Plus he could be elaborately deferential. He bowed, shook hands, called Tom "sir," inquired after his health, complimented, flattered, and laughed at all of Tom's jokes. Tom wondered if he was being humored or if he even minded. This gave him pause. Had he become pathetic? He didn't want to be pathetic. He forced himself to resume reading *Madame Bovary,* to listen to a concerto each day, to eat three meals, to do little exercises. One day he bought a *Herald Tribune,* the first he'd purchased for some time. He also bought a small notebook and a green felt-tip pen. He sat in the garden again, drank tea, and made himself read the paper from front to back. When he finished, he sat longer. Then he slowly opened the notebook, creased and folded it back on itself, took the cap off the pen, and carefully began to write.

Veldhoven, August 2007
The War, Part I

First of all, Nora, I got here and I am okay. I think I'll leave it at that for now. Second, I've decided to honor your request and tell you the story of my part in the second war and my relationship with a young Dutch translator named Sarah van Praag. I'm doing this, quite frankly, because I have time on my hands, but also because those long-ago times occupy my mind more and more these days. I hope that by writing about them I can relive and perhaps dismiss them, but doing so presents a special kind of challenge. This is a story that in all these many years I have never really told, so it's like speaking a language I once knew well but haven't used in more than half a century; I may have trouble finding all the words.

To start with, I was with the 101st Division of the United States Army, which parachuted into Brabant in the southeast of Holland with the 82nd Division and the British 1st Brigade in what was called Operation Market Garden on September 17, 1944. To give it a context, this was three months after D-day, three months before the Battle of the Bulge, and almost a year before the end of the war. The plan was to emulate the success of the D-day parachute assault and then connect with and be supplied by a column of Field Marshall Montgomery's XXX Corps that was coming up from the south into the city of Eindhoven, the home base of Philips and thus the center of the Dutch electronics industry. We were then to advance on Nijmegen and Arnhem to the northeast, taking the bridges that crossed the Rhine and using them to invade Germany. That was the plan, but many things went awry. A lot of gliders went down with heavy loads of much-needed cargo. Then the British got bogged down in Eindhoven because the Dutch people came out to welcome them, and there was much premature dancing in the streets and beer drinking. It was harvest time, and the Dutch people passed out apples to all the soldiers and clambered onto the trucks, jeeps, and tanks, stalling the convoy. During the night the Germans attacked from the air. The British vehicles, still strung out through the city center, were sitting ducks. In an hour of bombing, Eindhoven's business and industrial districts and the British convoy with its precious supplies were destroyed. This had a direct effect on me because I was a supply officer.

Our men up the line were isolated and low on everything. They had expected to be a strike force, to lead a three-day charge to Nijmegen and then be replaced by infantry troops. Instead Montgomery began using them as infantry troops, and they were ill-equipped for the job. Behind the lines we had to scramble. An airlift was started to drop in supplies. We had hoped to open up the port of Antwerp, fifty miles to the southwest, now that Montgomery controlled it, but it was heavily mined, and the long access route to it along the Scheldt River estuary was guarded by German artillery in southern Holland; this meant that supplies desperately needed to liberate the Netherlands and invade Germany itself would not come in through Antwerp at least until November.

As you can see, I was in the thick of things, but that was a sudden development. In fact, just one year earlier I had been a student in my sleepy little prairie college far, far from the war. My roommate and I had an old Philco radio, and on it, in that little school in that little town, we listened to news of the events that were about to lift us up and sweep us away. Toby enlisted in the Marines. He survived Anzio and became a dentist and then an orthodontist in Midlothian, Illinois. He once told me that sometimes with his fingers in the mouth of one teenager or another, he would ask himself if this was what God had saved him for.

I was sent to Officer Candidate School, and I remember almost nothing about it except big Tony Longo, after whom your Uncle Tony was named. How and why that happened is part of this story. Tony Longo was very Italian and, I think, the first Italian I knew personally. Before the war most of us lived in and rarely strayed from our own small ethnic communities. Ours was white, northern European, and mostly Protestant. There were some Catholics, but they were circumspect Germans and Irish. Tony was not. He was one of those fellows who stands too close to you and talks too loud. One day he and I were paired off to fight each other with pugil sticks, and we ended up in a pile on the ground, going tooth and nail. The next day on the parade ground I caught up with him and said, "Sorry about yesterday."

"Next time, I'll f****** kill you," he said.

I tried to avoid Tony Longo from then on, but we were constantly thrown together. He took to calling me "the little quartermaster" because I was being trained in logistics, which meant in all likelihood I'd be in the rear rather than on the front. To Tony that seemed to mean that I wasn't tough enough for combat or strong enough to be a leader of men.

By the winter of 1943 I was in England, which was both fright-
ening and thrilling, the busiest, most exotic place this small-town
boy had ever been. I was assigned to a logistics group at Division Headquarters of the 101st Airborne, which was located in a
manor house near Aldbourne. The house had already lived several
lives, including one as a boarding school that had left it thread-
bare and inelegant. And it was cold. Sometimes the drafts would
scatter papers on our desktops as if a window had been opened.
We worked in our woolen overcoats. Still, we knew we were engaged in a great cause, and we were impressed with ourselves.
"We" included another second lieutenant by the name of Earl
Karl Singer, some rotating noncoms, and companies of enlisted
men. Earl Karl was a stacker of coins, a collector of dandruff, an
obsessive brusher of teeth who color-coded his keys for quick and
easy access. He endeared himself to me by believing in his heart
that despite these things, a prematurely receding hairline, and the
biggest Adam's apple I'd ever seen, he would one day be presi-
dent of the United States. He called it his destiny and spoke of
it fondly, as you might a little brother or a pet. Earl Karl Singer
and I worked with British officers to accommodate the thousands
of American troops who were pouring off troop ships in Liverpool
and Portsmouth every day and spreading out across the southern
counties.

We lived in tiny servants' quarters on the third floor of the
manor house and in the evenings drank beer in a pub called the
Griffin, where we spent much of our time being beaten at darts.
When we finally got weekend passes, Earl Karl and I went to London. We ate small gray pieces of mutton with watery mint sauce
and boiled potatoes, sitting at a long communal table in a bleak
lunchroom, and later we looked in at the American Bar in Picca-
dilly Circus, hoping to find a couple of cold Miller High Lifes, I

suppose. There were none. Most of the crowd was British soldiers, and one of these who was quite drunk started asking us questions in a thick, slurred Cockney accent.

We couldn't understand him, and Earl Karl made the mistake of saying so. The soldier and some of his pals took umbrage at the suggestion that there was something defective about their English and by implication something superior about ours. They began to jostle us. I think the drunkard said (pardon my Cockney), "Take off your bars and les se'uhl this 'ere and now."

Then I heard a very big voice: "Well, if it ain't Lt. Tom Johnson." And there was Tony Longo. He said something corny like "Looks like you boys could use some help here," and then he grabbed a couple of Brits and, just like Moe used to do to Larry and Curly, clunked their heads together hard. This act created considerably more mayhem than it did for the Stooges; there was blood and screaming and reeling and we went out the door, down into the Tube, and onto a train. What ensued was a night of drunkenness and high jinks that involved another fight and several more bars and clubs.

By eight a.m. we were standing in the canteen in Paddington Station, trying to sober up on ersatz coffee, when Tony called me "quartermaster" and I remembered how much he'd always disliked me. I asked him why he had bailed us out.

He didn't know, said it was good to see a familiar face, even mine. Besides, he didn't much like the Limeys, and he'd gotten ditched by some "Ivy League SOBs." I tried to imagine what had happened and pictured a couple of trim, soft-spoken young lieutenants glancing sideways at each other and being embarrassed by Tony.

We were quiet a moment. Then Earl Karl asked if D-day was coming soon.

"'Course!" said Tony, waving a hand across the station waiting room, where there were literally hundreds of troops from half-a-dozen countries. "What do you think this is all about? All this leave?" He asked if we were being well fed lately. Real eggs for breakfast? Fried chicken? Spaghetti and meatballs?

So one day I was studying for my Shakespeare final, and the next I was drinking beer in London, and the next I was racing around farmers' fields in The Netherlands, dodging German machine-gun fire and trying to collect supplies that had been dropped in. I worked out of Division Headquarters in the village of Son just northeast of Eindhoven, where a depot of sorts had been set up to manage the meager supplies that were getting through. By then the Dutch underground had reported that the Germans had withdrawn to the north of the Maas River. The southern tier of the country had been liberated except for the westernmost province of Zeeland, where the Canadian First Army was beating back Von Zangen's Fifteenth Army, which had bombed the dikes and flooded most of the island of Walcheren. When Antwerp opened, I was given the assignment of developing supply lines from it, and I led the first couple of convoys there and back.

Just to the west of Eindhoven the farming village of Veldhoven had missed out on the bombing. We took over some farmland and buildings on its outskirts, and almost overnight there was a steady stream of trucks arriving from Antwerp and guarded convoys going up the corridor toward Nijmegen. My CO was a Colonel George McDougal. He had an easy, collegial style. He invited us to be creative and taught us to be respectful of the locals. He would say, "These people have had a hell of a time of it." Shortly after I got there he gave me orders to go see the mayor of Veldhoven. Now, here is one of those odd little quirks of fate that seem to determine so much in life; there were no jeeps available at that hour of that morning, and I didn't want to drive anything larger into the village, so I rode a bicycle.

On the main street, called the Kromstraat, there was a café that seemed to be the center of town life. It was full of cats and ferns and old men, some wearing wooden shoes, some smoking pipes, some even smoking clay pipes. I asked for the burgomaster and someone was sent to get him. The bartender put a glass of beer in front of me. "No coffee," he said, wagging his finger. "No tea. Beer. In Nederland, beer always." He smiled. The old men smiled. There was something I liked in this attempt at humor, in their self-deprecation, in their commonness, in their ability to have a light moment surrounded as they were by the ruins of their country.

The burgomaster came in with a slight young woman whose dark hair was chopped off short, parted in the middle, and pushed behind her ears. She was Sarah van Praag, although when the burgomaster opened his palm in front of her, he called her something else at first. She corrected him. That she would correct her elder not firmly but clearly, that she would know her mind so well and so comfortably, made her seem older than she was. She had a faith in herself, in both her beliefs and actions, that is rare in young people. It was apparent in everything about her, including her manner, which was to be inconspicuous, not in an obsequious way but as one does when one understands and accepts that one's part is ancillary. During our interview she never looked at me. (Perhaps it was then that my doubts about her began.) She looked at the burgomaster's face, and he looked at mine.

I explained who I was and that I'd been sent to offer assistance.

She translated, and the burgomaster nodded, thought and spoke.

Still looking at him, Sarah quite formally conveyed his thanks for driving out the Germans and freeing Brabant. He then asked for a few things. As I recall, these included flour, dried beans and peas, a little sugar, cooking oil plus insulin, penicillin, morphine, and iodine, and he wondered if we had any coffee. The Dutch had colonized Indonesia, introduced coffee to Europe, and were addicted to the stuff.

At a staff meeting later, Colonel McDougal said I'd done a good job with the townspeople. The mayor liked that I rode a bike. I was to be the liaison to the community. I was to give them all the help I could. I didn't know it then, but this meant I'd be spending most of the rest of the war in Veldhoven.

Each time I met with the burgomaster, Sarah translated. She seemed almost like a child who thinks that if she doesn't look at you, she can't be seen. I came to realize that she was actually quite young but both poised and frightened. She was hiding something. I wondered if she had, perhaps, translated for the Germans, or something graver.

On November 28th our beleaguered 101st was finally withdrawn after seventy-two days of unrelieved combat, but I stayed on with a quartermaster and a company of clerks and drivers to supply the English and Scottish divisions that replaced them. Then in mid-December the Germans launched the massive last-ditch offensive in the Ardennes in Belgium that grew into the Battle of the Bulge. Clearly they wanted to retake Antwerp, and if they succeeded, they would not only cut our supply lines but divide the Allied forces and either isolate those in the Netherlands or force them to withdraw. For five weeks the battle raged. If these were the Reich's death throes, as we all hoped, they were mighty ones. By late January Bastogne, around which the battle had been fought, was secured, but at enormous cost. Over twenty thousand Allied soldiers had died, and our entire supply operation was in tatters. It had to be rebuilt in order to fuel the push into Germany.

Back at the Supreme Allied Command Headquarters in London, the decision had been made not to attack Holland's German-held Randstad, which included Rotterdam, Amsterdam, the Hague, Utrecht, and most of the Dutch population. It was feared that civilian casualties would be too great, and it might mean getting bogged down in The Netherlands. Instead the Canadian First, which had been rushed east to the Bulge, would now push northward to Groningen. In this way the Germans occupying Holland would be surrounded by the Canadians, the British, and the sea, and their supply lines would be cut. The depot outside Veldhoven would be maintained and would supply the northern Allied divisions as they pushed across the Rhine and on toward Berlin.

My orders were not only to help run this operation but also to try to get some assistance to the occupied Dutch. "They're eatin' tulip bulbs up there," McDougal had told me before he had left. Intelligence said the German command in Holland was getting soft. There were commanders who might be anxious to ease their own way, make things better for themselves when the war was over. McDougal had said to work with the underground to try to locate a resistance organization called the Albrecht Group and get some relief to occupied territory by going through the network of wetlands, islands, and deltas called De Biesbosch. He had told me to hire Sarah to help.

I didn't want to. I was still suspicious. The only thing that recommended her was that she didn't want to be hired—that and the fact that she was the only good candidate. I reluctantly offered the job, and the burgomaster talked her into it. I'd keep her on a short leash and use our intelligence people whenever I could. They gave us a list of contacts. The first of these was a grocer, and I wasn't much taken with him even before Sarah said anything. He was too anxious to please. The second was a dairy farmer. I asked Sarah's reaction to the two men as much as a test of her as of them. She wouldn't give it. She said she was just a translator. But I pressed her and pointed out that intelligence said they could help us.

She said that they would help us the same way they had helped the Germans or would help anyone who paid them. She told me that they were not patriots, that they were not in the underground.

I asked her who was, but she was not ready to answer my question. Still, I sensed that she was right. I was not inclined to trust either man, but neither was I inclined to trust her. At the same time, I couldn't figure out why she would offer her opinion if she was up to no good unless it was part of the no good. The next day I asked her how to find the local underground.

She hesitated. She said she would help me but only if I didn't question her. She said to do so could endanger someone. I could see that she had thought this through thoroughly. I imagined her doing so while walking in the light drizzle that had fallen the night before. I could see she was taking a chance, so I decided to as well.

A few days later Sarah van Praag took me to see another Dutch farmer whose name was Van Helst. She gave me Dutch clothes and a Dutch bike, and just at twilight we drove out northwest across the farmland beyond Tilburg. Then we left the truck and biked into the night. We sat around the farmer's kitchen table. I said we wanted to supply the resistance with some medicine and food. And I told him we were looking for German officers who were sympathetic to the Dutch people. Sarah said all of this in Dutch and then a good deal more. The man leaned on his elbows, nodded, and told us to return the next night.

Riding back, I asked why all the secrecy? After all, the Germans were gone.

"Germans have a way of coming back," she said. "Like a bad penny." She said they were still watching, that not all Nazis were German.

I asked her where she had learned to speak English so well.

She said she had had a British teacher in school.

"But that's an American expression, isn't it? 'A bad penny'?"

She said she had probably learned it from a movie. Sarah liked American movies.

And with that, as if she'd somehow said too much, she pedaled ahead. Perhaps the British had taught her their reticence as well as their language, I thought. I watched her easy gait in the moonlight. It was steady, unhurried, strong, rhythmic, relentless like that of all Dutch cyclists, who never stood up on a bicycle, never coasted, just plodded on and on and on. She no longer seemed fragile to me, but what she seemed I could not say. She was changing as time was passing. I tried to imagine any possible way Sarah could do me harm, but I couldn't. What good would it do to turn one lowly deskbound junior officer over to the Germans? They wouldn't want me. And why wouldn't she leap at the chance to help her countrymen? Still, there was something secretive about everything Sarah did.

The next night we repeated the long, circuitous trip, and the farmer was waiting for us on his own bicycle. The three of us turned out of the gate and almost immediately into dense woods where the hard-packed path twisted, turned, and forked. It was dark, and we rode without lights so that my companions were only shapes, dark Dutch shapes loping, loping, loping. Who were these people, I thought, and why was I trusting them?

The farther away we got, the darker the night, the lower the clouds, the more foolish and vulnerable I felt. I was hopelessly lost. Was that the idea? We came to a short wooden dock and stopped. After a while another dark shape appeared. It was a small bicycle ferry. A couple of people got off, lifting their bikes onto the dock, and we lifted ours onto the ferry. There were no lights and no talk. We waited for something for several minutes, then crossed the estuary and were deposited on the other side. Once again we had a long, labyrinthine ride through dark woods and darkened villages until we came to more water and another farmhouse. We propped our bikes against the wall, knocked softly on a door, and entered a smoky little kitchen lighted only by oil lamps. We sat with a new man, who asked in English to see our papers. He was squat and solid with a very pronounced chin and a cap pulled low on his brow almost as if he didn't want us to see his face. We sat around a small table and drank shots of Dutch gin. Then we heard something outside, and I realized that we had been waiting again. The man handed Sarah's papers back but held on to mine.

"The boat's here," he said to me in English.

"I want her to come too," I said.

"I'll translate," he said.

I said I wanted Sarah to translate.

He said that wasn't possible. He said she might be in some danger. He had motioned to her and was unfolding her papers on the table.

I pointed out that if she would be in danger, I would be in danger, too. I said this very calmly. I thought my reasoning was quite clear.

"Oh, are you a Jew?" I remember him asking. "A Jood?" he said, this time in Dutch. Then he was tapping on the paper with one big farmer's finger. "See? Van Praag. She is a Jew. Besides, these are not German papers. They are old Dutch papers that are coming from before the war. They're no good."

This boat was a little fishing skiff. It was just the chin man, me, and the man at the tiller. No bikes. No farmer. No Sarah. We didn't speak, but finally the chin man pointed, and I began to see dark shapes with corners and edges and spires on the far shore. The skiff let us off at a wharf. We crossed to knock on a door in a wall and found ourselves in a café that, compared to everything else, was brightly lighted. Half-a-dozen men sat around a large table, drinking beer and gin. The three in the middle seemed military. True, they wore no uniforms, but they did so uncomfortably. The one in the very middle was glassy-eyed and swaying even as he sat. Chin man handed over our papers and did all the talking, this time in German. The others looked from him to me, listened, and spoke. Neither he nor I sat down.

Chin man turned to me and said that they wanted letters of passage and that I should agree to provide these.

I did. I asked for a guarantee that none of the goods would go to supply troops. The chin man didn't bother to translate this. He told me not to worry. Then my papers were returned, and we were outside again, stepping back onto the skiff. The whole business had not taken three minutes, and that seemed fine with everyone.

"What are letters of passage?" I whispered

He said he didn't know. "Make somesing looking official. It can be your job." Back on the other side, he told me they would use rowboats and skiffs. He said they'd start the next night.

And so began my part in Operation Manna during the Hongerwinter, as the Dutch people came to call it, of 1945. I rode the bicycle back that night with true joy in my heart. But it could be only partly explained by the mission we had accomplished and the danger, real or imagined, we had escaped. There was also a strong north wind now at our backs that made the journey shorter and easier, and then there was Sarah van Praag. I was so relieved to have an explanation of her odd behavior. Of course she was guarded, suspicious, nervous, even paranoid—she was a Jew.

But what did it even matter to me? Was this something personal, or had she become emblematic of a humankind I'd learned to doubt and distrust and now found worthy again? All the way back, as I watched her constantly shifting shape ahead of me, I realized that she had taken a great risk that night. And I realized, too, that I admired her for it. As I rode along I phrased and rephrased a little apology in my head. But when on the last ferry I finally found myself alone with her for a few moments and tried to deliver it, she stopped me, and for the first time she smiled at me. She said I had done what was right. The last leg of our ride and then our drive home was in a heavy rain. We got back to Veldhoven just before dawn. By then I was sick and a little bit in love.

Veldhoven, August 8, 2007
The War, Part II

That early spring my workload increased, and so did my hours as our supply lines stretched on toward Berlin and living conditions in the Randstad worsened. I worked at a big table in a little office that was really a shed. And whenever our dealings were in Dutch, Sarah sat and worked across from me. Outside the depot was a farmyard supervised by a warrant officer, defined by a perimeter fence of barbed wire and consisting of cartons and crates stacked on wooden pallets and protected by canvas tarpaulins. All day every day trucks brought supplies and other trucks took them away.

When Sarah was there she would make herself a morning cup of "English tea" with milk and sugar. She began to make me one, too. I had always associated tea with sickrooms because my mother had made it, stirred with honey and lemon, only when I was ill. Even during the months I spent in England, I favored instant coffee or chicory coffee. But Sarah converted me. I've been drinking tea ever since. Later we began to eat dark Dutch bread with unpasteurized butter and sometimes at lunch with very mild new white cheese. Later still, during breaks, we began to tell each other about ourselves.

I told Sarah about the house I lived in, the street I lived on, about the brilliant colors of the sugar maples in the autumn and how yellow leaves would stick to the wet bricks of the street, how ash logs split so easily and cleanly when you put an ax to them, how root beer tasted, how loons sounded. I told her about delivering newspapers before dawn, when the only sounds in the world were your footsteps and the papers thudding onto people's porches. I told her about the lakes where I lived, about paying five dollars to go up in a barnstormer's biplane once and seeing them all below me like shiny silver coins scattered on green felt. I told her how people drove cars out onto the ice and cut holes in it to fish. I told her about pan-frying walleye. And I told her that living on the lakes is a way of life out there.

Sarah told me about Holland before the war, about riding bikes along the dikes in Zeeland in the springtime when every field is filled with tiny white newborn lambs, about digging mussels in the wet sand, about empty Sunday streets and families walking their dogs in the woods after mass, about Belgian beers and Dutch cheeses, about Sinterklaas and Zwarte Piet and the various kinds, qualities, and potencies of licorice. Later, when the confectionaries opened again, she would sometimes bring little bags of these to try to educate me. She told me about horses and horse carts and guild parades.

I asked her if she rode. Everyone in Brabant seemed to. She said she had as a girl but didn't like to because horses scared her.

"But you rode?"

She said she'd had no choice. When she told her parents she was frightened, they said she had to master her fear. When she told them she wanted to quit, they wouldn't hear of it. Her grandfather even said he'd give her anything she wanted if she placed in the village competition. Sarah knew he meant her own pony. She trained and trained all year long and won the blue ribbon in the steeplechase. Her family was very happy. They raised three cheers for her and toasted her with champagne. Then her grandfather asked what she wanted as a reward, and she said she wanted to quit riding.

"Really? And did you?"

"I did. I never rode again."

I looked at Sarah a little differently after I heard that story.

In April of '45 new orders came through. I was to follow the supply lines into Germany to the village of Krefeld just north of Dusseldorf on the Rhine River, where lines from France and Belgium converged and where a major supply depot had been established. It happened quickly. I was to leave the next day. I remember we had a modest meal at Sarah's parents' house. We ate omelets. Her mother, who didn't speak English, smiled. Her father, who did, talked, and when I complimented him, he tapped his ear and said he'd learned English listening to the BBC. We may also have looked at photos from Sarah's childhood. It was all very awkward.

When Sarah and I parted at her front door, we shook hands. I remember that. I think we both doubted that we'd ever see each other again. But during the weeks I spent in Germany, I thought almost constantly about her. I told myself it was because I was lonely and far from home. I tried hard not to trust my feelings, but I had trouble denying them. I missed her terribly. I longed to talk with her. I dreamt of her. I feared I had lost her before I'd ever really known her.

The end of the war had left me with a kind of hangover. All that remained was rubble and poverty and an astonishing amount of death. Then in June I got a message from a field hospital out-side Cologne that made matters even worse. A Captain Anthony

Longo who was a patient there had asked to see me. I requested a jeep and went there as soon as I could. Tony's head was heavily bandaged and his torso was wrapped, but there was no mistaking his big nose and big teeth. He was groggy but coherent. We avoided talking about what had happened to him. I blabbed on and on until he interrupted me.

"Tom," he said, "can you help me go home?"

I told him I still knew people at Division and would try. Then he asked me to come back and read to him. Later I wondered if maybe his mother or father had read to him when he was sick as a kid, or maybe he just realized that I needed something to do as I sat at his bedside. That was what he really wanted, someone sitting there. On my way out I found his doctor. I lied and told him I was at Division Headquarters and that I could get Lt. Longo stateside if he'd approve him for evacuation.

"He's not going anywhere, Lieutenant," the doctor said. Tony had left too much of himself on the battlefield. Half his insides were gone, and he was badly burned. That night I wrote all of this in a long letter to Sarah. It was a letter I couldn't send because civilian mail service hadn't been reestablished yet.

Over the next couple of weeks I visited Tony whenever I could and read him *In Our Time,* the only book I had. I remember that he liked the "Big Two-Hearted River" stories about the young soldier fishing by himself in the woods and cool waters of northern Michigan.

Tony died on July 2, 1945. I wasn't there. A few days earlier new orders had come through—I was being sent back to Veldhoven to help prepare for the reverse flow of men and machines that would soon be coming.

Looking out the train window as we traveled through southern Holland I tried, not very successfully, to avoid thinking about both Tony and Sarah. I tried to focus on the familiar things we were passing: the long, straight canals, the wide, open pastures, the village church spires. Eindhoven was already being rebuilt. Piles of rubble and bricks had become neat stacks. Others had actually become walls again.

I caught a jeep out of Eindhoven toward the depot with a growing fear in my heart that Sarah would have gone to Amsterdam to be with her sister, or to England, or that she would have just disappeared, as people do in war, and no one would know anything about her. In the compound new men looked up from the table that had once been ours. New men worked in the yard. As soon as I'd thought of a reason, I took a jeep to Sarah's house. She opened the door.

"Oh, Tom," she said. She had never before called me anything but Lieutenant Johnson. Standing there in that doorway, we agreed that we were very, very happy that the European war was over, that the Allies had won, that the Nazis had been defeated, that Hitler was dead, that Holland was free. We agreed on all these things despite the fact that it had been eight weeks since VE day. Then we said what we really were thinking.

"I was afraid I wouldn't be able to find you," I think I said.

"I was so sure that you would be the last one killed," she said with tears in her eyes. That was the first time we held each other.

I guess I'm going to leave the story right there for now, Nora. Perhaps I'll tell you the rest later. I had in a sense come home to Veldhoven, and now I've come home here again, only this time I can't find Sarah van Praag. She is dead. The details don't matter. I've stood at her grave and read her name. I even put some flowers there, but it was a windy day and they blew away. I know that is the worst kind of high school English-teacher metaphor, but it's also true. I put them back two or three times, and still they blew away, so I brought them home and gave them to my landlady, Mrs. Waleboer, in whose garden I'm presently sitting. There is a pear tree in the middle of the garden, and the east wall is covered with wild roses whose scent is fresh and spicy and clean, especially after it has rained, which it does often here. Great Dutch bumble-bees lumber around from flower to flower and above swifts wheel and squadrons of starlings fly in formation.

It's a lovely garden, and that much does matter and perhaps that much is all that matters. The Dutch have a proverb for it: "If you want to be happy for a day, get drunk. If you want to be happy for a year, get married. But if you want to be happy for a lifetime, plant a garden." What that means in my life is that my great love, like my great goals, ambitions, and dreams, was made of dust, but I've long known that the grand things almost always are, and I've long known that it's the not-so-grand things that make life worth living: a cup of pea soup, a small glass of bitter beer, a new friend, an old memory, a warm fire on a cold day, a cool breeze on a hot one, the smell inside a dog's ear, putting one word after another.

I think I'm going to go on writing if you don't mind. It helps me. I think I'll finish the family history you started. I will not do it better, although I may do it differently, especially now. Your paper affected me deeply, Nora. Thank you for telling the truth. I guess I didn't know how complicit I was or how selfish and petty I could be.

Two minor corrections: it was a 1930 LaSalle that the Capone men were driving, and Tony actually managed the basketball team, not the football team, at the high school.

Veldhoven, Autumn 2007

Sometimes Dickie would teach Tom how to say a Dutch word or phrase, would model for him the guttural rattle that happened at the back of the mouth or the vowels that came off or out of the pursed lips, and now and again he produced a special strong licorice drop or a particular kind of sticky bun that could be purchased only at a certain bakery. Tom began to feel as if he was Dickie's project and wondered just a little suspiciously why the other man might be quite so available. Every few days Dickie telephoned or appeared with an outing in mind. Wearily Tom went along. He began to call Dickie his "camp counselor" and "the tour guide." Dickie smiled when Tom said these things, but it was hard to know if he was pleased or embarrassed. Whatever his self-appointed role was, he was conscientious in it. On one outing Dickie took Tom fishing in a canal and brought along an odd little quilted blue cooler and "a little something Belgian," two cold brown bottles of some rare Belgian beer supposedly brewed in tiny batches by a handful of old monks in some abbey or other, and two matching glasses bearing the brewery's insignia. "That's part of the ritual, old man. Never drink a De Koninck out of a Duvel glass." Dickie rolled a cigarette, the two men drank together, Dickie smoked, and I think Tom realized then how very sad he had been since learning of Sarah's death because for that moment he was a little less sad. Perhaps it was the beer.

Sitting there, he wondered again what to do next. He knew he was waiting, but he didn't know for what. He hoped it was for his path to become clear, but he feared it was simply out of habit or the lack of anything better to do. He wanted desperately to go home and hated the very thought of it at the same time. He had considered Paris, but it was too massive and amorphous. He could imagine only loneliness there. Or some BBC village in the Cotswolds if one still existed. No. Why not stay here? he thought more and more often. He had a room. He had a history. He liked the no-nonsense people and the quiet. He liked the beer. Or was this inertia, too? And would this place only feed his blues?

He wondered these things as he reread a letter he'd written to me about Dickie, about his journal, and about his indecision, as he carefully folded it and addressed its envelope, as he walked to the post office to mail it. He had always wanted to write; perhaps this was his chance. There were stories to tell, if only to himself and me. Perhaps I could be his muse and his audience. He knew I would read what he wrote. He thought I would understand it.

A week later Dickie took Tom on a "fishing expedition." They drove out of town in Dickie's old Citroën Deux Cheveaux with the windows rolled down and the sunroof rolled back, fishing rods protruding, and fished the Wilhelmina Canal west of Best on the way to Tilburg. Dickie whistled the theme from *The Bridge on the River Kwai* all the way, as if he'd decided to in advance and couldn't renege on that decision now when his lips and cheeks were tired. Sometimes too much about Dickie seemed forced.

Tom was invited to dinner to eat their catch and given special instructions to bring two chilled bottles of a certain French rosé. On the way to Dickie's apartment that evening, Tom saw the same round man he'd seen earlier that day when he'd walked Leo, only the man who'd been wearing a cap was now wearing a hat. Tom said, "Goede avond." The man ignored him, and Tom had the sinking realization that the man might be following him. He looked back, and the man was gone. Nothing. But when he entered Dickie's building, he waited a few moments in the vestibule, and here came the round man around the corner. "Oh, please!" he said. "Not this again." But yes, this again. He remembered his own words: "You were doing what you had to do, and now I am doing what I have to do." And they would all go on even though it would all come to naught. Nada y nada y nada. He was embarrassed when he thought such melodramatic things.

Tom sipped a glass of Belgian beer as Dickie, whistling again, bustled around the kitchen, and he looked at pictures of Dickie's wife, Olive. She had been quite stunning as a girl, beautiful later, handsome finally. How old had she been when she died? In the pictures of them together, Dickie was posing and she was not, and Tom saw then that that was about self-consciousness, not mania. And so was all of this; behind the role-playing and bravado, Dickie was self-conscious. How very little he knew about his new friend; he felt as sudden and fickle as a teenager.

Field's nocturnes began to play. Dickie came in and lighted the candles on the small table he had set with a white tablecloth in front of the great windows that looked out upon the fields and canals. He poured the rosé and served a bowl of mussels ("Just coming into season again. They're tiny and very fresh") steamed in a broth of wine and diced vegetables, then melon "to cleanse the palate" wrapped in prosciutto.

Dickie was agitated. He was a little loud, a little frenetic, perhaps already a little drunk. He poured more wine and drank it quickly. He served the sautéed white fish in a mild mustard sauce

full of herbs and tiny pink shrimp with very small parsleyed potatoes and Belgian endive on the side. There were a few halved
cherry tomatoes with a little vinaigrette and some carrots sautéed
with mint. The tastes fit together like puzzle pieces: the savory
sauce, the bitter endive, the sweet carrots, the acidic tomatoes,
the buttery potatoes. And the wine was perfect; they were already
halfway through the second bottle.

"My Lord, Dickie, this is just wonderful."

Dickie opened his eyes very wide. "Well, old chap, I am the
cook," he said as if it were an old joke, one Tom should have
known but didn't. Tom was reminded that they were pretending
to be better friends than they were.

"Chief cook and bottle washer," said Tom. "Do you know that
one, or is it an Americanism?"

"Oh, yes, chief cook and bottle washer."

"That's what we used to call Julia, the kids and I. Of course we
did so sarcastically. She wasn't much of either."

Dickie opened his eyes very wide again, perhaps surprised that
Tom would say something critical of his dead wife. "You know,
she's been gone a long time now, Dickie. Eleven years."

"Do you still miss her?"

And here was that moment Tom thought they'd both agreed
to avoid. He hesitated. "We didn't have a very good life together,
I'm afraid. We didn't have a very good marriage, Dickie. We got
on the same life raft and couldn't get off. Do you know what I
mean?"

"Hmmm." They were suddenly awkward.

"Do you miss Olive?"

"I do. She would have stopped me today." And again Dickie
was inviting something he had not before.

Tom waited and waited; the invitation seemed both perilous and unavoidable. Finally he asked, "What happened today, Dickie?"

"Oh, for God's sake, don't ask. Don't bloody ask," he snapped. "But she wouldn't have let me do it. She would have said, 'Dickie.' She would have said, 'Richard.' She would have put her hand on my arm, but she's not here, goddamn her soul." Then he was sobbing with his chin on his chest, sobbing without any intent to stop, perhaps ever. Tom had only been vaguely aware of Olive until now, hadn't even known her name for a long time, didn't have any idea when she had died but assumed it had been long ago because Dickie had rarely even mentioned her.

Then Tom saw everything, as you sometimes do when you are drunk, and even when you are not. Dickie did not speak of Olive because he had forgotten her but because he couldn't think of anything else. He was incomplete; he was half of something; a mirror image, a one-legged man in a three-legged race. He was desperately hanging on. He had been trying to save not Tom but himself. Tom had great pity for an instant, then great envy. In the face of the other man's pain, he felt himself small and dry and hard, wallowing in his own pool of self-pity over an ancient, imagined love after he'd never in eleven years shed a tear for Julia.

"You see," said Dickie, finally drained, "I'm not a stoic like you."

"I'm not a stoic," said Tom.

"I'm not paying you a compliment, old boy. She would have stopped me from saying that, too, wouldn't she? But then, she's not here. Not here. So." He got up and came back with a stone bottle of Dutch gin. "The elixir; the thing every real Dutch celebration must get to in the end. Jenever!"

"Is this a celebration, then?"

"It is, old chap."

"What are we celebrating?"

"I haven't the faintest idea."

Tom was not to recall much of what happened after that, nor for how long it went on. An hour? Perhaps two. There was some confession, some speechifying, a good bit of confiding. There were several toasts.

And it was that night that Tom heard Dickie's story, and Olive's. How Dickie's father was a great admirer of the British and the English language, even named his son Richard after the Lionhearted and called him Dickie after an English music-hall juggler and comedian he'd seen in London. How when Dickie was sixteen in 1938 his father sent him to study at a public school in Oxford and asked his father, Dickie's grandfather, to go along as a chaperone. How Dickie and his grandfather took rooms, really a room, in a boarding house on the Effley Road that was operated by a Scottish woman named Mrs. Mundell, who had a fifteen-year-old daughter named Olive. How Dickie and his grandfather got trapped in England when the Germans overran the Netherlands, and Dickie enlisted in the Royal Navy and, because he spoke both Dutch and German, worked as a translator in London at the Admiralty.

It was during that time that Dickie began to write to and see Olive Mundell. After the war Dickie came home to Veldhoven, but in the summer of 1946 he went to visit Olive, and together they bicycled all over Cornwall. He sang Dutch folk songs to her, they camped on the beach and the heath, and by the end of the month they were engaged. During the next year he returned on holidays to visit Olive, but the next summer she came to visit him, and this time they bicycled around and fell in love with Brabant, which, in those days before superhighways and fast trains, seemed idyllic and quite remote and very much divorced from the larger world they were not sure they trusted. In the spring of 1948 they were married by a Presbyterian minister in the parlor of Olive's mother's boardinghouse, and they settled in Veldhoven because Dickie got a job in Eindhoven as an editor and technical writer.

Tom did not remember walking home that night or early morning, and the next day counted himself lucky not to have fallen. He realized that he'd forgotten the round man and had no idea if he'd been followed again, but he did remember Dickie's words: "I'm not paying you a compliment." And he did remember Mrs. Waleboer opening her bedroom door a crack as he apparently made too much noise coming up the stairs. He remembered saying, "So sorry," and telling himself he had to learn more Dutch if he was going to stay here. The next day he didn't care a whit. Nor did he get out of bed until late afternoon. The hangover disarmed him and plunged him back and deeper into despair, reminding him of just how close to it he always was. He couldn't lift his head off the pillow without being dizzy. He sipped water. He ate the two chocolate bars he'd bought to give to Ilse and Nienke. He slept and listened to the BBC, to shows about politics and sheepherding and what records someone famous he didn't know would take to a desert island. He lay still and stared at the can of pepper spray on his nightstand that Dickie had forced on him for his walk home the night before: "Can't be too careful. The world has changed, you know."

Or is it we who have changed, thought Tom, *while the world goes on and on and round and round?* Again he embarrassed himself. He decided, perhaps in reaction or perhaps because he was feeling vulnerable, to carry the pepper spray with him from then on. His glasses, his wallet, his passport, his watch, his pen, his umbrella, and now his pepper spray. And what of Dickie? What did Tom have in common with the old Dutchman except their damned near adolescent need for another?

The second day Tom didn't get dressed or leave the house. He let Leo shit in the garden, ate soft-boiled eggs, and sat for a while in the sun like a patient in a wheelchair at a sanatorium. Slowly he began to pull himself back up, if only in chagrined deference to Dickie's real sorrow, and the next day he made himself go out. He was standing in a supermarket aisle trying to decipher the cooking instructions on the back of a box of rice when he felt a presence. He looked up, and there was the woman from the market standing stock-still at the head of the aisle, staring right at him. Then she was gone, just like that, and although he abandoned his cart and followed her, he lost her again. Out on the sidewalk he went one way and then the other but couldn't find her. Finally he gave up and started home. Then he saw someone who might have been her nearly a block ahead of him, and he followed her. She turned right, then left, then right again. He came around the last corner as she was entering a row house at the end of the block. Just before she did, she looked directly at him. It was the same woman. Tom kept his eye on the door and walked toward it. He rang the bell and waited. He rang and rang. He knocked. Then he began to call out: "Hello? May I please speak to you for one moment? Hello?" He rang and knocked and called until the next door opened and a man looked out.

"Sorry," Tom said. "Listen, can you tell me—"

The man said something in Dutch and closed his door.

The next day Tom went to Jan Dekker's office. The lawyer was surprised to see him. "Can you tell me who lives at this address?"

"Easily." Dekker turned to his computer. And a moment later, "Her name is Pim de Wit."

"Oh," said Tom, "I see."

"What?"

"Well, Sarah had a sister named Pim. It must be her sister." He could not hide his disappointment.

"Well, ja, there you have it. That explains it."

"So," said Tom a little reluctantly, "that explains it."

They sat. Finally the lawyer said, "Is there something else?"

"Maybe," said Tom. "Have you done immigration law?"

"Some."

"I am thinking of applying for residency."

Dekker smiled at him a little as if he'd won a bet with himself. He turned to his computer again. He found and printed the proper forms. He carefully went over a checklist of the things Tom would have to provide. "If you decide to apply, bring it all back and we'll send them in to the IND. You give your papers and wait. They are informing you by mail."

Turning the corner into Mrs. Waleboer's street, Tom walked past two men in a parked car and then heard them opening their doors and heard them come up behind him. He turned just as one man took him by the elbow. "Mr. Johnson," said the man in a British accent, "please don't be alarmed. We're friends. We just—"

"I know all of my friends, and I don't know you." The man was still touching but no longer holding his arm.

"We're friends of your family. We just want to have a word. They are very concerned about you. Everything they are doing is in your best interest, I assure you."

"How do they know that?"

"What?"

"How do they know what's in my best interest, and I don't? Is it because I am old? Isn't that kind of presumptuous? Did they ever think of asking me what I think is in my best interest?"

"Well, yes of course, and we can talk about that. ..."

Tom knew that that was all they wanted, to talk to him, to reason with him, to persuade him. He knew they were not going to bundle him into the car and jab a hypodermic in his thigh and force him onto a plane. He knew he wasn't in any danger, but when the other man took him by the other arm, he produced the pepper spray he'd been holding in his pocket and sprayed the man in the face.

The man screeched and grasped at his eyes, swearing loudly in Dutch. Tom turned to the first man and held the can toward him. The man leaped back. He hesitated as if considering his next move. Tom took one step toward him and sprayed some more. That was enough. The man helped his companion into the car and drove away.

A woman working in her front garden down the block was watching. Tom looked away, embarrassed for himself and his children and his family. A public spectacle. He wondered what he would have done if Brooks and Christine had simply left him alone. He saw their move and his countermove as parts of a board game that one day soon would be folded and put away on a closet shelf. What in God's name did any of it matter? How long would any of it be remembered? "Tom Johnson? Wasn't he the one who ran away as an old man?"

Tom knew he hadn't needed to do what he had done to the men, one of whom he realized now just might have been wearing a clerical collar, but at the same time he knew that he had very much needed to do it, and afterward he felt the same sense of relevance that he had felt after carrying Nienke to the doctor, and after that he felt the same dam-break of emotion so that he was crying when he opened his front door.

Johnson Family History Continued

For Nora

Julia's and my marriage didn't "effectively end" when Russ Lawton was killed in the auto accident, but it started to end. It was like a slowly sinking ship; we closed one bulkhead after another and settled deeper and deeper in the water until the only compartment left was the one marked "parenting." Still, there were times when I thought we might be able to right the thing, but that was all before Julia fell in love.

In 1963, having given up on me and his own sons and apparently without ever even considering Julia sitting there in her glass office, Russ hired a business manager named Tim Hodges from Dayton, Ohio, with an eye toward eventually making him a partner if things went well. Tim was an ambitious, progress-minded guy who wore a Princeton haircut, creased gray flannel slacks, a blue blazer, and the first tassel loafers I'd ever seen. He almost immediately talked Russ into abandoning his cramped old showroom and garage downtown and moving out to the edge of town, where they would have acres of land and lots of room for expansion. This was a good idea. He then talked Russ into buying out an underfinanced Ford dealership in the next town and incorporating his old and new agencies on their new site. Another good idea. Next he talked Russ into importing English Fords, not such a good idea, but one that made the agency seem open-minded and future-oriented. And it was Tim who recognized Julia's acumen and began to involve her in decision making.

It was about then that Julia stopped going on vacation with the rest of us; she became too busy. I'd take the kids up to a rental cottage in Door County, Wisconsin, for a couple of weeks as soon as summer school was over. We fished, hiked all over Washington Island, canoed on the bay, and ate fish boils. We spent all our money on go-carts, miniature golf, and batting cages. Then on spring break we'd go to a little motel on Treasure Island in Florida that had a pool, a grill, and shuffleboard. Christine got her own bed, Brooks and I shared one, and we put Tony on a roll-away. We had a kitchenette to make breakfasts and lunches and the grill for hot dogs and hamburgers, and we'd walk the beach for hours looking for the best grouper sandwich. It was all kids' fun, of course, and while I enjoyed it, sometimes at night, when they were in bed or watching TV, I'd sit outside in the dark, drink a beer, and wish Julia and I could be sitting there together, remembering the day, smiling about something one of the kids had said, planning tomorrow.

We became the "Jonnsons" on one of those vacations and while Julia was a part of us, she also wasn't. She was watching us through a window. It happened when Tony was about eight and Brooks was seven. Tony made a lanyard for me with our name on it at a little day camp in Door County, except it read, "the Jonnsons." Brooks was learning to read, and he picked right up on it. He said Tony forgot the "h" and didn't even know how to spell his own name. He laughed at Tony, and Tony got very upset.

"That's an 'h'!" he said.

"No, that's an 'n.'" said Brooks. He called Tony a dummy, and

Tony started crying. He said it was an "h" okay, an "h" with a short neck.

I gathered Tony in my arms, took him across the yard, and set him still blubbering on a picnic table. I took out the lanyard and examined it. To make it at all was an achievement because Tony had very poor small motor skills. "Yep," I said, "that's an 'h' okay. A little short in the neck, but that's definitely an 'h.'"

"See, I know how to make an 'h.'"

"Make an 'h'?" I said. "Tony, you made this whole lanyard, and I am very proud of you. This is the best present anyone has ever given me. And you know what I want to do? I want to put it on my key chain so that I'll have it in my pocket right next to me every single minute of every single day the whole rest of my life."

"'Cept when you have on your pajamas." One thing you had to always remember with Tony was that he was an absolute literalist.

"Then I'll get a pair of pajamas with pockets. And every single time I use my keys I'll think of our family, and I'll think of you because you gave it to me, and I'll think of the twenty-seventh letter in the alphabet, the one you invented."

He looked at me uncertainly. "Which one?"

"Why, the short-necked 'h,' of course."

So that's why Julia wasn't a Jonnson, not quite. I think she wanted to be but couldn't figure out a way. Perhaps she wouldn't let herself. Perhaps I wouldn't let her. I know she shared some of my regrets. Many years later, when she was dying, she said completely out of the blue one day, "I never should have stopped going to Door County with you." It melted my heart. She could do that. Every now and then she would show me that there were other places in her. Once she came down to sit on the dock on a warm spring morning, rare enough in and of itself, but then she said right out of nowhere, "I'm sorry you weren't able to finish your doctorate. You would have been a wonderful historian." Imagine that. I had no idea she knew or cared how I felt, but one part of her did. Trouble was, there were very few times I can remember that she showed me that part. I think it was just too dangerous to do. Perhaps for me, too. Perhaps it meant compromising roles we had made commitments to play no matter how disabling or destructive those roles might be.

When the next year I suggested that she might like to join us in Florida, she fixed me with a long, icy stare before saying, "You've got to be kidding." She was right, of course. My invitation had been unrealistic if not insincere, and we both knew it. In fact, we had long since begun the process of discovering just how far from perfect we could exist together with some measure of contentment and comfort, at least enough to allow us to go on, at least a little more than our measure of discontentment and discomfort, for the truth of the matter is that if you can win just fifty-one percent of the time, your potential is limited only by how much you have to invest, and most people who would never settle for fifty-one percent when it was first offered would if given a second chance. Fifty-one percent is not that bad, and a person can live a pretty good life on it.

When Russ died, Julia threw herself into the business. If she'd once been a dilettante, she was no more. She left it to her brothers, Warren and Frankie, to drive around in convertibles with dealer plates, play golf, and go to auto shows. She rolled up her sleeves and worked. That meant a lot of meetings, business lunches, and drinks after work with Tim Hodges.

For three or four years their relationship seemed to be nothing more than a great flirtation. Hodges was married, had kids, and was home every night for dinner, and there were precious few places in our small town for a tryst. I think that up to a point it was all theoretical. And in the beginning I pretended to be happy for her. In a way it was, after all, what I'd always said I wanted for her: a life of her own. Plus, she was happy in a way I knew I'd never made her, or perhaps lighthearted or even fulfilled. I realized that for the very first time, she was hopeful. And that thing happened to me that happens when someone else sees something in a person that you had missed altogether. I wanted to see it, too. When someone else wanted her, so did I. I think that during that difficult time I learned more about my very human nature than I ever had before.

When I told Mike McIntyre what I was feeling, he said, "Hmmm. I think you may be confusing possession and love. Tell me this: Were you ever in love with Julia?"

"Oh, who knows?"

"You would if you had been."

"Can you 'finally' be in love?"

"I don't know. Maybe."

"I guess the only time I was really in love was with that girl in Holland."

"Then I'd wait," he said. "See if this goes away." He said to stay out of Julia's way and let the thing play itself out. It was advice that I tried to honor until Julia told me that she and Hodges were going together to the national sales meeting in New York. That was in 1970.

"I don't think that's a very good idea," I said. She looked at me as if I didn't have the right to think that or anything else. Actually, she looked at me as if she hadn't seen me in a very long time, which I realized then was almost certainly the case. Funny because all along I had assumed that at least part of what was going on was for my benefit. Now suddenly I knew that I was the last thing on her mind.

"It's business, Tom."

"But I mean after the business."

"That's business, too. Mine, not yours."

"Julia, we still have a marriage here and a home and a family."

She looked at me again. She said carefully and not unkindly, "We have a home and a family, true, but we don't really have a marriage, Tom."

"Then maybe we shouldn't have a marriage at all." I said it to see if I could still hurt her, but the fact that she hesitated was about something other than hurt.

"You promised you'd never leave," she said.

"We both made lots of promises that don't seem to mean much anymore."

"No, we didn't," she said very quickly. "I never promised you anything."

It was true, and at least part of the reason was that I had never asked her to, something of which she seemed keenly aware and apparently always had been. I wondered then and wonder still if anything would have been different if I had asked for her word rather than just giving my own.

Julia went to New York with Hodges that winter, and I went to see a divorce attorney. But when Julia returned, something had changed. Not only was her hope gone, but something harder and darker had replaced it. She smoked more. She took long, aimless drives. She spent hours listening to the soundtracks of musicals she had seen on Broadway. She continued to go to the meetings, dinners, and golf outings, but something was different. Once while I was sitting in my chair in the living room reading the paper, I watched her through the open door to the kitchen staring out the window above the sink. She didn't move for perhaps two minutes. At first I thought she must be watching someone or something: a sailboat, a fisherman, a deer drinking at the shore. Later I thought she probably wasn't. Eventually I called the lawyer and told him to put things on hold.

The next year Julia went to San Francisco for the national sales meeting. This time she came home early, and Tim Hodges didn't come home at all. It was suddenly announced in the newspaper that he had taken a job in Middletown, Ohio, and he and his family were gone just like that. I never completely understood what had happened, but I think it fair to say that it was something between a love affair gone bad and a coup d'état. At any rate, Julia moved into the big office, the one that had been her father's and then Tim's, and in short order Warren and Frankie were back out on the floor rather sheepishly selling cars again. Neither lasted. Eventually Warren became a silent partner and moved to Florida. Frankie sold out to Julia and opened a bar and restaurant in town.

Julia now worked twelve hours a day and had little time for anything other than her job. At the same time her dedication was cheerless and angry. She left Tony alone, was even sweet with him at times, but she quarreled with Christine, Brooks, and me about selling the house and building a show place in town. When we wouldn't let her, she added another addition to our lake house even though Christine and Brooks were grown and gone. She made a lot of money, took a lot of trips, drove big, fast cars, became increasingly and somewhat famously profane, suffered no fools, cultivated her own small growing legend, and in time developed a kind of permanent smirk that seemed to say, "See, I knew all along that it was all just a bunch of bullshit."

As for me, I had a flirtation or two over the years and tried unsuccessfully not to think of Sarah because I was superstitious. If I thought of her she wouldn't be there, and some part of me needed her to be there somewhere. Of course I never really stopped thinking about her, but when I thought of her, it was still 1946 and Sarah was still a girl with slim legs and thick hair who smiled and smelled and giggled like a girl.

I don't know why Julia stayed in our marriage all those years, but I have a few theories. One is that she was a Hedda Gabler: larger than life and outrageous but strangely afraid of scandal even when divorce was no longer scandalous. Or perhaps she liked being angry and disappointed. Some people need those things. For some, disappointment confirms something important. Or perhaps behind it there was just a flicker of hope that before it was all over and against all odds, we'd somehow manage to figure things out and end up sitting at the end of the dock together. As for me, I stayed for several reasons. One was because I said I would. Oh, I can hear Julia now: "Gimme a break. Don't kid yourself. How noble." Fair enough. Another reason was inertia. I couldn't ever see myself sitting in an apartment somewhere watching a rented TV. It was also the children—I couldn't imagine myself explaining this thing to them. And for a time I stayed because I wanted to resent Julia. I didn't know it then or wouldn't have been able to admit it. In fact, I think I've only fully realized it quite recently. I resented her, and I resented her deeply. So there, we weren't so different after all. I wanted to blame her for toying with my naive little heart, for getting pregnant, for spoiling my dreams of a life with Sarah, causing me to forgo a doctorate, trapping me in marriage, the town, our life, even for having poor little chromosome-impaired Tony. And I resented her for not feeling guilty about any of it. Of course my resentment ended way back on the day Julia's father died because the books were balanced then. If resentment had ever been my due, it was no more. But in reading your paper, Nora, I see that bitterness took its place. Clearly I have blamed her for things that were my own damned fault.

Maybe Julia and I were more alike than I know, or maybe in some perverse way we complemented each other: her yin to my yang. I guess that's the main thing she and I did for each other; we were each what the other person was not. It's a dynamic I can't seem to escape even all these years after her death.

The year I retired, Julia got sick. Her reaction to the cancer that first go-round was pretty much the same as her reaction to anything: it made her angry. "Oh, right, now this." In the end she not so much denied as defied it. "Just you try!" she seemed to say. She refused to give up smoking or drinking, and although she allowed Tony and me to take care of her after the surgery and during the chemotherapy, she grew impatient with us after that. She did not like to be fussed over. So one day she just said, "Hey, why don't you take Tony and go fishing?"

"We did that yesterday."

"No, I mean take a fishing trip. Get out of here for a while."

"My Lord, Julia ..."

"Look," she said, "I just need time to heal. I need time alone."

Tony sat in the bow of the boat, and I sat in the stern, staring at his back, for a whole week. He had no idea that his mother might die, that I was going to die, that his own days were numbered. He had just turned forty. Suddenly it seemed that Tony hadn't much to show for his life. He'd worked at the IGA for twenty-four years, bagging groceries, stocking shelves, and collecting grocery carts in the parking lot. This latter task was his favorite because he got to sing while he did it, and he often sang at the top of his lungs. Most people quite liked his singing, although occasionally kids mocked and imitated him. It seemed to me that he didn't know, but I was wrong.

Late in the afternoon on Friday, with a cold beer and a fish fry in the motel restaurant on my mind, I said something about hav-

ing a good week, about being fishing buddies or the two Muske-
teers or something.

"Yep," he said, "just Tom and the retardo."

"What?" I said. "What did you say?"

"Nothing."

"No, Tony, tell me. You're not in trouble."

"I said, 'Tom Johnson and his retardo.'"

"Where did you hear that, Tony?"

"What do you mean?"

"Who said that to you?"

"Geez, Dad, everyone says that to me. People been calling me
that for years."

"What people?"

"Kids. Kids mostly."

"Oh, Tony, kids don't know what ..."

"It's okay, Tom." It was one of the rare times he called me by
my name, and I realized that he was comforting me. "It doesn't
bother me. It's just another word for Down syndrome; I know I'm
a retardo. It's okay."

"You know you are a man who has Down syndrome, yes, but
that's not all of you. You're much more than that."

"Oh, yeah?" he said, smiling hugely. "What more am I, Dad?"

"You're many things. You're a brother. You're a son. You're an
employee, an excellent employee. You're a local character."

"Oh, yeah? A local character?"

"Sure. Don't you know that people stop and shop at the IGA just
on the chance you'll be in the parking lot singing? Sure, they do."

"I like to sing, that's for sure. So what else am I?"

I looked at him for a long time. I looked in his eyes, and he
looked back. I'd never known him in all these years to look at
himself in this way, to introspect. Had he been doing it all along?

It was a bit like your dog suddenly saying, "Do I look goofy when I pant?" Was that what Tony had been to me: a glorified humanoid pet? What if he'd been like any other kid and just fallen off a motorcycle and hit his head? Wouldn't he still have a soul? Didn't Tony have a soul?

"I'm a pretty good fisherman!" he said.

"And you are an excellent fishing companion."

"How's that?"

"You're never in a hurry, and you're comfortable being quiet."

Tony got a big kick out of that. "I like being quiet!"

"I'm serious. Lots of people don't know how to shut up. Not you."

Tony threw his head back and laughed. I could see he was loving this. "That's why you're a good friend," I went on.

"I do have lots of friends."

"You're my good friend. Fact, I think you're my best friend." It sounded odd coming out of my mouth, like pronouncing a word I'd only seen written. I said it again just to hear it.

"Oh, no," he said, "Mike's your best friend."

"Nope, you are." And the amazing thing, Nora, is that he was. He really was. There was no one in the world with whom I was more comfortable. There was no one in the world I cared about more than this odd, chromosome-impaired little man-child sitting at the other end of the boat, smiling foolishly at me, this Tony Johnson.

"Nooo," Tony said. "You're crazy. You're nutso. You can't be my friend. You're my dad."

WHEN WE GOT home to Frenchman's Lake, there was a note on the kitchen counter from Julia that said, "Gone to Hilton Head."

"Hilton Head, South Carolina?" I asked Christine on the phone.

"Yeah. I guess they play a lot of bridge there."

"Well, how long's she going to be gone?"

"At least a month."

"A month?"

"Yeah, she rented a condo. Dad, listen, you know how she is.
…"

After a couple of weeks, I called Julia. I asked her how she felt, how the bridge was going, when she was coming home.

"Don't know."

"You don't know?"

"Listen, Tom, this is what I want to do, and I'm going to do it. I suggest you figure out what you want to do and do that. Don't wait around for me."

And that was pretty much how we lived the next nine years. Julia sold the dealership and bought a condominium in Hilton Head. She played lots of bridge and lots of golf, showing up at home when it pleased her and then spending much of her time at the country club. Every now and again she'd have us all over there for dinner as if it were her house. Brooks and Christine and all you kids were invited to South Carolina every year for specific and limited periods of time. She flew everyone in and flew them out. Tony and I sometimes stopped there for a day or two, coming or going somewhere else.

And what I figured out early on was that I didn't have a lot of choice. Tony and I were stuck with each other. Our mutual commitment was as absolute as it was involuntary. I could make either the worst or the best of the situation, and I decided on the latter.

One morning I said to Tony, "You know what I have a taste for?"

"What?"

"A grouper sandwich."

"Oh, yeah! A grouper sandwich. But you only get those in Florida, Dad."

"Let's go to Florida, then," I said.

Tony took a leave from the IGA, and a few days later we were sitting in Frenchie's on Clearwater Beach, eating grouper sandwiches. Then we started to work our way back. Slowly.

You couldn't be in a hurry traveling with Tony. You had to stop at every historical marker and almost every Dairy Queen for a butterscotch-dip cone and tuck a napkin in his collar so it didn't all end up on his shirt. In time there were other mandatory stops: scenic overlooks, drive-in theaters, water parks, petting zoos, demolition derbies, minor league baseball games, and Sunday brunches. We became masters of the brunch (eat eggs Benedict first, seafood next—especially oysters, shrimp, and smoked salmon—then meat and salad; avoid fried foods, breads, and desserts).

On the road you had to listen to either the Beatles, to which Tony always sang along, or English mysteries on tape. I was never sure how much of these stories Tony understood, but it didn't really matter because he just liked the way English people talk. We listened to some of the stories over and over, including *Taken at the Flood* at least ten times; we liked Hercule Poirot because he was little.

And we drove. I was the pilot and Tony was the navigator, always aflutter in unfolded maps that he didn't really understand. In those years we explored every corner of the United States, much of Canada, and a good bit of Mexico. There was something about the noise and motion of the car that made Tony happy and tired. He often fell asleep with his head on my lap. I would drive, smooth his hair with my hand, and sing "Danny Boy" or "Go Tell

Aunt Rhody" to him. Then when he woke up forty-five minutes or an hour later, he always wanted to know exactly where we were. I'd pull over, and we'd hold the map between us while I traced the route we'd driven and the distance we'd covered.

The trick to life with Tony was doing it on his terms. Otherwise it was all condescension, frustration, and impatience because he lacked many conventional skills. He could not walk, read, think, or bait a hook as well as I could, but he could do other things better. He could outwait a fish, any fish. He could lose himself in a song like no one I ever knew. He had an uncanny knack for knowing when a traffic light was going to change. "Now," he'd say a split second before it went yellow. And he could talk to animals, but this I never even knew until he was in his forties and we got Al Jones, which happened when we were driving in southern Illinois and saw a hand-lettered sign by a farm road that read, "Free Dog." Tony instantly wanted it. For twenty miles I tried to talk him out of it, but he would not be deterred, and I began to think, Why not? We went back and found the farmer working on the engine of his pickup. I told him we were interested in the dog.

"What dog?" the farmer said.

"The free one," Tony said.

"Oh, that. There ain't no free dog. That's the name of my place here."

"Why'd you name it that?" asked Tony.

"Well, my wife always called me 'dog.' When she was mad, which was a good bit of the time, she called me 'shit dog' or 'scum dog' or some such. Then she up and left." He smiled.

"So there isn't a free dog?" I asked.

"Just me. But there's a twenty-dollar dog."

"I guess I should have known."

The dog turned out to be a black-and-white border collie mix of indeterminate age.

"Is he housebroken?"

"After a fashion."

"What does that mean?"

"I've never let him in my house, but he knows not to shit where he lives."

I wanted to call him Twenty Dollar, but Tony insisted on Al Jones after a former produce manager at the IGA. Now it was the three of us. We lived like children despite the fact that the hourglass had been turned and our sands were running ever faster. Of course Tony was only vaguely aware of this, and Al Jones wasn't aware of it at all, much less that by virtue of his genes or the lengths of his telomeres, his lifetime would be squeezed into just twelve or thirteen years. Sometimes, driving along, I'd look across the car to where Al Jones had his head out the window, tongue lolling, ears blown flat, and Tony was singing "Yellow Submarine" too loudly, and then at my wrinkled old face in the rearview mirror, and I would wonder which of us was better off.

Tony loved Al Jones. He took him on long walks, fed him, groomed him, talked to him, taught him tricks, tried to teach him to walk on his hind legs, bathed him too often, always using Alberto VO5 shampoo, fell asleep with him in front of the TV, and fried eggs for him on Sunday mornings. And he talked to him endlessly. He sat on the floor with Al Jones in deep, heartfelt discourse, and the dog cocked his head and ears and looked every bit as if he were about to answer.

WHEN JULIA'S SYMPTOMS reappeared, she ignored them. By the time she went to the doctor, the cancer was everywhere. This time her reaction was entirely different. It seemed that the part of Julia that died first was her animus, and when it was gone, when she was stripped of anger and suspicion and resentment, there wasn't much left. When this happened, I knew that the thing had defeated her, and then I realized that for a long time I had thought she couldn't be defeated.

The children were very attentive to Julia while she was dying. Christine drove over three times a week to bathe her. She would sit on her mother's bed, and the two of them would talk quietly. Brooks was there just as often, striding around the room full of false cheer. Tony would tiptoe up the stairs and peek in at Julia's door. Sometimes they watched old movies together. Julia even took a brief if awkward turn toward me. One day when I was bringing her a tray of food, she gestured toward the book that lay beside her on the bed. She asked me to read to her.

It was Christopher Ogden's biography of Pamela Harriman called *Life of the Party.* I read until Julia fell asleep. The next day I read again, this time for two or three hours. The day after that, after I had read, Julia had me help her into a sitting position and brush her hair. She put her head back, closed her eyes, and let me gently pull at her hair and massage her scalp with the soft brush. It was the first time I had touched her with anything like tenderness in a very long time. But when I came to read again the following day, she rolled away and said she didn't think she could take it. I stood there saddened, embarrassed, afraid that I had, as I often do, given ten when only one had been requested or imposed something on her that I'd thought she was enjoying. I felt foolish. Of course she wasn't enjoying it; she wasn't enjoying anything. And what couldn't she take? Me? Intimacy? Pamela Harriman's gay, exciting life? Perhaps life itself. A few days later I was speaking to her, and again she rolled away.

"Julia?" I said.

She didn't answer me. I had started to leave the room before she spoke. "There was a letter for you from Holland." She said it as if it had come yesterday, and I was puzzled because she hadn't been downstairs in weeks.

"For me? When?"

"Back then. In the beginning. I destroyed it."

"You destroyed it?" I knew I couldn't ask her if she'd read it. I knew I couldn't ask her what was in it, but I also knew why she had accused me of having a "Dutch whore."

It was about a month after this exchange that Julia died.

Her funeral was not the celebration that many modern funerals try to be. Instead, people said careful things.

"I so admired her."

"She was always so stately."

"She was a presence."

Brooks was very emotional. Christine wept silently. Only Tony didn't show much feeling, and I worried some that he didn't know or understand what had happened. When I tried to explain, he wasn't very interested or he was impatient. I gave up, but one day more than a year later, when we were fishing, I saw that his cheeks were tear-stained.

I asked him if he was okay.

"Oh, yeah," he said. "I was just missing Mom."

As for me, I felt grief, but it was the grief of finality, that now there was no chance at all of a knowing glance or a whispered secret. I also felt the relief you feel with any death that isn't sudden and unexpected: relief from the illness but also from life itself, which at its sweetest and softest is still hard. "To die, to sleep ... 'tis a consummation devoutly to be wished." And I felt release, from my vigil, from our long mistake.

After Julia's death I made a conscious decision to try to find Sarah. I wrote her a letter and sent it to her parents' address. Sometime later it came back. I sent it again to Veldhoven, general delivery. It came back again with words that translated "address unknown." Still, I knew now that our dialogue had not ended with my letter to her. No, there had been a reply, and perhaps there was still a question to be answered.

I do not know why Julia destroyed the letter nor why she finally told me about it. Perhaps to torture me, perhaps to give me hope. Perhaps as an act of contrition or confession or forgiveness. I really do not know, but then there were many things I did not know about my wife.

In the years that followed Julia's death, Tony and I slowed down. We still traveled, but our trips were fewer and shorter. Perhaps it was because we were both getting older, perhaps because we had some health problems. I had my gall bladder removed, and Tony had high blood pressure. Or perhaps we no longer had as much reason to be away from home. We spent a lot of time sitting in our big pink chairs, fishing on the lake, and cutting and stacking firewood, although we finally had to get someone else to do that for us. In May we planted a garden of roses, impatiens, petunias, marigolds, lettuce, zucchinis, tomatoes, peppers, parsley, basil, and sometimes a pumpkin or two. We put onions, potatoes, and carrots in, too, to harvest in the fall, and when the weather turned we baked bread once a week. Tony was the kneader, kneeling on a chair and pushing and pounding the dough with his hands and fists while listening to the Beatles turned up loud. Sometimes we baked oatmeal cookies or butterscotch brownies, too.

For my eighty-fourth birthday, Tony gave me two third-row box-seat tickets for a Cubs/Pirates game at Wrigley Field. That was a big deal for both of us, so I told him we'd make a day of it. After the game we'd eat outside at Penny's Noodles and drink cans of Guinness with the hot food.

"Oh, yeah!" he said.

I let Tony sleep in and cooked him a special Mexican breakfast. When I heard the dog whining, I opened Tony's bedroom door to let him out. Al Jones lay on the bed beside Tony, who had been dead for some hours. His mouth was open and twisted.

I sat on the edge of the bed and touched his cool hand. I smoothed his hair. Al Jones nosed at me and whined. I let him out the back door, got the phone, sat back down, and started calling people. After a while I called the undertaker.

So that's the story of our family, Nora. Julia and I didn't have much of a marriage, it's true, but we made three children, and they hit doubles in the gap, flunked out of college, got pimples, bought houses, bagged groceries, had five more children, and those children won medals, earned degrees, got arrested, broke legs and hearts, and they'll have children, you'll have children, and it will go on. Julia has been dead for a while, and I'll be dead soon, but for the moment I'm still here, and as long as I am, I'm going to keep going because even after eighty-five years, life can still surprise me. I'm not ready to give up on it quite yet. In fact, I've decided to stay here in The Netherlands if I can. I'm in the process of applying for permanent residency.

Veldhoven, Autumn 2007

How long should it be until we hear?" Tom asked over the phone.

"How long since we submitted the application?" replied the lawyer. "Two weeks? Shouldn't be long."

"I also wanted to ask you if you can find out more about Pim de Wit."

The lawyer hesitated. He seemed about to offer some advice but asked instead, "What do you want to know?"

"Anything. General information."

Again the lawyer started and stopped. "I shall need two or three days."

But he called the next day. "Ja, I have your information. Quite interesting. Pim de Wit was born in Veldhoven in 1922."

"Not in Rotterdam, then?"

"Hmmm? No, here. A teacher of English at two schools in Eindhoven and one here. Married once, divorced long ago. Lives in a rent-controlled house that is owned by a housing association. Two children. A female named Ella, who is a dentist and lives here at Draaiboomstraat 37, which is also her clinic, and a male named Joost, who died in childhood. Now, here is the interesting thing." Then Tom heard papers shuffling.

"Go ahead."

"Just checking this to make certain. The daughter's name is Ella Mostert, but according to this, her maiden name was not Ella de Wit like her mother nor Ella van Praag. It was Ella Johnson."

TOM RANG THE BELL again, knocked on the door, and then banged on the door. "Pim de Wit. Please. I must talk to you. Pim, I know about Ella. I know. I would like to know more about her. Please." He banged some more. When the neighbor opened his door again, Tom smiled and stopped. He put the slim envelope he carried through the mail slot and left.

Tom went back twice more before the children came home from school to ring, knock, and call out, but to no avail. By late afternoon he was sitting in the garden with a book he wasn't reading. Ilse and Nienke were at the dining room table doing their lessons and taking them very seriously, as children sometimes do, turning work into play or play into work by pretending that they were small adults, and Tom was watching them from outside through the plate-glass window. What did they know of their mother's worries and heartaches? He had come down to the kitchen one day and found Saskia in her apron crying. She had pointed to the onion she had just cut, but hers were not onion tears. Instinctively he had put his arm around her, as he would have Christine, and she had leaned into him, cried against his shoulder for a few moments. Now Tom looked at the first floor, where Saskia had cranked the windows open and hung the bedding across the windowsills to air and thought that the house would likely get cramped and stale in the winter. He knew that change was coming. He did not know what it would be.

Tom saw Ilse slip off her chair and go into the hall, and he turned to his book. A moment later she was standing beside him. "Meneer," she said, "er is een vrouw voor u."

"A woman … ?"

Pim de Wit stood outside the front door. She held an envelope in her hands, which he assumed was the one he had left at her house earlier. She was quivering. Her lips and hands were quivering. Her hair was mussed, and she had been crying, but when she spoke, she did so with forced, enforced control. "What are you doing here? Why have you come here after all these years?"

Even if Tom might have answered, he didn't have time.

"I do not want you to be here. I want you to leave Veldhoven immediately. Do you hear me?"

This time he chose not to reply.

And this time her voice broke and her eyes overflowed. "And you are to never, ever speak to Ella. Do you understand? Never! Or see her. I want you to have nothing to do with her."

"But I need to know—"

"All you need to know is that after you left, I raised Ella alone, I had a hard time, we had a hard time, Tom Johnson, but that's behind us; I've made a good life and a good family and now, now …"

"Sarah …"

"Please leave them alone. Please leave me alone. Please do not do this to me again." She caught and calmed herself. "I want to be as clear as you were in this," she said, handing him the envelope. It was the letter he had written a couple of days after Tony's birth.

"Sarah …"

"I am not Sarah. Sarah is dead. Now, please, I beg you, go away."

Tom watched her go across the street and around the corner, and he watched the street long after she had disappeared. He didn't move or speak. Sarah. But she wasn't Sarah—yet she had to be. Many things converged in him then. One was the sound of her voice, which he'd not forgotten but now remembered quite viscerally in the pit of his stomach and in the middle of his head and the center of his chest. Another was the pain that voice could not conceal; her use of the word "beg" had not been merely a formalism. Another was the sudden, certain knowledge that of course she could not have been dead or he would have known. Perhaps he had always known that somewhere in the world she was alive because he could feel her there. And another was the thing that had brought him across the world and the years to this place and moment.

Finally Tom took the letter out of its envelope, unfolded it, and read it. He barely recognized his words. He barely recognized his handwriting. It seemed a very different letter than the one he had written so long ago. Could he ever have been so impersonal? Had it been some stiff-upper-lip attempt at sounding noble? And had he really used the phrase "look to the future" as if he were writing some Chamber of Commerce brochure? Did he have to say "very much"? And why "I'm sure you will understand"? He hated people who said that. And he hated people who said, "they say." Only the last sentence made any sense at all, and he'd forgotten he'd ever written it.

> *Dear Sarah,*
>
> *After shipping out I wrote you several times while still in England. When I didn't hear from you, I assumed it was because you didn't want to continue our relationship. I decided to look to the future. I came home, found a job, fell very much in love with a girl I knew in school, and married her. Recently two important things happened. Your letter was delivered almost a*

year after it was written, and our son Russell Anthony was born.
I'm sure you will understand that my life is now here with Julia
and our baby.

They say that fate works in strange ways, and this must be one
of them. I am sorry. If I live to be a very old man, I shall remember
you always.

Tom

TOM WOULD HAVE BEEN amused by the two policemen standing in Mrs. Waleboer's parlor if they hadn't frightened him so.
They both played the Dutch "We're just a small country" card;
the elder as in "I'm sorry to be wasting your time on something
so insignificant," the younger defensively, as in "Don't think just
because we're small you can come over here and push us around."
He made a production of studying Tom's passport, although it
was all but empty, scanning each line horizontally with his little
finger and then half turning away to say something in Dutch to
the other man. Fortunately it was the older cop who addressed
Tom. "There is a complaint against you by a citizen of the Ned-
erlands"—he pronounced the country's name quite pointedly in
Dutch—"accusing you of"—here he hesitated and spoke to the
other man, who answered him behind his hand—"of harrassness.
It seems that you have been molesting her. Now, I don't know—"
he continued with a note of qualification in his voice, but the
younger man interrupted him.

"You can be losing your visa over something like this," he said.
"Your residence here is temporary and privileged. You can be exported."

But they did frighten him so. They "scared the hell out of me,"
he told himself later, walking Leo. But why? When they had spo-

ken the name—Pim de Wit—it hadn't even registered with him for a second; it wasn't her name, not the girl he'd once known. It was her sister's. He realized that he hardly knew who this woman was. All he truly recognized in her was an ancient history and a desperate present, for the only thing they now seemed to have in common was the disproportionality of their reaction to each other, and it slowly dawned on him that this was something more than a last hurrah, an old man's final lark. No; the stakes were higher than he had known. He became aware that he could now see the vanishing point on which he had apparently always been advancing, the place at which his reality and his destiny would finally meet. The grandiose terms in which he found himself thinking alarmed him, but they also made everything much clearer. *It's just this simple,* he thought. *It's what everything boils down to. It's as simple as that.*

He sat down on a park bench because he was a little light in the head and weak in the knees. There was no turning back. No. There was no longer choice involved, only inevitability. This was how he was going to spend the rest of his life, and for the first time he wasn't sure he was up to it. Perhaps this woman Pim was just as daunted. Perhaps this explained her vehemence and anger and fright; did she somehow know what he had just realized? And what was that thing? That he had set something in motion that he could not stop?

And what in God's name was he to do now that he could not knock on her door, couldn't write her or talk to her or come within "fifty meters" of her without fear of "exportation"? He laughed out loud at that, sitting there on the bench, and Leo turned to him, nuzzled his hand, and wagged his tail. Tom Johnson had not felt this vital in a long time.

But that was before the letter arrived from the IND. Jan

Dekker leaned back in his chair, raised his brow, tapped his lips, and studied it. "Hmmm," he said. "You have been denied."

"Is that common?"

"Not in my experience. Not when all your papers are in order and you are having health insurance and a private income."

"Then why ..."

"Let's see. It refers to a pending legal action in Illinois."

"Yes, my son is trying to obtain guardianship of me."

"Ja, well, that probably means nothing here. Still, I think I might take most of your money and put it in a bank box."

"A safety-deposit box?"

"Yes. In a different bank. Protect it, but don't close your account. Now, this also refers to a letter your family wrote challenging your petition."

"My family? How did they even know I'd applied?"

Dekker tapped the letter. "They are having an advocat, a Dutch attorney. Anton Smits in Rijswijk, where the IND offices are. Probably an immigration specialist."

"Okay, but what are the grounds of the denial?"

"I don't know, but it's easy to guess. Something to do with your competence, physical or mental, your ability to handle your own affairs."

"Okay, Jan, what next? Is there an appeal process? Is there anything I can do? I need time."

"Well, yes, you can appeal, and they'll probably extend your visa if necessary. Otherwise you'll be required to leave the country when your visa expires, I'm afraid."

"Does an appeal stand a good chance?"

"If Ella Johnson Mostert is your daughter and Pim de Wit is her mother, it stands an excellent chance. If you are willing to use that information, it is all you need."

"And if I'm not?"

"Well, then, you haven't anything new. They'll reach the same decision."

"But I may buy some more time?"

"Perhaps. We can ask for a hearing. If it's granted, we can go together, and I can ask you questions, and, ja, the commission can see for itself that you are not incompetent. It is a bit of a small chance, but it is the only one you have. And it should give you some more time."

"And a hearing isn't part of the process?"

"No, not usually. We would have to request one."

"Not usually or not ever?"

"Let me look in it. Let me do a little research. I doubt that it would be without precedent."

Veldhoven, Autumn 2007
The War, Part III

Well, Granddaughter, I'm back. Again I have time on my hands, and again I'm going to fill it by writing (I can only hope that your request was sincere). This time the rest of my war story, which really begins when the war, at least the war in Europe, was over, although you'd hardly have known it. Everything was still olive drab, delayed, rationed, and top secret, but the shooting had stopped, and Sarah van Praag and I were in love.

After returning from Germany, I was billeted in a guesthouse that was more or less on the way to Sarah's home, so we often walked to and from the compound together. Then we began to take weekend bike rides into the countryside. On one of these we rode along the Dommel River to the village of the same name where they had a little brewery that made a crisp, bitter beer. It was late afternoon and quite warm, with the soft golden hues of summer in the air. People had brought chairs out of the cafés to sit beneath the linden trees, to drink and talk, to relax, to feel the oblique rays of the sun on their faces, to lean toward each other and smile or laugh, to not feel fear or anger this day. We joined them. We drank beer and ate young cheese, still-warm bread, and some of the vegetables that were coming in with the harvest: radishes, scallions, maybe beets and cucumbers. In front of us men in caps and women in scarves rode their bikes back and forth to the shops. An old bus creaked to a stop. A big farmer who somehow had managed to remain fat during the war rode a big workhorse bareback right down the middle of the shaded street, his legs splayed and knees locked, clogs bobbing on his big feet. Two other farmers dismounted from bikes to sit across the way, nursing beers. They looked like old friends who had not met in this way for a long time.

I asked about Sarah's sister in Amsterdam. She was an artist. Perhaps she could come to visit. Perhaps I could meet her.

"How did she escape the Nazis?"

"How do you mean?"

"I mean being a Jew."

Sarah said that her sister was not Jewish, that they were half-sisters, and while her father, who had died when she was a baby, was Jewish, Pim's was not. He was the man I had met, Sarah's stepfather. She told me that she had hidden in their vegetable cellar for more than four years, that she had not left their house from May 6, 1940, until September 17, 1944.

"My gosh. What did you do down there?"

"I studied English." She smiled. "I read books in English and French." She told me that she loved languages, that they came easily to her. She said she had always assumed that she would become a teacher of languages, but that now she had a new ambition. "I want to do what I do for you. I want to be a translator." She said she loved helping people who spoke different languages and came from different places understand each other. "I particularly like translating humor, like when you can help one person laugh at the other person's joke. I like when there is nuance, and you have to take distinctions. Like between 'slim' and 'skinny,' for instance. Or between 'rich' and 'wealthy.'"

"What is the difference?"

"Wealthy people have had their money longer."

"Is that true? I'm not sure it is."

She laughed and blushed at this. "Oh, dear. Perhaps I have been misleading you all along. Is there a difference between 'poor' and 'impoverished'?"

I loved watching her. The summer sun had tanned her skin, and it stood in striking contrast to the whites of her eyes and her white, white teeth. I had not known about her teeth for a long time because she hadn't smiled or laughed for a long time. This day she did both. She twined her legs around each other, crossed her arms, cocked her head, leaned back into her chair as if she knew that it could not fail her, and smiled and laughed. She had slender arms and legs, and when her hair fell over her eyes, she blew it away. I was amused by this because it seemed so casual or tomboyish, and everything else about her was quite elegant.

Later in grad school I would read Wordsworth's line about "spots of time" to which we return all through our lives because they contain something essential and restorative. I remember sitting in the main reading room of the Deering Library watching the motes of dust in the great shafts of sunlight coming in the tall windows and thinking of Sarah on that August afternoon, of her words, her smile, her dreams that now seem even more wonderful and magical because they were so young.

"Perhaps I will live in Den Haag or Geneva or even New York," she said. "Perhaps I could even help prevent another war."

What I said to Sarah that day was mostly youthful foolishness. I told her I wasn't sure I could go back to the flat, guileless

Midwest after all I had seen. I wasn't sure I could sit in church and sing "Faith of Our Fathers" with a straight face or pledge allegiance to any flag or rake leaves into a pile and burn them on an autumn afternoon. What would be the point? I said. What I think I meant was that I wanted always to be right there, right then with her.

That warm evening we dropped our bikes beside a farm canal and lay on our backs in the late northern twilight looking at the new stars. They were gleaming and sparkling and shooting. They were putting on a show just for us. I remember laughing out loud, they were so wonderful. I remember telling each other everything. Just everything. I remember falling asleep and waking at dawn with a new fact in my life, knowing with certainty that I was in love, and despite many years of trying to doubt and deny and negate it, I've known it ever since.

I think it fair to say that the next eight months were the happiest of my eighty-five years on earth. Sarah and I discovered that for all our differences, we saw life in the same way. We agreed about values and people. If someone was phony or genuine or interesting or manipulative, we both knew it and usually at the same time. And the people we agreed about included us. After that night with the resistance fighters and the Germans, we never doubted each other again, at least not until our very last night together.

And yes, of course I've wondered how my relationship with your grandmother would have been different had I never known Sarah. I do not know the answer to that question, Nora. What I do know is that what I never had with your grandmother is what I always had with Sarah. But even that is problematic because what we also always had was a deadline.

The war was over. We were shipping people home. My turn was going to come. We both knew that. Oh, sure, we talked of my coming back to Holland, and she talked of coming to America, but I'm afraid I discouraged this latter notion, and that led to our big fight, which in turn led to our breakup. I gave her the impression that I didn't want her to come, and by extension that I didn't want her. It wasn't that at all; it was just that I couldn't quite see Sarah in the church basement on Wednesday nights eating deviled eggs, baked beans, and Jell-O salad. Apparently she couldn't quite see me living in Veldhoven, either. At any rate, for all our pledges and promises, her coming to northern Illinois sometimes seemed impossible to me, and my coming back to Holland was fraught with difficulties I tried not to think about. If I were honest with myself, I knew I had had nothing to do with getting there the first time. Every single detail right down to the color of my socks had been arranged for me. Still, I had come to appreciate and identify with the Dutch people; they were nothing if not practical. Yes, they'd suffered great losses, been deeply wounded, even left for dead. But someone still had to bake the bread. Slowly they were puttering around, putting their country back together again, and I thought perhaps I could help them do that.

Sometime after Christmas Sarah announced to me that she had to go to Amsterdam to see her sister. "Good," I said. "Let me engineer some leave. I'd like to meet her, and I'd like to see Amsterdam."

"No," she said cautiously. "Listen, Tom, I have to do this myself and to ask you to let me and to not question me. Can you do that for me? Please can you trust me?"

She said she'd be gone five days, and she was gone nine. In that time I imagined many things: her sister was in trouble. Perhaps legal trouble. Her sister was a Nazi. She was pregnant. She was pregnant by a German. She was one of those pathetic, disowned women wandering around with her head shorn.

When Sarah came back she was chastened. After a time I asked her, "Is your sister all right?"

"Please don't ask me, Tom. Please understand that I can't talk about it."

"Sarah," I said, "it's not good for us to keep secrets."

"I know, but I have to. I made a promise."

"Don't you trust me?"

She turned then and looked in my eyes. "Let me tell you a story."

"Is it about your sister?"

It turned out to be about Sarah when she was a thirteen-year-old schoolgirl. There was a student in her form named Bep who was immature and quite unpopular. Bep did things that invited teasing, like picking her nose and being inappropriate. Also, she was fat, and she smelled because she didn't bathe often enough. So people teased her, and then she'd make matters worse by crying or fighting. One day the headmaster called Sarah to his room. Naturally she thought she was in some sort of trouble, but what he wanted was for Sarah to be Bep's friend. He said things about Bep as if Sarah were an adult. He asked her to sit with Bep during breaks and to include her in her group of friends. He seemed to think that Sarah was well adjusted and could help Bep.

I said that that must have been quite flattering.

"It was awful. No thirteen-year-old is well adjusted. I was just as insecure as everyone else."

"So what did you do?"

"Nothing. I didn't do anything, and then I had great feelings of guilt that grew and grew the longer I did nothing. It was terrible. He never should have asked me to do it. I was a child."

Was she telling me that she was not as strong as I'd come to believe she was? "And now I shouldn't be asking you to tell me about your sister, is that what you are saying?"

"Yes." Then she said slowly, "I shall tell you about my sister when you leave. I shall tell you on that day."

My leaving was on both our minds. In the final weeks, Sarah began to teach me Dutch quite purposefully, and I began to really work at it. It was as if we were trying to forge some more permanent connection, something I could take with me or something I could bring back.

One spring weekend we took a trip to Antwerp, and the train was full of GIs headed for Ostend to ship out. Three sat in our compartment, and I remember that they started to talk about home, about cold beer and hot showers and thick steaks. About angel-food cake, strawberry shortcake, and cold watermelon. Then they talked about baseball, about all the ballplayers who had enlisted, about the retired players and kids who'd replaced them. One said that the St. Louis Browns even had a one-armed outfielder and the Reds had a fifteen-year-old pitcher.

"Fifteen?" the other two asked each other.

When the GIs left, I caught Sarah watching me. It was as if she'd learned something new about me, something she didn't quite understand or perhaps even trust, as if she'd seen me in my element for the first time. She asked me if I felt like the young soldiers.

The little I remember about that weekend isn't very pleasant. I remember a lot of bombed-out buildings, elegant old buildings ruined. I remember the whores of Antwerp. They were also old and damaged-looking. I remember our bleak little room and that we quarreled and went to bed angry with each other. I remember that we walked beside the River Scheldt which was still littered with war wreckage: things floating, things washed ashore, the burned and half-sunken shells of launches and barges. I remember Sarah saying, "What's wrong, Tom? Are you all right, darling?"

I was quite sure she'd never called anyone "darling" before. I was quite sure she'd been waiting a long time to do so.

I remember that I ate mussels for the first time, that we dipped hunks of bread into the broth they'd been steamed in, that Sarah gave me a lesson in dark Belgian beers, that I called her the docent of the beer museum. It wasn't all bad, but it wasn't the romantic escape we had planned; we had wanted it to be a gay occasion.

Everything that came afterward was anticlimactic. We were waiting, and waiting is an anxious state. One evening we rode our bikes to the café in Dommels, hoping to recapture the good time we'd had there, but our effort was forced. I was trying to speak Dutch, which I did then at the level of a very young child, and Sarah was laughing at me good-naturedly. She wanted me to say "Scheveningen," which is a place name so hard to pronounce that it has been used in the past by the Dutch army to unmask spies.

I tried and tried. "I'll get it," I said.

"You'll never, ever be able to say it," she said, laughing, "not like a Dutchman." And then she was serious and honest in a way I was not prepared for. She said that Holland, unlike the United States, was not a nation of immigrants, that everyone there was Dutch and had been for a thousand years, and besides, now it had been bombed to bits. She wondered why we would not logically go to my home in Illinois. "I know you think I'd be bored. ..."

"It's not that."

"Then try to help me understand what it is, Tom."

What it was was that I was twenty-four years old, had been the first in my family to get a college degree, and now I'd been to Europe. I was quite impressed by how far I'd come and quite embarrassed by where I'd come from, by my father saying "right cheer" for "right here" and falling asleep in front of the fire with his shirttail sticking through his fly, by my mother putting canned soup in the meatloaf.

"It's not that you'd be bored, really. You just don't understand," I said, wanting very much for that to be the fact and not that she'd wounded my pride by being amused by my Dutch. "The people I live with are farmers. They're very, very provincial. They're worse than that. They're small-minded, narrow-minded. To tell you the truth, half of them are German, if you know what I mean. ..."

"No, I don't know what you mean."

"Of course you do. They're German. Don't make me spell it out."

"Because they're German and I'm Dutch?"

"Because they're German and you're a Jew, for gosh sake. There aren't any Jews in the town."

She said that she was half Jewish and that no one would have to know.

I said everyone would know. For that moment I wanted to have authority over her, to know something she didn't.

"They're all anti-Semites? Are your parents?"

"No, of course not. They just don't know any Jews."

"Have you told them I'm Jewish? I don't think you have. What have you told them about me?"

"Well, you know, just general information."

"General information? Like my name, rank, and serial number?"

"Oh, Sarah, no, of course not. Like you work for me. Like I've been a guest in your home."

"Have you told them that we're talking of marrying and spending our lives together?"

"Look, I thought I'd—"

"Have you told them about me at all? Do they even know I exist?"

"Of course they do."

"They don't, do they? You haven't even told them about me. Are you embarrassed by me?" She stood up suddenly with tears in her eyes. "I'm sorry," she said, "I'm sorry. I can't be with you. I must go." I thought she'd gone to the toilet, but then she was pedaling her bike right past me. I looked for the waiter. I called for the check. I dug money out of my pockets. I rode after her, but she had sprinted ahead or turned off.

What I realized as I rode along was that I'd never really thought about taking Sarah home with me because I'd always assumed that I'd stay here, that I'd become a Dutchman, that we'd wear Wellingtons into the woods and ride bikes and drink beer in cafés for the rest of our lives. I thought that the status and standing I had as an American officer would somehow continue after the war. I'd never thought at all about making a living or pronouncing "Scheveningen" or how inchoate and unrealistic my fantasy had been, and as soon as I saw it, I was too embarrassed to admit it. So I didn't. Now, riding faster and faster, it was all I wanted to do. *Of course we can live in America,* I wanted to say. *Of course my parents will love you, and yes, I've told them all about you, especially that I love you and want to marry you. I don't care where we live as long as we are together.*

I was so lost in all of this that I missed a turn and was a long time getting to Sarah's house. When I finally did, I knocked several times at her door before her stepfather came. "She is not here," he said. The next day, when I knocked again, he said, "She has been called away to Hilversum."

"But my orders have finally come through. I'm shipping out

now. Possibly tomorrow." I must have seemed desperate to him because he was a little frightened.

"But she is not here. It is the truth. She is gone. I am very sorry."

And that was it. I never saw her again. I rode in the back of a jeep to Belgium half in a daze but still sure we'd reconnect. Then I was in England, writing endless drafts of a letter saying everything to her that I had said to myself on my long bike ride and finally "Please, please forgive me. Please, please write me. Know that I do love you so." Then I was on board a ship. Then I was home.

For the next sixty years I wondered what had really happened. Did I somewhere in my deep recesses harbor ancient, atavistic fears and hatreds? And what had Sarah meant by "I can't be with you"? Now? Had she meant "I need a moment alone," or had she meant "I can't ever be with someone like you"? Had she discovered that thing in me that we all fear will eventually be found out?

I still don't know, Nora, but I think I may soon. Sarah is alive after all. The details aren't important except that her name isn't Sarah van Praag at all. It is Pim de Wit; don't ask me why because I don't know. What I do know is that she's here, she's very angry, and she wants me to leave. So, strangely, I have hope. What I also know is that all these years, I've never spoken of that time, but neither have I forgotten it, and I've never forgotten Pim de Wit and the night we invented love.

Veldhoven, Spring 2012

Much later Pim would also remember that night for me and would laugh when I used Tom's phrase "we invented love." "That man," she would say.

We would be sitting in her spring garden amidst budding flowers, drinking tea. She would speak with the candor and directness for which the Dutch are famous. She would, despite the differences in our ages, speak to me confidentially as one woman to another, leaning a little toward me as if we were two people who knew something that one-half of the human race did not, and I guess maybe we did. She would look at me with those steady, very blue eyes, those still-water eyes that surprised me at first because Tom had never written about them, but then maybe eyes are one of the things that men don't know about or understand. She would say to me, "Of course I liked him. He was tall and handsome and had that wonderful smile, a bit too wonderful if you know what I mean. There were stories—we had been warned about Americans that they were, oh, I don't know, glib and insincere. I kept waiting for him to be those things, kept expecting him to be. That smile. I thought he used it as a weapon, and here he didn't even know he possessed it. And yes, I was falling in love, but reluctantly. I was fighting myself over it. I was angry with myself about it. I just didn't trust him. Not until the night you've asked about. And oh, yes, I remember it. I've always remembered it.

"We were coming back from somewhere on our bikes. We were riding along a river, and we stopped to adjust something on one of our bikes and started to look up at the stars. All day long I had thought that he was going to try to make love to me that night. And I had thought of what I would do, how I would turn my face from his, how I would say no. But then he was so frightened and uncertain that I felt awful. I felt guilty and cynical, I guess, and—well, yes—in love for the first time in my life. And though I knew nothing at all myself, I suddenly knew that I knew much more than he did.

"We had put our bikes down. We were standing on the banks of the river, and he tried to hold me. Awkwardly. He put his arms around me, and I started to put my arms up between us as you do—I'm sure you've done it—but before I could, I felt his heart beating. I felt his heart beating against my breastbone, and I felt him trembling, and, well, it disarmed me." She said it also thrilled her and frightened her and sent a surge of desire through her like an electrical current. "I had felt desire before that night, but I'd never known what to do with it. That night I did. I could feel my body preparing itself for love." And her defenses dissolved. They were gone. "I looked at him again. He was a man-child, a little boy, a baby. He, too, was scared to death, so I took a step back and looked into his bewildered eyes. And then I smiled at him as you might smile at a little boy or a puppy, perhaps, and I said, 'Touch your hands to mine. Go ahead.' And then we were holding hands like that, just hands, face to face. 'Feel my hands,' I told him. He was uncertain, so I said, 'Now touch your forehead to mine,' and then I said, 'Touch your nose to mine,' and then he said, 'Oh, Sarah,' as I'd always wanted someone to say my name even though it wasn't my name, and then we were kissing." Now Pim laughed and shook her head. "Oh, my, did we kiss. The next day my face was a little chafed, and my lips were swollen. Do you know what I mean?"

I should tell you that at the moment when Pim asked me that question, I did not, but I should also tell you that I do now; that is also part of this story.

"And then, I don't know … I'm sure we did it all wrong." She laughed again. "We hadn't any idea what we were doing, neither of us. I lifted him with my hips, and he entered me, he parted my flesh as if he'd always been waiting for me and I'd always been waiting for him. And then I quite suddenly felt everything I'd ever wanted to feel, and I knew in an instant what I'd always wanted to know. We didn't stop kissing for a long time." Those blue eyes had a faraway look in them now. Then they looked at me, and Pim smiled and asked a bit incongruously, "Can I pour you some more tea, Nora? Would you like a biscuit?"

Part Two

Veldhoven, Autumn 2007

The first woman was too young. She was pretty in that uncomplicated, sanitized, spearmint-scented way of dental technicians, and she had the easy patter about pets and children and holidays one step removed by good but not perfect English. She'd been to Chicago, stayed in a hostel "near the university," gone to a free concert in Grant Park, and eaten deep-dish pizza. She took x-rays as she told him all of this, scraped and polished and flossed his teeth.

The second woman was older, shorter, and plumper. When Tom said he'd never had a female dentist before, she said all dentists should be women because their hands are smaller and their fingers nimbler, and he knew they were having an exchange that she'd had a thousand times with a thousand patients. She studied his mouth, and he studied her face; how else could he have gotten so close? Her chin doubled as she leaned over him; her eyes were magnified by safety glasses and her pores by proximity. Her smallest finger was sharply tapered at the end, just as his mother's had been. That made him take a little breath. She was taking little breaths, too. They were breathing together, Tom and his daughter, alone and together in that little room.

"So you are an American, then?"

"Uh-huh."

"Why are you living in Veldhoven?"

"I'm staying with my son. He works for Philips."

"Do you like it here?"

"Uh-huh."

"My father was an American," she said.

"Uh."

"Soldier in the war. He abandoned us. Not really me. I hadn't been born yet. He abandoned my mother. You are having a cavity. Make an appointment, and I'll fill it."

In the days between the appointments, Tom thought mostly about two sentences. The first was "He abandoned us." He tried to put together all that he knew and all that he could assume. The letter Julia had destroyed must surely have told him of Ella's existence, and when he hadn't answered it, the rest of the narrative was easy to imagine: Cavalier American soldier impregnates trusting Dutch girl and leaves. Takes no responsibility. Offers no support. No wonder Pim de Wit was so hurt and angry. And all these years that he'd been remembering her with fondness and longing, she had been hating him. She had hated him for decades, fifty times longer than she had loved him, if she ever had.

The second sentence Tom couldn't get out of his mind was "My father was an American." What would he have done if he'd gotten Sarah's second letter? Well, certainly supported Ella, maybe gotten to know her, possibly helped raise her. He imagined her visiting during the summers, saw a ten-year-old Ella in the rearview mirror sitting on the backseat of a station wagon, reading to Tony, Brooks, and my mother, Christine. But of course Julia never would have tolerated or allowed this, which was why she had destroyed the letter, he was sure. What would have happened then? Trans-Atlantic phone calls. Long letters. Yearly trips to Holland.

Or perhaps it would have precipitated the break that never came and maybe should have. The undivorced.

Each time Tom passed a mirror or a store window, he looked a little more closely at himself, like a man with a new hat or one growing a mustache. All these years he'd had four children and never even known it. He thought about that most intimate and personal of facts that many of us are not privy to but the rest of the world is: how and when we die. "My father was an American." Past tense. He wondered how he was supposed to have died and also what else he didn't know about himself: some weak-walled blood vessel, secret tumor, genetic predisposition, as yet unrevealed fatal flaw, accident waiting to happen, some kindness or unkindness or miracle or devastation he was destined to deliver or had already delivered without even noticing. The world had changed just like that. For Tom now, every single idea, act, fact, thought, and feeling was itself and one thing more, was itself plus Ella Johnson. Nothing was the same. Not his last night with Ella's mother. Certainly not. Not his first night with Julia, oh, my, no. Not bliss or clarity or certainty or love. Nothing.

"Hard to be an American now," said the doctor, sitting above him during their second session.

"Uh-huh." And when he could speak, he said, "This damned cowboy."

"You weren't believing in the weapons of mass destruction?"

"No, I didn't buy that. I used to teach debate, and any first-year debater could tell you there wasn't enough evidence. Some aluminum tubing, a couple trucks, and one questionable informant. Besides, there is only one real reason for war, and that is because it is necessary. This one isn't."

"You are sounding like the voice of experience. Were you in World War II?"

"Yes."

"In Europe?"

"Yes."

"Where?"

"In France, Belgium, and Germany," he said cautiously.

"In Holland?"

He couldn't lie to her again, although he'd planned to. He'd made up a son and a name, but when she asked him directly, he said, "A little."

"Where?"

"In Eindhoven."

She had her back turned to him, although he could have touched her. Her head was bent, her elbows splayed, her hands engaged. Tom was still trying to assess if the silence in the room was awkward when she said, "I am thinking you may be my father."

FROM THE BEGINNING there were ground rules. They were not to be seen in public, at least not in Veldhoven. He could have no encounters with Pim, not even accidental ones; he was to turn and go the other way. Pim was also off limits in their talks; he was not to ask about her. Any information Tom came by, Ella volunteered. And he was to tell no one. Of course he had to tell someone, and it pretty much had to be Dickie. Besides, the other man seemed to be slipping away. Perhaps he'd been embarrassed by their night of drunken intimacy, or perhaps Tom had said something offensive that he hadn't remembered afterward. Dickie wasn't picking up his phone and was less often in the park. On a day when he was, Tom blurted out the whole story, in part to say it and in part to confide it, to signal to Dickie that as far as he was concerned, nothing between them had changed.

"Bloody hell," said Dickie.

"I had no idea," said Tom.

"Rubbish," said Dickie, and in just that word, there was some slight asperity or impatience. "'Course you did. Something brought you here."

"Yes, her mother."

"And something else, I think. You must have considered the possibility."

"You don't understand," said Tom. "I was the condom king; that's what they called me. I had crates of the damn things. Of course I'd never used one before. I'm not sure I would have known had one failed."

"Apparently not."

His meetings with Ella were all initiated by her, each for a limited time and covering a specific subject. For a while they took place at Mrs. Waleboer's when neither Saskia nor the children were home. The first thing Ella wanted to know about was her half-brothers and half-sister. They sat at the dining room table. He had a stack of Kodak packets, and he emptied these one by one, laying the pictures out in front of her in rows almost as if he were dealing cards. She studied each intently, and Tom watched her. Some of the photos she picked up to see more closely or to hold in the light. First she wanted to know about my mother. Tom had already decided that if this moment came, he would have no secrets. "The only trouble we ever had with Christine was when she was a teenager. She went with this wild boy I never liked. She got pregnant, but she miscarried. They quarreled over it and broke up." He told her that my mother was generous, genuine, sensitive, high-strung, and conscientious, a worrier who would be worrying about him right now. Saying it made him feel guilty and then immediately defiant, as if guilt were a trap laid by his children. *Goddamnit,* he thought. So he told her a little less sympathetically about Uncle Brooks. Big, funny, loud, gregarious. Always falling out of trees. Always landing on his feet. Not much work ethic but lots of charm and a big heart.

"And this is Russell Anthony?"

"We called him Tony."

"When was he born?"

"Same year as you: 1947. You're a few months older."

"How did he die?"

"He had a weak heart. Down syndrome people often do."

"Did he live in a hospital or rest home?"

"No, no. He lived with us and then with me after Christine and Brooks grew up and Julia, my wife, died."

She wanted to know everything about him, so Tom told her. He told her about Tony the classroom helper, the grocery bagger, the fisherman, the baseball fan, the dog lover, the singer of Beatles songs. She wanted to know his favorite. "'She was just seventeen, you know what I mean' ... 'Yellow Submarine,' 'Sgt. Pepper's Lonely Hearts Club Band' ..."

"Was it difficult to care for him?"

"Sometimes."

"Do you think he was happy?"

Tom didn't want to answer this too quickly or certainly. "I think so, and so was I. He was my pal."

She wanted to know what "pal" meant, and he tried to translate: "Buddy, friend, little friend."

"Little friend," she said. "Vriendje." She looked at more photographs and asked more questions: Did anyone ever make fun of him? Did he know he had Down syndrome? Did he like girls? What did he like to eat?

"His favorite thing was a grilled cheese sandwich."

She wanted to know what it was.

"Like a tosti," he said. He made them each a grilled cheese. They ate them with pickles and chips and glasses of cold milk, just as Tony used to. Ella sat with her ankles crossed and chewed so thoroughly and earnestly that Tom had to chuckle at her.

"Why do you laugh?"

"You're reminding me of someone. Maybe my father."

IT WAS AFTER the first visit that Tom decided he needed to check on Brooks and my mother. Perhaps because he wanted to make sure that just because Ella had suddenly appeared, they hadn't suddenly disappeared, or perhaps because since the pepper-spray incident things had been strangely quiet. Could they possibly be content just to know where he was and that he was well? Maybe my mother. Not Brooks. No, Brooks was up to something; Tom just knew it. He began to feel the annoyance a parent feels toward a child who has disobeyed him: "But I told you ... I instructed you!" But when he allowed himself to think of Christine, he felt the alarming ache a parent feels for a child who is in pain. When she didn't make cheerleader in junior high school and cried herself to sleep in his lap. When her second baby was stillborn and she came home to sit in a lawn chair and stare at the lake for hours and hours under a quilt on a chilly day; how many times had he looked out the window at her?

He dialed half her numbers before stopping, thinking, replacing the receiver, going for a walk along the little canal behind the church. Maybe that was a line he mustn't cross. Maybe that was the one door he couldn't reopen. If he did, then they would be here or he'd be there, and after this great fiasco, this colossal Toby Tylering, they'd lock him away so fast. They'd handcuff him to his bed. They'd never rest easy again.

He went back and used a calling card to phone his lawyer, Jerry Santoro. "They're worried about you, Tom. Can they contact you?"

"No. Did you see Brooks?"

"Yes."

"Did he ask you about guardianship?"

"No," he said carefully, "but then he wouldn't, would he? I'm *your* attorney. But I heard something across the table at the Rotary luncheon last week you might be interested in. It's on the QT, but apparently Brooks has applied for a rather large home equity loan."

"What? Why would he do that."

Jerry didn't answer, but neither did he have to.

"Wouldn't Christine have to sign for that, too?"

"For it to be legal."

Afterward he sat a long time, worrying about what was going on. Would Christine ever have agreed to sign the loan application? He didn't think so. Did that mean Brooks had forged her signature? And how much trouble was Brooks in, anyway?

At their second meeting Ella brought the photographs. The first few pictures were of Ella through the years. Tom would later call this small collection self-effacing: carefully selected, representative, modest in number, more modest in what the photos depicted—Ella the infant, the toddler standing knock-kneed and openmouthed, the tiny, pudgy broomball player in a swarm of others, with pigtails, giggling, looking embarrassed in a two-piece bathing suit, looking awkward with a teenaged boy, looking mysterious and intense with other girls who looked the same at a table filled with beer bottles in a room filled with cigarette smoke, graduating from dental school, wearing a lab coat in a clinic, with a baby in her arms, caught off guard and looking over her shoulder. Next were photographs of her garden and her house: all windows and open space, which surprised Tom. Then there were pictures of Ella's husband, Henk. And of the children. There was a boy, Robby, and a girl, Hanneke. Both kids were blond. The girl had the delicacy of her grandmother, a certain fineness of feature, a certain grace in movement that could be seen even in still photos. It was in the way she sat, stood, held her arms and hands. The boy was also delicate, perhaps even frail, when he was young, but in adolescence his shoulders broadened, he grew tall, his hair became a tangled mop that hung over his eyes, and Tom wondered if he ever blew it away as his grandmother once had. There were many pictures of Robby playing tennis. Tom could tell, as he was poised beneath a serve he had tossed high in the air, as he cocked himself to hit a two-handed backhand, that Robby was an accomplished player.

At their third meeting Ella explained her mother's two names.

During World War I Ella's grandmother had married a local boy named Ard van Praag, who was Jewish. They had gone to live in Rotterdam, perhaps because his parents or hers had disapproved. They had a child named Sarah; then van Praag died of influenza, and the woman came back to Veldhoven with her infant daughter. There she married another local boy, a young clerk named Alfons de Wit, and they had a daughter they named Pim after Alfons's brother, who had enlisted in the Belgian army and died in the war. "That's how she got a boy's name." Years passed. World War II broke out. Brabant fell to the Nazis in the spring of 1940, and Sarah, now twenty-two, went into hiding in the vegetable cellar; the family told their neighbors that she had got out just in time, that she had gone to England before the fall. The subterfuge worked, but during the course of the war, Sarah became ill and weak. As soon as the Americans liberated Veldhoven, she was rushed to a doctor and diagnosed with tuberculosis. The best treatment and the best doctors were at a sanatorium called Zonnestraal in the town of Hilversum. The problem was that Hilversum was in the part of Holland that had not yet been liberated and that was still behind German lines, but Sarah would die if she was not treated, and her parents didn't trust the Belgians or the French or the English. "They were very provincial," Ella said. "Only a Dutch doctor was good. Besides, at that time the Germans are fleeing and the Allies are coming fast; everyone thinks that the war is almost over. Of course it is not." Pim, who was twenty-three, made contact with the underground and arranged to smuggle her sister into German-controlled territory. "This is how she knew to be your guide a few weeks later. Already she had done it once." But of course Sarah was half Jewish, so the two girls exchanged identities and papers. Sarah became Pim, and Pim became Sarah. The plan worked. Pim, of course, was safe because Brabant was under Allied control. "Safe, so, until you come along and ask her to work for you. Now her harmless deception looks not so harmless, especially to her parents. What if it is found out that she is carrying false papers? Someone can think she is a spy."

"Why not just tell us the truth in the beginning?"

"It is wartime; the truth is not worth for much, and besides, five years under the Nazis and my grandparents do not trust all authorities. Also they feared that if Pim is revealed, Sarah might be in danger. So Pim lived as Sarah, and she fell in love with you as Sarah van Praag." There was something important in this to Tom: an acknowledgment that Pim had been in love with him, something the daughter could know only if the mother had told her. So she must have said the words years afterward.

"But why not tell me after the war was over?"

"She wanted to, but her parents are still frightened. Trials are going on in Nuremberg. People are hanging, and my mother has lied to you. They are afraid she will be accused of espionage."

"Then I have been looking for the wrong person," he said.

"No, just the wrong name. Sarah never got better. She never left hospital. She died only a little after the war."

"Then your mother, Pim de Wit, is the same woman that I knew as Sarah van Praag in 1946."

"Yes and no."

"How do you mean?"

"She is the same person many years later, and that is not the same person. When people go away, they think that what they leave behind stays the same, but it doesn't. It changes." Now Ella smiled at Tom. It was a cautionary smile. There was in it a component of curiosity and perhaps one of warning, as if to say, "There are things you don't understand."

Northern Illinois, Autumn 2007

The part of academic life I was beginning to think I didn't really like was the academic part: the academy, academe, belonging to a group of people I wasn't sure I belonged with. This occurred to me one dreary afternoon in a seminar on Marxism as I watched the students across the table from me nodding their heads almost in unison to something obvious and unbrilliant that the professor was saying. He was a slouch who could barely bother to show up, let alone teach, a task he farmed out to us; we spent the quarter reading our papers to each other, laughing at his bad jokes, currying his favor, and kissing his ass. I'd mortgaged my future in loans and was working my butt off waiting tables at Bar Louie for this? And here was the real joke: the half-dozen Marxists in that class were about the only ones left in the world. The thought of spending the rest of my life with them in these little rooms that had once thrilled me now scared the shit out of me, but not quite as much as the thought of what I'd do if I didn't have these little rooms.

I got someone to take my shifts at the restaurant and went home for the weekend, but that wasn't much better. My mother tried to impress me by cooking coq au vin, something she'd never, ever done before, and my father by engaging me in an intellectual discussion of an episode of *Law and Order*. After dinner I gave up and went to meet some friends in a bar, but that was worse yet. They seemed consumed with talk of boys, cars, and clothes, almost as if they were still in high school. I watched from a growing distance until I realized they, too, were trying to impress me, and that really got me down. If I didn't fit in one place and I didn't fit in the other, where did I fit? I felt very much at sea.

When I got home my parents were still up. My mother was in tears and my father in a rage. Apparently Uncle Brooks had been using my mother's car all week because his transmission had gone out and was supposed to return it that night, but he had called at nine o'clock with some fishy story about his car not being ready, so he was going to have to keep hers until Monday.

"He's up to something," my mother said.

"Didn't even ask," said my father. Now my mother was going to have to use my father's car to go to work, and he was going to have to change his plans to go to the botanical gardens.

"Take mine," I told him.

"That's not the point."

"Then don't."

"Well, no need to be snippy."

But that's what I was: snippy. Maybe it wasn't that I was at sea but that I needed to go to sea, like Ishmael when he feels like knocking men's caps off. The next day, with the house to myself, I turned the music up, lit some candles, and took a long, very hot bath. While I was soaking there, I had an idea. When I got out

I got on the computer and looked up my mother's I-pass. There was the whole record. Three times since Monday Uncle Brooks had crossed the Chicago Skyway and the Indiana Tollway to exit 10 in Gary.

"Shit," I said aloud. Then I e-mailed Tom and told him, "You know what that means: riverboats."

Brabant, Autumn 2007

Tom looked for traces of himself in Ella. He held her hand in his and touched her tiny, tapered finger, explaining that it was identical to his mother's. She was visibly affected by that, as she had been by his letter.

> *My dear Ella,*
>
> *I must tell you that never in all these sixty years have I ever even thought of the possibility of your existence. What an awful thing for a father to say to his daughter. And yet it is true. At least I think it is. My friend Dickie Druyf says that somewhere on some level I must at least have wondered. He says that's why I came to Veldhoven: to see you. Perhaps he is right. I don't know.*
>
> *What I do know is that finding you, however accidentally, and now getting to know you is the most wonderful gift I've ever been given.*

Tom thought a good bit about how to sign it. "Your father." "Your dad." "Love, Dad." All seemed presumptuous. In the end he signed it "Tom Johnson."

There was something about the way Ella stood up from a chair that was also like Tom's mother, and her sudden, surprising burst of laughter that recalled his father's brother, and her candor. One day she said, "So what do we do now?" There it was. There was the evidence of him in her. It was the exact kind of question he would ask, and he almost heard her say it in his own voice.

"You mean now that we've exchanged pictures and life stories and all of that?"

"Yes."

"I'm not quite sure."

"I don't know, either. Are you planning to stay here in Veldhoven?" And he wasn't sure if it was an invitation to stay or one to leave.

"I have planned that, but I may not be able to." He told her about his application for residency, its denial, the letter Brooks and Christine had written, the hearing Jan Dekker had requested.

This conversation took place on a Friday evening in a rather swank restaurant in Den Bosch, the next city up the train line. They shared a meal, a bottle of wine, and a certain familiarity born of their mutual honesty, which Tom was tempted to think of as intimacy (walking back to the station, she did take him by the arm, if only for a moment or two, and said the word "father" in both English and Dutch). Tom was afraid to think of it as affection and did not want to think of it as flirtation, although later he would have to admit that the evening had had something of the feel of a date about it.

They had come on separate trains but made the mistake of sitting together on the return train. Someone must have seen them, so the next day there wasn't any ambivalence at all when Ella said, "You must leave Veldhoven at once."

"What's happened?"

"She knows, and you must go. I am not asking you to leave. I'm telling you that you must leave. She is extremely upset."

"My God, Ella, why does she hate me so?"

"She doesn't hate you. She fears you."

"Fears me? Why would she fear me?"

"She thinks you've come to take me away from her," she said with characteristic candor and a bit of impatience as if he should have seen this.

"But Ella, I couldn't do that if I wanted to."

She looked at him and said tentatively, "My mother and I, we've had a difficult life together. For many years we did not talk."

"I didn't know that," Tom said quietly.

"Of course you didn't. You didn't know anything. You have imagined all of it."

"Then tell me."

"No!" Ella answered almost shrilly. "You haven't the right to know. You would have to ask her."

Tom was taken aback by Ella's severity, and he realized that in focusing on Pim's reaction, he had overlooked Ella's, and hers was one of anger that to his surprise was directed at him but, also to his surprise was not directed only at him. "Do you know how hard it was growing up without a father or one who was a myth and with a mother who cared more about a lost memory than me?"

"Oh, Ella, I don't know. I'm sorry. I—"

"Just go away. You have no idea the trouble you have caused here."

He did not have any idea. In fact, up until that moment, despite Pim's reaction to him, he had thought of himself as a messenger of love and hope, a romantic emissary from the distant past. But now he recognized again in himself, as he had so often, a tendency or perhaps a need to turn life into a drama in three acts with villains and victims and heroes when he knew full well in his heart that no one is all of one of these and everyone is part of all of these. Now he also realized that he was somehow a threat not only to Pim but to her daughter and her family.

Oddly, viscerally, selfishly, also he knew it was better to be a problem than an afterthought or a footnote. Still, or perhaps therefore, he went away. He was looking for the thing he could do for Pim and Ella, and here it was. He could leave, and he would have left that very day if it hadn't been for the bank account he had to clear and Mrs. Waleboer's need to find someone to watch the girls after school and the phone call he felt he owed Dickie, which after several failed attempts turned into a phone message that he would later think was too cryptic to be of any worth at all. So Tom didn't leave for two days, and that was fortunate, or this story might have ended very differently.

The morning of his departure he put his bag by the front door and stood in the living room looking at the street and waiting for the taxi. He put a couple hundred euros in an envelope, sealed it, wrote "Mrs. Waleboer" on it, and left it on the dining room table. He hadn't told Jan Dekker that he was going. He planned to call the lawyer from the small hotel in Amsterdam near the Museumplein that he had booked for a day or two. When the taxi honked and he was stooping to pick up his bag, he found a small envelope addressed to "Tom Johnson" that had come through the mail slot. He slipped it into his breast pocket on his way out.

In the taxi he thought about Pim standing disheveled at his door, holding his letter in her shaking hands. Through all these years she had become an abstraction to him, a theory, an idea. And then there she was, saying his name again, explaining something so desperately again, raising her brow in earnest again, crying because of him again. And her presence. Her physical presence—his sense of which, his memory of which, had become smeared or smudged by time—was instantly real and immediate, and he felt like a child looking through his fingers at someone who had never gone away. The silky, supple timbre of her voice only slightly diminished, her still-perfect posture, her high, smooth forehead, her long fingers, her eyes, which searched and seared his just as they had the last time he had seen her. Why was he going? But he had to leave, didn't he? He would go someplace where he could think. Not here. He stared out the taxi window, where Veldhoven was giving way to Eindhoven. So many millions and millions of bricks. A world made out of bricks.

Standing in line to buy a train ticket, he reached for his wallet, and the little envelope that was on the floor came out of his pocket with it. Inside was a small embossed card. On it were these words in neat typescript: "You have not done what you came to do." That was all. He turned it over. He looked inside the envelope. It could only have come from Ella. No one else. Or Pim. But that seemed impossible. Both seemed impossible.

"Can I help you?" the ticket clerk was saying.

"Uh, just a moment, please. Een moment, alstublieft."

"Please step to one side, sir."

He leaned against the counter. Of course it was from Ella, but why hadn't she said it in person? Because that would mean seeing him, and maybe she couldn't risk that. But she certainly would not have changed her mind, would she? What could the note mean?

"Sir, are you all right? May I help you?" It was a very tall young policeman.

"No, no. I'm fine. I'm all right."

"Do you want to buy a ticket? May I assist you?"

"Well, yes, except I suddenly don't quite know where I am going."

"Are you a little confused, sir?"

"Oh, I'm more than a little confused."

"Perhaps you'd like to have a cup of coffee. We have some here in our reception."

"Do you have tea?"

He sat in a small office down a corridor. A dark-haired, dark-skinned woman wearing some kind of uniform opened the door with a key and handed Tom a cup of tea.

She sat opposite him. "How are you feeling, sir?"

"Better than an hour ago."

"May I ask your name?"

"Of course. Thomas Johnson."

"You are an American?"

"Yes," he answered a little warily, afraid that requests for addresses and phone numbers might follow.

"Mr. Johnson, are you traveling alone?"

He would not mention Ella, he decided. Not when all he had to go on was the card. No, keep it simple. "I'm traveling alone."

"Can you tell me where you live?"

"Well, that's a little hard to say just now. Let's just say that I am betwixt and between."

"Mr. Johnson, will you do me a favor?"

"Of course, my dear."

"Will you count backward from a hundred? In English."

Tom put his cup down with a little clatter. "Are you evaluating me?"

"I'm just trying to help you, Mr. Johnson."

"I live in Veldhoven. Dotterbeek 1. I moved in there on July 9."

"Of what year?"

"This year."

"And what year is this?"

"2007. May I please call a friend?"

"I thought you said you were traveling alone."

"I am, but I have Dutch friends, and I'd like to phone one of them to come and get me." He imagined Dickie's phone ringing and ringing and going to the answering machine.

But then a nurse was taking his blood pressure and making a phone call herself, and two paramedics were outside the door with a gurney. "Your blood pressure is a little high," the nurse was saying. "We'd like a doctor to have a look at you." And then he was sitting on the end of an examination table in a hospital gown. "Your blood pressure is quite high," a young doctor said. "Do you take medication to control it?"

"Well, I used to. I ran out, and I haven't had a chance ..." Tom was given a shot and some pills.

"We need to watch your blood pressure for a while," a nurse was saying. Then a social worker with a clipboard was asking him questions. She was kind and sympathetic and seemed genuinely concerned for him. He was guarded, especially when she said, "May I ask you who is Christine Panco?"

"I don't know."

"We found her name and address among your things. Is she a relative of yours?"

Tom didn't answer.

"Mr. Johnson, part of my job is to evaluate your mental state, and with someone your age it is routine to look for signs of dementia. Now, I'm not finding any until now, but you're not helping yourself by not answering."

"I do not want to go home. Christine will come and get me and take me home. I do not want that." He surprised himself by

how forcefully he said the words and more so by how forcefully he
felt them. He thought of Brooks and my mother, of phones ringing and wheels turning.

When the social worker got up to leave, Tom said, "Are you
going to call my family?"

She smiled at him but evaded his question. "That is not a decision for me."

"Am I going to be released?"

"The doctor is going to keep you here until your blood pressure
is coming under control. It was dangerously high." Then Tom was
in a four-bed ward with a TV that droned in Dutch and a window
that looked out on a drab street. He ate some hospital food and
went to sleep almost immediately. He slept to the middle of the
next day and was only vaguely aware of being given pills in the
night. He had a dream about Pim riding a bike in a wood and
wailing in anguish. He must have been riding behind her, but he
wasn't gaining on her. When he awakened, he knew what to do,
and when the nurse came he asked if there was a library or a way
he might send an e-mail. An hour later there was a laptop computer sitting in front of him. He sent this message to me: "Nora,
I need your help. Somewhere I think in my old file cabinet is a
folder marked 'Sarah van Praag.' In it I hope is an envelope addressed to Sarah that should be sealed and have a dated postmark.
DO NOT OPEN THIS LETTER. It must remain sealed. Send
it as is in its envelope to Pim de Wit, Evestraat 23, 5503 XM,
Veldhoven, The Netherlands. Here's the hard part. I don't know
where the file cabinet is. It may be where I left it in my study in
Frenchman's Lake, but it may have been moved or even placed in
storage. See if you can find it. I know I'm asking a lot. Thanks,
your Granddad."

In the afternoon the young doctor was there looking at his

chart. "Better," he said. Then the doctor was sitting on the edge of the bed. "You know about your heart condition, I think?"

"Yes."

"How much do you know?"

Tom told him. He described his conversation with Roger Daugherty, the diagnosis, the recommendation of surgery.

"Hmmm," said the doctor. "That would be riskier now. Your heart is weak. Probably weaker than—"

"Doesn't matter," said Tom. "I don't want surgery anyway," although he felt a little lightness in his stomach and head.

"So it is even more important that your blood pressure is controlled. Let's see if it is staying down. If so, I'll release you tomorrow." The words gave Tom relief; he had feared the doctor would want to keep him. Now he imagined himself standing up from a wheelchair at the hospital door and walking away. He looked out the window at the colorless street in the rain and felt stupid for having neglected his medication, but he'd felt fine since he'd run out of pills and hadn't known quite how to go about getting a new prescription. He had intended to ask for Ella's help, but he hadn't. Now he imagined Brooks and my mother on a plane, getting closer and closer to him. He saw the little blinking blip on the tiny screen advancing across the Atlantic, and his fear seemed to be confirmed the next morning when he asked the nurse who took his blood pressure and temperature if he could go home.

"Ja," she said. "Soon as the doctor looks at you. Your daughter is coming."

He felt a little weak. They were probably moving his stuff into Hanover Place already: his chair, some books, his old four-poster bed. Maybe it wouldn't be so bad. He couldn't quite imagine seeing Brooks, looking him in the eye, being sucked back into the whirlpool of his troubles and demands. Christine, however, Christine he suddenly realized he missed terribly.

But it was not my mother who came through the door at half past ten that morning. It was Ella. In the car on the way to Veldhoven, they didn't speak for a while. Finally she said tersely, "Something has changed. You mustn't go yet. We haven't finished." Even so, he didn't mention the note. It seemed too chatty to do so. "Oh, by the way ..."

He didn't say anything, and all she said was, "Saskia Waleboer still has your place."

Brabant, Autumn 2007

Tom sat in his room, waiting for something or someone. Ella? Not really. Not yet.

The social services people? The IND? The Mutt-and-Jeff cops? Maybe. He had to admit that he was paranoid. He had to admit he often felt that in Holland social planners were peeking around corners or over the tops of clouds, that committees were meeting in windowless boardrooms, that conference calls were being made, and that someone somewhere had a file marked "Tom Johnson." When he heard Mrs. Waleboer coming up the stairs in the middle of the morning with a man, he wondered if they had come for him before he wondered if she had a lover and then for a troubled moment if she could possibly be selling herself.

But he couldn't worry about her. For a time he couldn't worry about anything but himself; he knew that he must not leave, but he knew practically nothing else. What had changed? He felt foolish: the guy who finally got the joke everyone else in the room had been snickering about. "Oh, I see. I haven't really been free after all, have I? Perhaps I've never been free. Perhaps no one has. Freedom is an illusion, is that it?" Had the policeman almost taken him by the arm before? Had the social worker been waiting just offstage all these years? He even wondered about Jan Dekker until the lawyer called to say that he had been granted a hearing in early November and his visa had been extended until then. Tom told him in turn what had happened, but not that he'd been in the process of leaving at the time. "Is that a problem? Will it influence the decision?"

"It depends on what the doctor and the social worker write in their reports. Let me see if I can get copies."

After three days Tom went into the bathroom, closed the door, and looked at himself in the mirror. "Okay," he said, "what do you know for sure?" He had done this first during a hard time in the war when he'd been depressed and lonely, and it had made him feel less lonely. He had done it throughout his life, but sparingly because he knew or perhaps feared instinctively that he was only allotted so many such encounters, and they were not to be wasted. "Well, for one thing you know that things don't always turn out well. For another, you know that almost nothing is urgent and only death is final." He took a deep breath and felt as if he were really talking to himself now, a self who had been away. "You know that life is both tragic and beautiful, that you are entitled to nothing, and that every day is a carefully wrapped present, including this one." He went back to his room, sat with his palms upturned in his lap, and listened to *The Marriage of Figaro;* then he called Dickie. No answer. Tom was anxious to reconnect; he hadn't even told Dickie about his aborted departure or about being in the hospital. He thought that the little concert being given in the park that night might be neutral ground on which to meet.

In the end he was happy that he went alone; he felt a certain proprietorship he hadn't felt before. People nodded to him. A couple of them spoke to him in English. The old American. He drank French wine, ate Dutch cheeses, listened to a string quartet play

Mozart and Vivaldi, and answered the question no one had actually asked him. "I came here because you are a refined, cultured, genteel, and generous people." He knew that wasn't really why he'd come, and he knew that he only said or even thought such grand things after drinking wine. He'd had two, no, three glasses. Would he pay for them tomorrow? Did they make his heart beat faster and harder? The very fact that he worried was something; it meant he wasn't just sitting around waiting to die, as he had been before or as he would have been at Hanover Place. Or was that also an illusion? Was all this just moving about and dislocation? What, after all, did he have to live for? One wounded, lonely friend or maybe erstwhile friend, a clean, well-lighted place, a lifetime of memories that would last only as long as he did. And had he really escaped anything at all? Sometimes it seemed as if he thought more about Brooks and Christine and the house on Frenchman's Lake than if he'd never left.

That feeling was compounded by the e-mail he got from me the next day when he walked to the library. "Tom, Carly says Uncle Brooks has filed a criminal complaint against you with the State's Attorney for the misuse of Uncle Tony's funds. Apparently anyone can file a complaint about anything, so in and of itself it doesn't mean much and won't unless the State's Attorney files charges. Still, I thought you'd want to know. Nora."

Tom did not want to know. He did not want to think about his old life. He wanted to live in Holland, walk Leo, throw sticks with Dickie, wait for Ella, and hope for Pim. That afternoon he got dressed up. He knotted his tie, buffed his shoes, smoothed his jacket, clipped his nose hairs, and walked to Dickie's building. Someone let him in, and he went up in the elevator and knocked three times on Dickie's door. He knew the third time was out of frustration. Dickie wasn't home. A man came down the hall and paused. "Hospital," he said. "Heart. Sorry. Bad English."

"Heart?" asked Tom.

Tom took a cab directly to the hospital in which he had been a patient only days earlier. He sat at Dickie's bedside.

"Bum ticker," said the Dutchman. "Okay now." But he made no effort to lift his head.

"Can I call anyone?"

"No one left. One nephew in South Africa."

Their exchange was desultory and awkward to the extent that Tom wasn't sure he should even have come, but when he was leaving Dickie said, to his surprise, "Do come again. Please." So Tom went every day. He did so with some chagrin, knowing that the sick man was an easy mark and his own attentiveness was self-indulgent.

On the second day Dickie was restless. He had trouble getting comfortable. He asked Tom, "Do you ever worry about death?"

"Not much anymore. I used to when I was young. You?"

"Never," said Dickie with some feeling. It was a little bit as if they were strangers on a plane that was crashing who looked at each other across the aisle. Or was it as in Hopkins's poem himself for whom he grieved? Or was it displacement? Was he like one of those people who lavish their attention on dogs and cats because they can't figure out how to have real relationships with people? And was this true with Saskia, too? One day he had found the refrigerator standing open and empty. "Kaput," she said, and Tom went right out and bought a brand-new bigger, better one. When it was delivered, she seemed a little nonplussed, and he realized that his extravagance made her uneasy. Did he make everyone uneasy now, or was it mostly himself? Would he ever feel comfortable with Ella or ever see Pim again? "These things take time," he heard Dickie saying, Ella saying, a woman in the café saying to a friend. It was a Dutch mantra, one said automatically and in just such a way and to which Dutch ears were apparently inured, and he wondered if Americans had mantras of their own: "It will all work out in the end," "Everything happens for a reason," "It's all good." No, it isn't. He felt suddenly hopeless, or was he just tired? Very, very tired. Death was very much on his mind, and he wondered if it would be okay to die now, if he could go in peace.

"Never been religious," said Dickie the next day. "Don't believe in an afterlife. Except children. They're your afterlife." Was he commenting on the fact that Tom had three and now four or the fact that he himself had none? "That's Aristotle, you know: producing children is as close as we can come to participating in the eternal and divine."

Tom did not know and was impressed that Dickie did. He thought it an odd thing for a childless man to remember. Perhaps not.

"Love's eternal, too, you know," said Dickie as if he had once believed it a little more resolutely.

On the fourth day Dickie complained about the food and talked of going home, and Tom thought that maybe he was turning the corner. That evening he shopped for cheeses, meats, bread, fresh fruit, and even a bottle of Rosé d'Anjou, Dickie's favorite. The next day a nurse stopped him with a hand on his arm as he was about to open Dickie's door. "Wait," she said. "He died, your friend. I am very sorry."

"Richard Druyf? Are you sure?"

"Yes, I am sure. It just happened."

Dickie's clothes and bedclothes and hair were mussed, apparently by attempts to resuscitate him; a portable defibrillator still stood at the foot of the bed. Tom tried to imagine the scene: the paddles, the nurses leaning over him, doctors hurrying in. Dickie looked at peace now, but as if he recently hadn't been, as if he had, perhaps, just come in out of a storm. He was Dickie and then again he wasn't; in fact, he was the farthest thing from Dickie.

Tom went home and had the picnic by himself in the garden, including more than half the bottle of wine. That night he lay with his head against his pillow, listening to his heart beat in his ear, or perhaps listening for it to stop beating. Was he next? Was Dickie just a tired bit of foreshadowing in Tom's story? Silly. Presumptuous. Nonetheless, Dickie was gone, and Tom was alone again.

He was alone at the funeral, too, sitting in a pew by himself. The patterns and cadences and prayers were the same, though the words were Dutch. A soprano sang something he didn't know in a plaintive voice. Sunshine came in through the high, clear windows of the little church. There were more people there than he expected. Some cried. Dickie had had friends.

Tom walked home through the park where he and Dickie had so often met. He saw Pim on the bench long before he knew who she was. When he did it was because of the familiar way she was sitting, holding her head, crossing her ankles, and he stopped. "Hello," he said.

"I am sorry about your friend," she said.

"Thank you."

"I knew him, too."

"Dickie?"

"His wife, really. Not well, but you get to know who the native English speakers are."

"Of course. You would, wouldn't you?"

After so much and so long, their talk was easy and ordinary, or seemed that way. He might have been on his way to the grocery store, and she might have been reminding him to pick up a thing or two. *"Butter?"* *"Yes, and some fresh parsley; I want to make those potatoes you like."* For just an instant it was possible to imagine that they had never been apart.

"I have some photographs of yours. Ella gave them to me." She sifted through them and put one down on the bench beside her.

"This was your son Anthony?"

Tom knew which picture it was even at that distance. "Yes."

"I want to tell you something," she said. "Once I saw an American movie with an actor in a red sports car. I think perhaps it was James Dean. The top was down. The wind was blowing in his blond hair. Well, all this time, all these years, I thought that was your son. I hated you for choosing him over Ella."

"I'm sure you did."

"And now this." Beside the photograph she was laying the letter Tom had written after Julia's death, which I had recently found and sent as he had asked me to. "I'm not sure what to make of it, Thomas. I guess you didn't know about Ella. I guess that wasn't your fault. Okay, but I'm not sure what difference that makes."

"It means I didn't come here for her. I came for you."

"You don't have any idea what you are saying."

"I know exactly what I am saying."

She laughed then, not cruelly but knowingly. "You don't know me, and I don't know you. I barely remember you. You had a romantic soul, that is what I remember, and I loved you for it once, that's true, but I was twenty-three, and now I am eighty-four, and it seems like foolishness. And believe me, you do not know who I am. You know nothing about me. I am here to ask you to leave it that way. To leave me alone. I truly want to be left alone, Thomas. Do you understand?"

"Yes, I understand. I do. And I will leave you alone. I promise.

But in case you change your mind, I shall be right here on this bench every day at one o'clock."

"Thomas, please ..."

"Do not worry," he said aware that she had now spoken his name three times. "I sit down somewhere every day about one to read my paper anyway. Now it's going to be here."

He didn't look at her, and she was silent for a moment. Then she said, "That's from a movie, isn't it?"

"What?"

"About being on a bench at the same time every day. Oh, Thomas, you still think life is a movie."

"All I mean is—"

"Listen, when I was a girl and I heard the parable of the prodigal son, I always identified with the other son, the one who stayed and worked hard and did his duty."

At first Tom thought that this was a non sequitur, but then he knew it was not, that it was something she had wanted to say for a very long time, perhaps all these many years. At the same time he knew that she immediately regretted saying it. Perhaps that was why she was now walking away. And there was something in all of this that suddenly gave him a little hope. Maybe that they had had the same feeling at the same moment, that they had both known that she shouldn't have said what she had just said, that for an instant it had compromised the dignity he had always thought uncompromisable. Surely she knew that as well. Surely they knew it together, as they had once known so many things. He felt like hurrying after her, like taking her by the shoulders and turning her toward him. Instead he watched her until she was gone. She was old now, but there was in her step the same feline grace grown a little fragile that she had had as a girl. What was it that she so desperately did not want him to know?

Tom picked up the photographs Pim had left on the bench. He shuffled through them absently. He touched the letter she had left there with his forefinger. He held it for a while, trying to remember what it said. He couldn't. He knew what he had wanted it to say ten years earlier and what he wanted it to say now, but he wasn't sure what it said. In fact, he was a little afraid of what it said. Finally he took the letter from its envelope and slowly unfolded it.

May 11, 1998

Dear Sarah,

I am writing to tell you I recently discovered that many years ago you wrote me a letter I never received. It was destroyed. I think it must have been the last letter you wrote me. I think you must have written it in 1948. And while I do not know what it said, I spend a good bit of my time these days thinking about that. I guess I hope it said good-bye. I guess I hope it said you had fallen in love with someone else, and I guess I hope you've lived happily ever since.

I have not. I have had a long and healthy life, but I was never able to replace the love you and I once had. It has been through all these years very precious and important to me. I have always regretted that we quarreled, that we parted, and that I never came back for you.

I would love to hear from you. I would love to know all about you, and I would love to know that you are well, but if this letter is an intrusion, please forgive me and forget it. Just know this much: other than my children, you have been in many ways the most important person in my life.

Respectfully,

Tom

Later, in fact much later, Pim would admit that in the days that followed that day in the park, she often passed by his bench on the street behind him, sometimes on a bus, sometimes in Ella's car, always hoping he would not be there, and each time she felt frustration and anger until one day he really wasn't there, and then to her surprise and embarrassment she felt something like concern, and then she knew that this thing was not going to end easily. "Damn your soul," she said at the time. "Damn your soul!" But that was later.

Now a man passed Tom's bench, riding along the path on a bicycle. He was holding a sheet of plywood perhaps four feet square against his back with both hands down low behind him and turned backward. Tom wondered what he would do when he had to stop. Perhaps the world would see what he was doing and stop for him. Cars would come to a halt at green lights, crossing guards would hold up their hands, and pedestrians would step back onto the curb. Another man came along, walking two dogs, one large, one small, one black, one white, neither on a lead. Tom thought about Leo; he'd need to go out soon. Coming the other way, a young mother on a bicycle rode by with two small children. One sat in a seat behind her; the other sat in a seat suspended from the handlebars in front of her.

Tom would never see the plywood man again, but he would see the dog walker from time to time, and he would see the bike woman and her children often. Eventually they would nod and say "Goedemiddag" to each other. In time the older child, the one on the back, would watch for him and open and close her hand to him, and he would have become a tiny part of her life: the old man on the park bench with the friendly smile. De oude Amerikaan.

Veldhoven, Autumn 2007

O f course in the matter of reading the newspaper, Tom had dissembled; he usually saved it to read later in the garden or by Mrs. Waleboer's little blue enamel potbelly stove with a glass of beer. So what? Now he read it a little earlier on the park bench. What was the difference? In the rain he read it under an umbrella. In the wind he folded it into quarters.

Dickie's nephew from South Africa was a big, bewildered man anxious to bury his uncle, finish his business, and go home. Tom helped him inventory Dickie's possessions and select the papers, letters, paintings, books, and jewelry he would take with him; he welcomed the opportunity to seem capable. For everything else, including furniture and clothing, Tom introduced the nephew to Jan Dekker, who arranged an estate sale. In thanks the nephew presented Tom with a box of everyday, practical items, probably the contents of Dickie's desk: stationery, pens, pencils, paper clips, rubber bands. It was the gesture of a niggardly, inept person, and it made Tom feel even more capable, which was, he supposed, the real gift.

Sometimes Tom looked at the photographs that Ella had left with him, especially those of her daughter, Hanneke, because she reminded him a bit of the Pim he had once known, although she was much thinner, and her hair was lank, maybe unwashed, so that Tom wondered in a detached way, as you might about someone you saw on a train, if she used drugs. Sometimes she held an infant, but, at least in these pictures, she had no partner or ring on her finger. In one she wore a tank top that revealed a sleeve of tattoos resembling Hieronymus Bosch figures on her right arm. Harry Bosch. Tom thought of Michael Connelly's tough-guy detective, and for just a moment he was homesick for hard-boiled, hard-baked American idealism—the hell with this always sensible Dutch practicality—and for another moment he missed corn dogs, flag lapel pins, trailer parks, "God Bless America," and all the other silly American detritus he'd left behind. And he thought of his trip to Amsterdam to buy books, of the kid from Indianapolis he'd come across sitting cross-legged on the pavement, his guitar case open in front of him, tuning his instrument, telling rambling, funny stories in that easy Hoosier drawl to a crowd of almost a hundred people. As Tom had looked over people's shoulders, he had been proud of that kid. And why hadn't he remembered Harry Bosch when he was going up and down the aisles of the American Book Center? He'd give anything right now for a good Harry Bosch novel. Harry in his cantilevered house dangling over the expressway just miles from the San Andreas Fault in the mad, amorphous jumble that is Los Angeles, where nothing matches, nothing goes together, everything is out of place. Perhaps he'd grown a bit tired of Dutch uniformity, of bricks. If they could stand for stability, they could also stand for monotony. And he'd grown a little tired of people who wore drab clothing and drove discreet cars and hid their big houses in the woods. He wouldn't have minded seeing a bleached blond in a big Cadillac convertible with vanity plates that said "Look at me" or "36D" or something else outrageous.

But this appreciation was distant and nostalgic. He knew he couldn't leave. Not now. Not when Pim was upset, when she was feeling something, when she was not feeling nothing, which was what he half expected and feared after their two lifetimes had passed—that they would have a cup of tea, sum everything up in half an hour, and have nothing else to say. But that was not what had happened, and now he knew two things with certainty: that was not what was going to happen, and something else was going to happen. He also felt that Pim knew these things, that they knew them in common; they knew them together. He hoped like hell he wasn't crazy, that he wasn't making all this stuff up like some mad stalker.

Once a week Tom trooped off to the library, smiled at the librarians, sat down at the computer, and checked his e-mail from me. Occasionally he sent a short reply, if only to prove he could do it; it did not seem to him a very civilized form of communication. Then one day he got this note from me: "Tom, Heads up. Carly tells me that Mother and Uncle Brooks are making plans to come to The Netherlands in December. I'll let you know the dates. Nora." At about the same time Jan Dekker told him the hearing had been postponed until December.

"Do you know why?"

"No. Maybe because of the end of the year. Maybe they are having, ja, too many cases. But the new date is the day your visa extension expires, so if you are denied, you might have to leave the country very quickly." What worried the lawyer was that for Tom to reveal his assets was to risk them because Brooks might try to attach them. But if he didn't reveal them, his case would be that much weaker than the one made by petition that had already been denied. "That may be the reason for the postponement. Their advocat may be trying to find out what you have and where it is."

"I haven't much of a chance, have I?"

"Not really. Not unless you are willing to reveal that you have a Dutch daughter."

"I'm not."

"Then I am thinking that maybe your best chance is to go alone."

"Without you, you mean? Why would I do that?" Tom feared suddenly that he had offended the other man with the abruptness of his response.

"Because if I am there, I will have to speak for you. It's my job. And your best chance is to speak for yourself. Only then can they see you are not incompetent."

"Is this about your fee? I'll be happy to pay you. I think I should be paying you."

"No, strategy. I'll charge you if you want, and I'll go with you if you want, but I don't think it is a good idea, and I would like to see you succeed. You have opened my eyes, you see, and I am thinking that perhaps you can open the eyes of the hearing officer, but you'll only have one chance, and it's a bit of a small one; hearings are brief. The officer taps the gavel, and, well, it is over."

Then Pim came back. She stood in front of his park bench as if summoned or sent, and her tone had changed. There was some graciousness in it and perhaps even some contrition, like someone who had wanted too badly to win and now had won and was a little embarrassed about it. "I know you are leaving, and I want to thank you; it is for the best." To this intelligence Tom did not react at all, did not disagree or even look quizzical, and later he would think that fortunate. What he did do was imagine the conversation that must have taken place with Ella, and it added something to the picture he was forming in his mind of his daughter, which existed largely in the negative, as much of things that were not there as of things that were. What was not there in this case was strict adherence to the truth, impulsiveness, unwillingness to manipulate or to sacrifice the ends for the means, and, surprisingly, distrust of him; she must have gambled that he would understand and not give her away. "She wants to be able to see you before you go," said Pim, "and, well, I think that's fair." Here it was clear that she had been convinced that to acquiesce in this was to be generous. "And she wants me to tell you the things about her that only a mother can know, and, well, I said I would." And now Tom saw Pim's half of the conversation, saw her leaning slightly, saw her listening carefully and watching and nodding. He remembered her once doing all these things with him when they had talked of the life they would lead together.

Pim told Tom about Ella. She sat down on the edge of the bench quite tentatively at first—still holding a book she had apparently brought for him—and talked, also quite tentatively at first, but then less so. He welcomed the opportunity to watch her without feeling like a voyeur; he had forgotten just how elegant she was: her raised brow, her squared shoulders, the movement of her hands.

Ella had been a quiet child, not shy, but someone who didn't want or need to say very much. She had spent much of her childhood in her room, drawing pictures of horses, so that Pim had feared she was antisocial, but she wasn't. She was just naturally confident. She had always known her own mind. She had gone on being a little plain, a little plump, largely unconcerned about her appearance and quietly happy in a self-contained way most of the time. Pim described a day when she had looked out the window to see the seven-year-old Ella coming down the street through a sudden heavy downpour that had sent other kids running in all directions, bicyclists racing for shelter, mothers in their aprons hurrying in their doors. Not Ella; she trudged along, red slicker buttoned to her throat, rain hat pulled down over her eyes, lugging her book bag, until she trudged right through the front door that Pim was holding open for her. "And that's how she's gone through life."

Pim smiled at the memory, and Tom recognized her smile as you might a voice on the telephone many years later. It was the smile he had remembered for so long and then forgotten for longer, the one that began as a tiny crease, a comma, a momentary dimple on one side of her mouth, and then, with a little bob of her head and the crinkling of her eyes, migrated wryly across her mouth, opening it and exposing her teeth. And suddenly she was a girl again, the girl who all those years ago had squinted into the sun and first shared the smile with him. It was a playful smile, and he recalled now her playfulness, which had surprised him at first because it contrasted with her patina of refinement. He remembered her ability to turn almost anything into a game: thumb wrestling and who could read the most pages in an hour or kiss the longest or swim the farthest underwater. He remembered admiring her resourcefulness, her refusal ever to be bored at a time when he had often been. It was this as much as the competence with which she'd guided him to the underground and the Germans that he admired in her.

But there was more to Pim, too. There was sadness, there was vulnerability, and there was fear. And sitting there, listening and watching, he realized he hadn't known these things were in her, or perhaps they hadn't been in her or he had been too young or too much in love to see them. And maybe what she was afraid of was his image of her. So gilded. So romanticized. This woman sitting before him was brittle. She was tarnished and damaged.

When Pim and Bert Hendriksen separated, Ella was eleven.

She was badly hurt, and it was only then that Pim began to tell her about her father—that he was an American soldier who had died in the war. From that moment on Ella was in love with all things American. She played with hula hoops and Barbie dolls and wore a baseball cap. She loved Disney movies, especially *Old Yeller.* She watched *Gunsmoke, I Love Lucy,* and later *All in the Family.* While other girls her age were devoted to the Beatles, she loved the Monkees. She went to Amsterdam to march in protests against the Vietnam War and dressed like American teenagers she saw in magazines. She practiced Americanisms in her Dutch accent: "cool," "far out," even "y'all." She called her friends and family "you guys" and smoked Marlboro cigarettes.

Tom wasn't sure why Pim was telling him all of this. Perhaps because she'd promised to. Maybe to say he'd always been part of their lives, or maybe to say he'd never been.

When Ella went to university at Utrecht, she had a boyfriend from California named Don Williamson. She was forever dragging home Americans whom she met at the university, in train stations, at campgrounds: skinny, stoned, long-haired kids with gigantic backpacks stuffed full of dirty, smelly clothes.

"And you took them all in?"

"Her grandparents did. Ella was living with my mother and father then." She did not say why, and again Tom was aware of missing chapters, of things unspoken.

At some point along the way Ella figured out that she was too young to have a father who had died in the war, so Pim had concocted an even more elaborate lie. In it Ella's father was a fighter pilot whose plane had been shot down during Operation Market Garden. He had been found, sheltered, and nursed by the Dutch underground, of which Pim had been a member. Their plan was for her to join him in the United States, but he'd been stationed in the Aleutian Islands and then Korea, where he had been shot down again and killed.

"Oh, that," Ella said to Tom later, rolling her eyes. "I never believed any of it. It was obviously made up. But I did have a fantasy that you would one day try to find me, and now I have found that you didn't even know about me at all."

I know about you now, he thought as he studied her across the table, this solid, strong-willed little woman with her sudden smile and brash laughter who had quietly begun to crawl into him somehow. Or trudge. What he felt for her was very different from what he felt for Brooks, my mother, or Tony, something he'd become aware of since he hadn't been able to see her. Was this feeling because he had just met her? Was it because he had missed out on her whole life? No history. No scar tissue. They were an experiment in the laboratory of love. A case study. A *National Enquirer* headline: "Man Has Sixty-Year-Old Baby at Age Eighty-Five." Or was this a different feeling because he had loved her mother and hadn't loved Julia? She was very slowly beginning to fill out in front of him, to inflate like a balloon. He could now recognize her handwriting. He knew what she took in her coffee and how she answered the phone.

"Do you still read?" Pim was asking, standing now, presenting him with the book in her hand. It was the first time she had acknowledged anything from their past or that they'd even had a past, had once traded books and read them aloud to each other.

"Thank you," he said. I'm sure it was the present itself, combined with her softer demeanor when she was speaking of Ella, that allowed him to relax a little and try to engage her. Only later that evening, when he'd finished the novella she'd given him, did he realize that it was not a present at all but a warning, a cautionary tale, the story of a couple of their age and time who were absolutely destroyed by love. Now, however, he was hopeful and said, "Do you remember the first book we read to each other?"

It took her some time to answer or to decide to answer. "*A Tale of Two Cities*," she said finally.

"'It was the best of times, it was the worst of times.'"

"War always is, they say. Anyway, I'll not object if you see Ella."

"You know it wasn't Ella I came here to find."

"I know, but it's been too long, Thomas. ..."

"Well, I didn't know you were going to change your name and hair color and fake your death."

Suddenly she looked away. Quite unexpectedly he had made her smile.

Tom wanted to return Pim's favor by sending her a book that he thought particularly American and a thank-you note, so he looked in the box of desk contents that Dickie's nephew had given him. Beneath some stationery he found a small sleeve of embossed cards. Familiar. He took one out. It was a match to the one that now sat on his nightstand that read, "You have not done what you came to do."

He sat on the bed holding the two cards. Damn. Dickie. Dickie Druyf. But he did not think for even a moment that this was Dickie the sentimentalist, Rosé d'Anjou Dickie, no, no. This was desperate Dickie, dying Dickie, Dickie who needed one more time to believe in love even if it was someone else's.

Veldhoven, Autumn 2007

Ella came back, too. She brought along her husband, Henk, a big, flat-faced man who needed something to talk about and talked about the elaborate system of dams and bridges that had saved Holland from the sea. Then she brought her children, Robby and Hanneke, who shyly called Tom "Opa." Hanneke had her baby in a stroller, and Tom held him. But mostly Ella came alone, and mostly she was interested in Tony. So Tom told her all the old stories he could remember. He told her about De-Wayne Purchase, who befriended Tony when he was captain of the high school basketball team and Tony was the manager, and how DeWayne took Tony bowling and to a church youth group and one time camping overnight with his Scout troop. And how, when he was studying at the University of Iowa, he invited Tony for a football weekend, how Tony went to Iowa City alone on a Greyhound bus, both quite scared and very proud of himself, how he came home full of tales about parades and marching bands and drinking beer for breakfast at a fraternity party before the game, and how he also came home with a black-and-gold University of Iowa sweat suit that he wore every day for weeks and weeks, refusing to wash it.

Ella had told her mother that Tom would be leaving when

his tourist visa expired, although she knew it had been extended. She said Pim had sat down with a calendar and circled October 9, which was ninety days from the first time she'd seen him. It was less than three weeks away.

When Pim came back to return his book, Tom was ready for her. "Pim," he said, "you once wrote me, 'I love you, and I always will.' I've believed that all my life. I think love is like wisdom, and once you have it, you can't lose it. I've never lost the love I have for you and cannot imagine having lived this life without it. You once wrote, 'If you can come back, I shall be waiting for you.' Well, I've come back, and here you are. I don't think it is a coincidence, Pim. Life's given us one more chance, late and confusing, I admit, but I just don't think we should turn it down. I made a terrible mistake once; I didn't believe in you enough. I'm not going to make that mistake again."

Tom knew even before he'd finished that he was too proud of this speech, that it sounded a little too much like something from a movie again. But he was to realize then and appreciate later that Pim wasn't really listening to him very closely. She nodded and smiled a little. "Thomas, there are things you need to know."

"I don't need to know—"

"Hush," she said. "Listen. I had a little boy who died when he was just eight. Little boy. I insisted on having his tonsils out because I was tired of his getting sick all the time. My husband objected. He was old-fashioned, and I thought I was being modern. We quarreled, and I won, but the doctor gave too much ether. My husband blamed me. I blamed myself. I had a breakdown, Thomas. I tried to commit suicide. I tried more than once. I was in the hospital for a long time. I had many treatments. Even now I take medication. I take it every day. I need it." She paused then and waited, watching him. "I lost my son and my husband, and I nearly lost Ella; in some ways I've never gotten her back, you see. Thomas, forget me. Go home and live your real life, not your old dream." She watched him as if to say, *Do you understand? Do you finally understand?* but she didn't say that. What she did say was "Life didn't work out the way I thought it would." Then she stood up carefully, like someone about to step out of a canoe. "Thank you for the book," she said. "I enjoyed it. I know you think I've stereotyped you, but that hasn't been it at all." She said this kindly, but still it swept away what now seemed his mawkish sentiment and rhetoric. He wished he hadn't spoken, hadn't put his naïveté and self-centeredness on display for her to be kind about.

Tom found himself alone, sitting on his park bench for what was likely the last time. He was embarrassed that he'd understood so little, that he'd forced the glass slipper of his delusion on this poor woman, that he'd insisted so mindlessly that his compulsion be hers too. He had tried to make the words she had spoken a detached recitation, but they insisted on being a confession, and then he knew that he was her confessor, that the words had never been spoken before, perhaps had never even been thought, because they had never needed to be. But now they did because he had come here and she had failed to send him away. A confession that was framed thoughtfully and delivered dispassionately, like a précis or a synopsis. A lifetime in two hundred words or less. A reduction. An admission of failure and shame. And why? For him? Certainly not just for herself. To release him? To spare him? Perhaps even to forgive him? Or maybe to invite his condemnation of her secret, ancient sin, which seemed, as do all private sorrows that are long buried, so pedestrian and somehow unterrible when it was finally sitting there for all to look at? Tom thought of Brooks. He thought of Julia. He thought of how easily we can forgive another that which we can never forgive ourselves.

In the morning he lay in bed until nine thirty, wondering why he didn't get up, finally realizing that it was because his compulsion was gone, that the sense of urgency that had been planted sixty years before, that had germinated with his discovery of the letter he'd never received and been growing ever since, had dissipated. This concerned him at first because he had come to depend on it so much, and it saddened him, too, because he assumed with some reason that to lose it was to lose Pim as well, and it was, but it was to lose Sarah van Praag, really, the Pim who had never truly been there, or not for a very long time, the Pim who both you and I have suspected all along was perhaps only two-dimensional. And almost certainly Tom was not alone in his misconception. Sometime later Pim herself said to him, "You aren't what I imagined."

"You imagined me?"

"Of course I did."

"But inaccurately?"

"No, just incompletely."

"Are you talking about imagination or perception?"

"What's the difference?"

Tom wasn't sure if her question was linguistic or philosophical. "Do you mean that imagination is what you think you see and perception is what you actually see?" he asked her.

"Isn't what you think you see what you see?"

THAT WHICH WAS happening to Tom now made it impossible for him to think any longer of Sarah van Praag. To do so was both fantastic and puerile. Instead he thought of Pim de Wit, the old woman who had so matter-of-factly described her wounds and revealed her scars. What, he wondered, had that cost her? He felt like a schoolboy shown lines by a master poet that rendered those he'd labored over doggerel.

Grace. She had spoken without any pause or inflection that might invite pity or even compassion but somehow offered both. Perhaps it was in the way she leaned slightly toward him, or was that to say, "Please look at me; please see me"? Suddenly he realized that those very words were what he himself had been saying to Brooks and Christine and the world. And he thought again that Pim had probably never before put all those words and feelings together at one time.

And he finally had seen her, not the pale, distant reflection he'd been trying to grasp for so long but the white-haired, straight-shouldered old woman who'd been standing there all along. And it was she about whom he couldn't stop thinking now, although he really did try, in defense of himself and deference to her. He tried while baking bread, something he'd once done every week but hadn't done since Tony's death. He tried when he sat in front of the computer in the library, checking airfares, and when he wrote long, rambling e-mails to me that he probably hoped sounded wise.

Finally he went back to Pim's door, where he hadn't been since before the Mutt-and-Jeff cops had visited, and he wasn't at all sure she wouldn't call them again or slam the door or scream or faint or die.

"Would you have a cup of tea with me?" he asked.

Standing there, she looked into his eyes for a long time. Finally she said, "Let me get my umbrella." It had started to drizzle.

TOM AND PIM were never to talk of their last evening together so long before; she was never to tell him that she had found out she was pregnant that day, that she'd doubted him for the first time and run scared, that when she'd gotten home there had been a telegram from the sanatorium saying that her sister was hemorrhaging, that she had gone immediately on the last train because her parents just couldn't do it. She would not tell him any of this, and he would not ask about what had happened that day. It didn't seem to matter to either of them anymore.

What they did talk about, at least at first, were the kinds of things you'd discuss on a plane with a pleasant stranger: music, movies, best vacations, favorite foods.

"Indian," she said.

"I see Indonesian but not Indian here."

"No. I eat it in London."

"Do you go there often?"

"As often as I can."

He knew nothing about her. He didn't even remember that she was left-handed. He didn't know that she sang or gardened or whether she drank wine. He knew she'd once wanted to die and decided against it. Sometimes he thought "to be or not to be" was the only question.

The next day he knocked again and steeled himself. "Going to the market. Do you need anything?" Again she hesitated; again she fetched her umbrella. So most days it was something: a trip to the library, a bite of lunch, or just a walk. And in the same way they had agreed tacitly not to speak of the past, they agreed not to speak of the future. Instead they talked of the books they were reading. They described plots and characters, and they talked of their families, not of histories and explanations but of doctors' appointments and stolen bicycles. Or they didn't talk. They sat and listened to music together. They sat side by side on the couch in Saskia's parlor and listened to Bach's sonatas. They sat, they walked, she went down one aisle in the market and he another, and when they parted, it was without any kind of plan or promise. All of this was strangely comfortable; although Tom had been given to them all his life, he found life easier without grand designs and pronouncements.

One day he went to the library alone again. Perhaps he was hoping for an e-mail from me, something that would persuade him to leave or something that would persuade him to stay. Nothing. He sat looking at one-way fares: Amsterdam/Schipohl to Chicago/O'Hare. He would have to eat crow, he knew, but that could not be the reason for not going home. At the same time, could this fragile, damaged old woman be the reason? He thought of Dickie's card. Was she what he'd come here for? And how often is what happens not what you think is going to happen if not usually or maybe always? And isn't that exactly what Pim herself had meant?

No, saving face could not be his reason for not leaving, but neither could proving Pim wrong be a reason for staying. He thought of her delicate dichotomies: frailty and strength, sadness and contentment, fright and fearlessness. And what if they had married and it had been their child who had died? Would he have abandoned her as her husband had? It was too easy to say no. And was that what he had done to Julia? Left her emotionally stranded until her angst had turned to anger?

For what felt like a very long time, he'd known exactly what to do, and now he hadn't any idea at all. Not today, not the next day, not at all. There was this woman, and if he let it, his mind kept coming back to her, and if he didn't, it came back to her anyway. Still, she was a different woman, the wrong woman, at least not the one he'd expected to find.

"You're different, too," she would say to him.

"Am I? How?"

"You are rueful and needy."

Rueful. Disquieted, maybe, but he wasn't troubled. He was oddly free of trouble or anxiety or almost anything at all but a desire to knock on Pim's door, to see her one more time, to make her smile again. He would tell her about the two cops. "You can be, well, ja, exported," they had said. She would surely smile at that. As for remorse, he might finally be finished with that, too. What good does it do to regret anything if nothing is what it seems? If those things you've always regretted should be celebrated and those things you've always celebrated turn out to be disasters?

Oddly free. Liberated by Dickie's death from any concerns about his own. Liberated by delusion, by illusion, by deception. How easy it all is then. *I was misinformed. Oops. Forget everything I've said until now.* Go back to square one. Start over.

He knocked on her door. "Do you drink wine?"

'Yes."

"Would you have a glass with me?"

October 9 came and went. He didn't mention it, and she didn't seem to notice at first, but then she did. "Hasn't your visa expired?"

"It's been extended."

"Extended?"

"I need to tell you something, Pim. I've applied for residency. I have a hearing coming with the IND, but what I want you to know is that no matter what happens, I won't stay in Holland without your permission." He phrased this carefully. He very intentionally did not say "unless you want me to" or even "if you don't want me to," nor did he actually ask her permission, and he anticipated several possible answers, but not the one she gave.

"Did you come here to die?"

"To die? No. No, I didn't come here to die. I may die here, but that's not why I came."

"How long?"

With someone else (Ella? My mother? Me?) he might have pretended that he didn't understand, but with her he found that he couldn't. "A year or so."

ELLA HAD LEFT them alone for a while, but as the date of Tom's hearing approached, she reappeared, and with a new agenda. She always seemed to have one, and Tom was both amused and impressed by the compartments of her mind and the ease with which she moved from one to another. Now she seemed to want him to know about her without being quite sure what she wanted him to know, so she talked of her travels and travails. She talked politics and expressed opinions, some as if she knew he'd approve, others as if she was afraid he might not. She had been to North America just once. She liked Toronto and Santa Barbara. She thought Americans were too fat. She was disturbed by people sleeping on park benches and begging with hand-lettered signs at traffic lights. She loved Mexican food.

"I make some very good enchiladas," said Tom.

"I like them with green sauce, and I like chile rellenos."

"I can make those too if I can find poblano peppers."

They both realized at the same time that that wasn't going to happen now, that they weren't likely to start cooking for each other, and that there wasn't time anyway. Ella talked then about the future. In ninety days he could come back, and then it would be springtime; "The flowers are best in the spring." Or perhaps she and Henk would come to the States. She seemed to be saying that she wanted this to end at the same time that she didn't. Tom knew that feeling well, but he was not thinking of endings or next times. He was thinking of roasting poblano peppers over an open flame.

Veldhoven to Eindhoven to Rijswijk
and back, Winter 2007

Tom got up very early on the day of his hearing, but Saskia got up earlier, and when he came downstairs she served him a breakfast of rolls, cheese, ham, and marmalade, something she had never done before. "Good luck," she said to him in English.

"Thank you, Saskia, thank you very much," he said. What was he to her? Something other than the old man who lived in the spare bedroom or a profligate stranger? The old American? Perhaps.

Ella gave Tom a ride to the train station at dawn. Their moments together were pregnant with unspoken words. I'm not sure what Ella wanted to say to Tom, but what she said was "I've never had a father before. I don't know very well how to do it, but I want you to have these things," and she gave him a manila envelope. "Read them on the train. They may help. I ... I hope ..." It was all fairly awkward.

"Thank you," Tom said, holding the envelope, turning it in his hands. "But I can't use these. Not unless your mother knows you are doing this. Does she know?"

"Shh. Go, now. Good luck." Ella kissed her father on the cheek and squeezed his hand.

"Does she know, Ella?"

Ella hesitated before answering. "She knows."

"Are you having second thoughts?" Tom had asked Jan Dekker three days earlier.

"No."

"Neither am I."

"I think your path is clear. There is nothing to concern you in the doctor's report or the social worker's."

Tom was feeling the same sharp, perhaps fatalistic sense of equanimity he'd felt on the day in 1944 when he had parachuted into Holland. After weeks of anxiety, he had been calm even when flak had begun exploding around them.

He'd felt then, he felt now, that the thing was out of his hands. He was prepared, he would do his best, and then it would be over. Even Dekker's call the day before the hearing hadn't rattled him. "Their lawyer has asked to be present. The hearing officer says that it's your hearing, so you may make the decision. Your children have no standing and no rights in the matter. All you have to say is no."

"It means they're coming, Jan. I had an e-mail from my granddaughter."

"Okay, then, I think you should give permission. Place all cards on the table."

Nor had his parting from Pim the day before unsettled him. He had turned back. "Pim," he had said, "my hearing is tomorrow."

"I know. Ella told me." He had wanted her to say, "Good luck." She didn't.

At the IND building in Rijswijk, Tom found the room and looked through the window in the door. There was a long table, on one side of which sat a man with an open briefcase. Brooks and my mother sat to his right, and though Tom had thought he'd prepared himself for this possibility, he felt a little lightheaded and had to sit down. He was still sitting there when a woman and a man came briskly down the hall. "Mr. Johnson?" the woman said.

"Yes."

"I am Jeanette Braden, the hearing officer. Let us go in, shall we?"

When they did, my mother jumped up and Brooks stood up. Tom went to them. He took them both in his arms.

"Daddy, Daddy ..." my mother said.

"Shh," Tom said.

"I just want ..." said Brooks. "I'm just trying to do—"

"Shh."

Then they were all sitting down, facing the stenographer and the hearing officer, who was saying, "Very informal here. Not a court of law. We are here to hear the petition of Thomas Johnson that he be granted a Provisional Resident Permit in the Kingdom of the Netherlands. I am IND Deputy Commissioner Jeanette Braden, and I will be hearing Mr. Johnson's petition. And are you Thomas Johnson?"

"I am."

"And you are?"

"Anton Smits, representing Brooks Johnson and Christine Panco." He gestured to them. Jeanette Braden had them identify themselves, then went on, "First, since Mr. Johnson and those who contest his petition do not speak Dutch, we will conduct these proceedings in English." This she said with a certain reserve that may have been disapprobation. "Second, those who contest this petition are here at Mr. Johnson's indulgence. As you know, his petition has already been reviewed and denied once. Your written challenge was considered and duly noted at that time. Do you bring anything new or additional to today's hearing?"

Anton Smits did not, but he plugged ahead with the same old catalog of Tom's high crimes and misdemeanors—his accidents, his oversights, his forgetfulness, his contentiousness, his losing his way in the woods, his "confusion and apparent disorientation"—and Tom noted that the hearing officer let him. Smits passed one document after another across the table, all the time using a kind of formal legal English, speaking almost as if he were in a classroom. Tom could see that he was very nervous, but he did not like him anyway. He talked as if Tom were not sitting less than five feet away. Tom went over in his mind all the things Jan Dekker had told him he must not say to the young lawyer.

Then Braden was asking for evidence from Tom. He handed across his bank statements. "As you can see, I have a private income in the form of a pension through the Teachers' Retirement System of the State of Illinois."

Smits was speaking again. "The commissioner should know that there is a court order in Illinois that the funds in Mr. Johnson's possession be seized. My client contends that they were stolen, that Mr. Johnson illegally appropriated those funds from the trust fund of Anthony Johnson, his elder son, now deceased, of whom Thomas Johnson was guardian. A criminal complaint to that effect has been brought in Illinois."

"And have charges been preferred?"

"Not yet."

"Well, if no charges have been preferred, Mr. Smits, you know as well as I do that an individual's complaint will have little or no bearing on this proceeding."

"Commissioner, Brooks Johnson and Christine Panco have no other motive in pursuing this action than to protect their father and their father's assets, both of which are in clear jeopardy because of Thomas Johnson's foolish, imprudent, and dangerous actions. All my clients want to do is to take their father home so they can care for him as only his children can. What other possible reason would they have to go to such lengths and expense?"

"To gain control of my money," said Tom.

"Commissioner, it is a common and widely recognized phenomenon that parents who are aged, infirm, and losing control of their faculties—"

"What money?" asked Braden. "I see a record of funds in the original petition, Mr. Johnson, but not in the documents you have submitted today. Do you still control those moneys?"

"Some of them. I've used some to pay legal fees, some for rent and living expenses, some for gifts and charitable contributions."

"See," said Brooks, "this is what—"

"Commissioner," said Smits, "this is a matter for discovery—"

Braden held up her hand. "Save it for the courts, Mr. Smits." She then turned to Tom. "Mr. Johnson, I very much respect your desire to be independent, but from any objective point of view it is difficult to be seeing how you would not be better off at home with your family. I'm sorry, but unless—"

"May I ask my son one question?"

"I object," said Smits. "My client is not on trial here."

"No one is on trial here, Mr. Smits," Baden said in some pique. "Again, this is not a court of law. I will allow a question."

"Have you recently applied for fifty thousand dollars in home-equity loans on the property at 26 Lake Road in Frenchman's Lake, Illinois, that I gave you less than six months ago?"

"What?" said Christine.

"No," said Brooks.

"And do you need that money to pay off gambling debts?"

"I have not—"

"Stop!" said Christine. "You mortgaged our property?"

"And do you have a serious gambling problem?"

"Absolutely not. This is—"

"Stop!" said Christine again. "You know that's not true! You know—"

"Commissioner," said Anton Smits, still not looking at Tom, "this man's wild accusations are further evidence of his dementia and incompetence. It is in his best interest ..." He had begun to lose his way. Braden was not holding the gavel. Tom decided to say what he knew he probably shouldn't; if she gave Smits latitude, perhaps she'd give him some, too. "I mean, it is not in his best interest ..."

"Son, may I ask you a question?"

Smits ignored him. "Uh ... in the best interest of Mr. Johnson ..."

"You don't mind if I call you son, do you, Mr. Smits?"

Smits stopped. "Yes, I do."

"Kind of diminishing, isn't it?"

Smits didn't answer.

"Well, now you know how you are making me feel. After all, I'm sitting right here, and you are treating me as if I am not present."

"Commissioner," Smits fairly pleaded.

"Do you know me, Mr. Smits? Have we ever met before?"

Smits had his eyes fixed on Jeanette Braden. He nodded once as if at a signal, but Braden was looking at Tom. "Commissioner ..."

"Answer Mr. Johnson's question, Mr. Smits."

"No, we haven't met."

"Then how in the world can you presume to know what's in my best interest? Mr. Smits, I may be old, but I'm still a human being, and I still have opinions and feelings and desires, and one of my desires is to live in Holland. Is that too much to ask?"

"I'm pleased that you like it here, Mr. Johnson," Braden was saying, "but so do many people, and if we let them all stay, we'd be quickly overwhelmed. I'm sure you understand. So, in the absence of further evidence ..."

"I have further evidence," said Tom quietly. "I have a daughter who is a Dutch citizen. Her name is Ella Mostert, née Johnson. She is a resident of Veldhoven. I've brought along her birth certificate," he said, sliding it across the table. "There."

Tom did not look at his children, but he heard my mother gasp and Brooks say, "What the hell?"

"You can see here that I am her father. And I have two Dutch grandchildren." Now he slid pictures and more birth certificates across the table. "Robert Mostert and Hanneke Mostert."

Jeanette Braden studied the documents and photographs through half glasses. At the other end of the table, there was only silence now. Tom looked that way and smiled and nodded as if to say, It'll be okay. My mother was covering her mouth with the fingers of both hands and staring at him. Brooks was looking straight up at the ceiling. "Do you live with Ella Mostert?" asked the hearing officer.

"No. I have a room of my own in a house near hers, but I see her and my grandchildren often."

"Then Ella Mostert wants you to take up residency in The Netherlands?"

"Yes." The word caught for just a moment in his throat.

At this Braden looked up quizzically.

"She says she does," Tom said, pushing a letter across the table. "You see, I only met her a few weeks ago. I'm only getting to know her."

Braden studied the papers. "You are Ella Mostert's father. Is that correct?'

"Yes."

"And Pim de Wit was her mother?"

"Is her mother. She is still alive."

"She is still alive? And do you have a relationship with Pim de Wit?"

"I know her," Tom said carefully.

"Well," said Jeanette Braden, sitting back and looking at Tom Johnson for a long time as he had hoped that she would look at him, "a family constitutes a good reason to grant residency, Mr. Johnson, perhaps the best reason, and you and Ella Mostert do constitute a family. I have little choice but to approve your Provisional Resident Permit. Congratulations."

Now they were outside on the street. My mother and Brooks had brief, harsh words; then she was crying on her father's shoulder, holding him tightly under both arms, her hands curling up to grip his shoulders, and Brooks was saying with resolve, "Look, Dad, I'm not going to stop until you are safe at home with us. I am not going to give up. This is not over yet." And then he was lighting a cigarette in cupped hands and walking away to the end of the block to stand and smoke. Tom felt only sadness as he held his daughter and watched his son because he knew suddenly and finally that it never would be over, not by way of resolution. That was not to be.

"I just can't believe this," my mother said. "I can't imagine it. You and this woman had a child, and you never even told anyone?"

"I never knew, Christine."

"Then why in God's name did you come here?"

"I came to look for Ella's mother, for Pim de Wit."

"Oh," said my mother after a moment. "Oh ..."

"Yes."

"My God, Dad. Can we meet her and ... ?"

"Ella. Ella Mostert."

"Can we at least meet these people?"

"No, not yet," said Tom. "It's too early. Maybe someday."

"So what are we supposed to do? Just go on home?"

"Yes," said Tom. "Give me some time. I need some time, so, yes, please go on home, but hold me a little longer before you do."

There was more, of course, but I'm not going to tell you very much of it. There was a cab ride, an awkward lunch in a hotel dining room, some recrimination, some pleading, an intemperate outburst, some more tears, finally some soothing words and reassurances that may have been sincere or may have only been expedient. But finally Tom was on the train alone; it took some time, some deep breaths, and some staring into the middle distance for him to return completely to Holland, but when he did, it was a different Holland. This one in some small part belonged to him. As he crossed the rivers moving south toward Brabant, he had for the first time the feeling that he was nearing home. My Lord. He'd done it, and it meant more to him now than he'd known it would. It legitimized him for a little while longer, and that, he thought, was about all any of us can hope for.

Part Three

The Netherlands, the North Sea
and England, 2008

The seasons are subtler things in Holland. Summer's not so long, autumn not so colorful, winter not so deep. And spring sneaks up on you; one day you look down, and grass is growing in the cracks in the sidewalk. Tom had forgotten that about the Dutch spring. He'd forgotten the low gray skies, the long, cool rains, the smell of ammonia coming off the dairy farms, the daffodils and crocuses, the tulips in so many colors and such profusion.

It was very early spring when he started making the pink chairs. He'd been thinking of it ever since Pim had seen them in a photograph, Tony sitting in one, Al Jones lying in the other, said she liked them, said they were "colorful." On Easter morning, when he had Henk and Robby sneak them through her garden gate and she found them sitting there "like big Easter eggs,'" she clapped her hands and laughed aloud.

They had begun as a sketch he made quite absently and then one he made not so absently and then a design he drew carefully with a straight-edged ruler. He had the lumber delivered and stacked behind Mrs. Waleboer's shed, drafted Robby to cut it and drill it but assembled and then painted the chairs himself, just as Tony once had: a coat of primer and two of pink latex. He did all of this quite deliberately, as he found himself doing everything now. One step at a time. One foot in front of the other. Do the next right thing.

So it was with Ella. Things had stalled out. His residency permit hadn't freed them to move ahead, as he had hoped and expected. They started repeating themselves. Perhaps she had gone as far with him as she was willing or able to go, or perhaps they had needed urgency to make things vital. Now they were flat, and sometimes he felt like a nuisance, like the long-lost birth parent who after the initial flush of discovery makes demands and asks to borrow money.

So he invited her to go to London. She had translated a local newspaper review of a revival of *My Fair Lady* for him, and he bought tickets. He thought that perhaps a little vacation, a day of leisure, would shake them loose. The day started out poorly for one that would come to mean so much to them both: Their crossing on the ferry was choppy, and the luncheon buffet for which he had paid a good bit was tired, mostly yesterday's fare. Even the glass of white wine he'd insisted they have turned out to be a tawdry midday gesture that only gave him a headache. Their B & B was also a disappointment. The photos he'd seen had been taken with a wide-angle lens some years earlier; their rooms were tiny, and the Laura Ashley wallpaper was peeling. Then when he lay down for a nap, he slept too long and too hard so that he woke up late and groggy and they hadn't time for dinner. But the performance was surprisingly fresh and relevant, and the little bistro they found afterward was good. They shared a big salad Niçoise with good bread and a chilled bottle of wine. For the first time all day Ella was animated; she had been distracted, distant, moody, preoccupied, perhaps even a little hostile. Now she relaxed and talked enthusiastically of the play, which she had also seen in London as a young girl.

And when they stepped out the door of the restaurant at almost midnight, she suggested they walk. "We'll hail a cab if we get tired." Instead they walked all the way. She hummed and sang some of "On the Street Where You Live" as they crossed Trafalgar Square; then she was quiet.

He wanted to prevent her from withdrawing again. "Frost forming," he said, nodding at the grass.

"Do you ever regret having children?"

He started to say no, thinking she must somehow be asking about the two of them. But he didn't.

"I thought there was something on your mind."

"Yes."

"Isn't that one of those questions we don't allow ourselves to ask?" he said. "Sure, I've wondered what my life would be like without children." He avoided saying "without them" because it seemed to exclude her and "without you" because it included her perhaps gratuitously.

"So do I, sometimes. I spend all my time worrying about them. Robby lives to go to the cafés on weekends. He drinks too much and then brags about it. He thinks it is a great accomplishment. And Hanneke ..." She sighed. "Hanneke's going to have another baby. No husband, no job, no education. Just babies."

They turned and walked alongside St. James's Park.

"There's a little cottage in Zeeland," Ella said, "just beneath the dike that we bicycle by on holiday. Sometimes there are an old man and woman working in the rose garden. Lovely roses. Sometimes I wish Henk and I were they. It's quiet there."

Tom thought of the quiet of the house on Frenchman's Lake, of the morning glories climbing trellises, of the yellow rosebushes on the east wall. He wondered if Brooks had pruned them in the fall.

"I don't think I'm ever happier than when I'm working in the garden."

"Tony and I had a garden."

"You miss him, don't you?"

"Yes."

"Do you miss the others?"

"Yes and no."

"Do you think of me as your child?" she asked abruptly.

"I keep having to remind myself that you are my daughter. I try not to force you into a box. I try to focus on the fact that I'm still getting to know you and be content that you are becoming more and more important to me."

He would think later that his candor and lack of hesitation encouraged her. At any rate, she went on to talk about her functional if imperfect marriage, to tell him things about Henk that made him a little uncomfortable, to talk of her awareness of her own mortality, her weariness with her work, her weariness generally—all much in the way that my mother used to launch a screed of complaints at him and Brooks used to rail at him—until he realized exactly what Ella and he were doing: she was being his child, and he was being her father. He took her hand in his.

When they turned onto their street, Tom thought perhaps she'd said everything, but she hadn't. "When I was forty-one I had breast cancer. Mastectomy. My mother came every day, and that's the way it has been ever since. I don't know why she comes, and I don't know why I let her; it's just what we do. I've quit trying to understand it." A moment later she asked, "What are you going to do about her?"

And he said, "Ella, I'm trying not to think about her tonight." In fact, he was trying not to think about Pim at all. After many years of thinking about her too much, he was trying simply to enjoy being with her when he was able, to appreciate her soft voice, her asymmetrical smile, the scent of her shampoo or perhaps lotion when she passed by him through a doorway. That spring they began reading and exchanging mystery novels, leaving them in each other's mailboxes, meeting in the park to talk about them, even discussing them on the phone once or twice, which made him feel like he was in high school again and trying to think of a reason to dial the number of the girl whose name he could no longer be sure of: Nelson didn't sound quite right. Nielson? Karen Nielson?

It was also that spring that Tom and I started to e-mail each other in earnest and Tom and Ella started to break bread together. The first time was an awful, awkward dinner at Ella's house that no one was quite ready for and that he aborted as an act of mercy as soon as he politely could, relieved to the point of exhilaration to be walking home alone in the chill air. Thank God. That was another thing he and Pim came to realize they agreed upon. "I like being with them," she was to say, "but the best part of that is when I leave them." It was true. He was always his own best company. Was she warning him not to get too close? he wondered. Or was she inviting him to be just that confidential himself? He told her that Brooks and my mother and perhaps even Ella ran on a different speed than he, that he was too slow and made them impatient, and they were too fast; they wore him out and made him nervous.

Another time, quite out of the blue, she started talking about a friend she had made in the hospital, a woman named Evelyn who developed cervical cancer and died. "Her death made me want to live. I hadn't wanted to for a long time. I was in the hospital for seven and a half years. At first Ella came to see me; then she didn't. When I got out she was at university. I had hurt her. She felt abandoned. She was very angry. We had an awful scene, and she told me she wished I was dead, that as far as she was concerned I was dead; that I was just as dead as her brother, Joost, whom I had always loved more than her anyway." Listening, Tom realized with some relief but also some disappointment that the little boy Joost—and not he—had been the lost memory that Ella had referred to.

"She didn't speak to me for almost twenty years. You'd have thought that that's when I would have given up hope, but it wasn't. It became my mission and maybe my penance to wait her out. If there was one thing I'd learned in the hospital, it was to wait."

Tom wondered if she was also talking about him and them. He thought that his relationship with Pim was even more complex than his relationship with Ella, existing as it seemed to at the confluence of imagination, memory, and perception. It was often hard to know where one began and another left off. What Tom saw ever more clearly as time passed was the keenness of Pim's mind and the deepness of her wound. He had nearly forgotten the first of these, and he did not know what to do about the second. But in fairness, neither did she.

And it was in the springtime that Tom began to cook and bake for Pim. The first time was actually for the whole family, including Robby and Hanneke, on Easter Sunday, when he roasted a perfect leg of lamb and made a pecan pie the texture of which the others found "interesting." The second time was out of necessity. Pim hadn't eaten breakfast and felt faint. . He made her an omelet that she thought was very good. Then he began to bake bread and make soup for her. He would boil a chicken all morning, throw in whatever vegetables he had and egg noodles at the end. She loved it. He made the soup and bread once a week. And when he stumbled on poblano peppers in a village market in Waalre, he made chile rellenos for Pim, Henk, and Ella. After dinner he walked her home, and at her door Pim kissed him three times on the cheeks: left, right, left. This is how Dutch men and women greet and part from each other. This is how they come and go. It is done millions of times each day, but it was the first time Pim had done it to Tom.

So it was that Tom and Pim started touching each other that spring. Their early gestures were tentative, simple matters of politeness: a grasped elbow, an extended hand. Then they were clearly expressions of fondness. A hand on a shoulder that lingered there, an arm that was offered and taken. One day over tea Tom reached across the table and touched the back of Pim's hand with his fingers. This touching was a casual-appearing, momentary gesture but one he had been thinking about for weeks. She turned her hand over to receive his fingers in her palm.

"What are we doing, Tom?"

"I don't know," he said.

Then there was the dance band that played in the bandstand behind the Kromstraat early on a Saturday evening. There were saxophonists and clarinetists in sparkly dinner jackets and a portly, animated director who encouraged everyone to dance, and everyone did: husbands with wives, sisters with sisters, grandfathers with granddaughters, young kids, even teenagers. Pim hooked her arm in Tom's as they stood watching. "Come on," she said.

"No, no. I don't dance."

"Of course you dance."

"No, I really don't. I don't dance."

"Okay," she said, turning to face him. "Okay," she said, taking his hands.

"What are you doing?"

"Shhh," she said, putting her palms against his. "Just close your eyes. Now, see if you can feel energy coming from my hands into yours."

He did close his eyes, and when he opened them again, she was watching him and smiling at him. "Do you remember?" she asked.

"I remember," he said.

After a while she shifted, and as her hands began to move, so did his, and as she began to sway, so did he. And when the song ended, she leaned close to him and said, "That was dancing, mister."

On another day Tom gave Pim a volume of Emily Dickinson's verse. That evening, in her kitchen, with soup makings all around them and loaves of bread just out of the oven cooling on the countertops, she stretched up to kiss him on the cheek, and he kissed her back on the cheek. But their mouths came together—you know how it is—and they stayed together. He was wearing an apron and she had a carrot in one hand and a paring knife in the other, but they went on for quite a while.

IT MUST HAVE BEEN at about this time that Tom sent me his journal without comment or explanation. It was in an exercise book, carefully written in longhand using green ink. At the same time his e-mails became even more frequent and detailed. It was almost as if he were trying to hang on to something—me, us, his old life, even life itself. Maybe he thought that by writing about his life he could preserve or extend it. Or maybe he just wanted to be sure we got things right.

On the morning of June 17th, Pim came home from the market to find Tom sitting in her garden. He had turned the pink chairs to face the sun. She made tea, made toast and buttered it, opened a jar of orange marmalade, put it all on a tray, and backed through the kitchen door. "Tom," she said.

He didn't answer. His paper had slid off his lap to the ground.

"Tom," she said.

"Oh," he said, waking. "Yes."

"Well, good morning. Would you like some tea?"

"Yes. Thank you, Pim."

"Tired?"

"Yes, I guess I am."

"Here," she said, laying a book and a small envelope on the arm of the chair. The book was a Harry Bosch novel. The envelope was a birthday card. "Happy birthday, Tom."

"Oh," he said, "how in the world did you know?"

"How? I remembered."

"All these years ... ?"

Pim sat on the other pink chair. "Tom, I have always thought of you on this day. Every year."

And then he was pressing his eyes with his forefinger and thumb.

"Darling," she said, "are you all right?"

"Hmm," he said, "old women don't say 'darling.'"

"This one does. Drink your tea, and let me read you something." Pim opened the slim volume of poems Tom had recently given her and began to read.

Now she crossed one ankle over the other. Now she leaned on her elbow. Now she caught a stray strand of gray hair and twisted it around the tip of her index finger a time or two. She might have been a schoolgirl reading something a little risqué in *w* or maybe Emily Dickinson herself. Yes, Emily Dickinson. That was it. Tom watched her as she tilted her head, as she raised her brow, as she smiled a little wistfully, as she looked up.

"Isn't that lovely?" she said.

"It is. Read another."

"Which one?"

"How about 'Hope is the thing with feathers.'"

"Okay." Afterward she said, "That's very nice."

"Read some more," he said.

So she did.

Epilogue

You know the rest of Tom's story. One day he died. Another day I got a completely unexpected check in the mail from his estate administrator, and I knew instantly what to do with it. I used it to tell Tom's story. I talked to everyone who knew him or remembered him at all, including all of us but also his colleagues, friends, and neighbors. I even talked to waitresses and cab drivers. Then I flew to Holland and did the same thing there. I went to the places Tom went and met most of the people Tom knew. I have broken bread with them and drunk wine with them. I like them.

And I'm still here. I'm thinking I might stay. Maybe part of me is Dutch—the practical, sensible, down-to-earth, no-bullshit part. I like bikes, I like tall, bony men—one especially—I like good bread, cheese, and beer, and I'm told I can even do a passable job of pronouncing "Scheveningen."

NORA PANCO
Veldhoven
December 2014

Acknowledgments

Thanks to Donald Burgett for his history *The Road to Arnhem,* Walter P. Maas for *The Netherlands at War,* Warner Warmbrunn for *The Dutch Under German Occupation, 1940-1945,* Cornelius Ryan for *A Bridge Too Far*, Harry Mulisch for his novel *The Assault*, to Ann and David Jonitis for teaching me about Down syndrome and to Wendy Strothman for her belief in this project and guidance with it. And thank you to the many people who have read and reviewed the manuscript in its many stages of development: Carolyn O'Connor Ferry, Dave Eggers, Connie Mc-Taggert, David McTaggert, Asa Ferry, Griffin Ferry, Lizzie Ferry, Laura Heffington, Corinne Mostert, Klaas Degeling, Frank van Sambeek, Bill Kent, Debbie Hammack, Gopal Vyas, Patrick Snyder, Carolee Snyder, Brenda Perkins, Charles Perkins, Gene Brooke, Mark Osing, Mike Piersol, Jane McGoldrick, Katherine Shonk, Sally Wasowski, Andy Wasowski, Dick Thuma, Pam Haferman, Richard Haferman and Janice Knight.